Through a Camel's Eye

A SEA-CHANGE MYSTERY

DOROTHY JOHNSTON

'Full fathom five thy father lies:
Of his bones are coral made:
Those are pearls that were his eyes:
Nothing of him that doth fade,
But doth suffer a sea-change
Into something rich and strange.
Sea-nymphs hourly ring his knell:
Hark! Now I hear them - ding, dong, bell.'

Ariel's song from *The Tempest*
by William Shakespeare

First published by For Pity Sake Publishing Pty Ltd 2016
www.forpitysake.com.au
10 8 6 4 2 9 7 5 3 1

Book design by The Scarlett Rugers Book Design Agency
www.booksat.scarlettrugers.com
Ms. Johnston's portrait by Lindsay Kelley - www.lindsaykelleyphotography.com.au
Printed in Australia by Griffin Press - Accredited ISO AS/NZS 14001:2004
Environmental Management Systems Printer.

National Library of Australia Cataloguing-in-Publication entry
Johnston, Dorothy, 1948- author.
Through a camel's eye / Dorothy Johnston.
9780994448521 (paperback)
9780994448538 (ebook)
Johnston, Dorothy, 1948- Sea change mystery
Police, Rural--Fiction
Detective and mystery stories
Queenscliff (Vic.)--Fiction.
A823.3

Also by Dorothy Johnston

The Sandra Mahoney Quartet
The Trojan Dog
The White Tower
Eden
The Fourth Season

Tunnel Vision
Ruth
Maralinga My Love
One for the Master
The House at Number 10
Eight Pieces on Prostitution (short story collection)

About the Author

Dorothy Johnston was born in Geelong, Victoria, and lived in Canberra for thirty years before returning to Victoria's Bellarine Peninsula where *Through A Camel's Eye* is set.

She is the author of ten novels, including a quartet of mysteries set in Canberra. The first of these, *The Trojan Dog,* was joint winner ACT Book of the Year, and runner-up in the inaugural Davitt Award. *The Age* gave it their 'Best of 2000' in the crime section.

Two of Johnston's literary novels, *One for the Master* and *Ruth,* have been shortlisted for the Miles Franklin award.

She has published many short stories in journals and anthologies, along with essays in Australia's major newspapers and she reviews fiction for the Fairfax Press. For more information about the author, please visit her website: http://dorothyjohnston.com.au/

For my mother, Ivy Johnston (1920-2014)

With grateful thanks to those who have helped in the writing of this novel, my family and the team at *For Pity Sake Publishing*.

ONE

In the pale green twilight, a woman was leading a young camel round a paddock. Camilla Renfrew stopped on the seaward side of the fence to watch. The woman was wearing jeans, a T-shirt, riding boots, and looked distinctly youthful too. Her short hair caught the light and glowed green-gold. She seemed intent on what she was doing and did not glance in Camilla's direction

It was a trick of the twilight, Camilla thought, to make of fading a lasting brilliance, stretching the day out longer than it had any right to be. And this girl, with her long legs, striding with her long-legged beast, drawing him behind her on a rope - across a paddock in which new growth was just beginning to make its way through last year's dead grass - this, too, was a trick of the light, to hold the scene taut in an attitude of praise.

The animal's gait was coltish and uneven, but every few steps he seemed to get the hang of being led, and found a proper rhythm. Camilla's eyes became used to the mixture of brilliance and shadow. She bent forward, peering under the branches of the Moonah, which were grey and nobbled, dusty in their grooves.

Some said the Moonah was threatened with extinction, but Camilla knew better. The small, tough, grey-green leaves, the stoop away from the prevailing south-westerlies, marked the plant as a survivor, able to outlast exotic creepers when the droughts came.

The young camel pranced, pulling at the rope as though he wanted to run away, then submitting with good grace.

Camilla recalled the way he ran to the fence when the trainer wasn't there, the way he stopped suddenly, all four feet planted boom! She remembered the feel of his downy hump, and the way he looked at her with great, open curiosity, head high, dark brown eyes taking her in entirely. Even her son, these days, preferred not to meet her eyes.

Camilla was interested in metamorphosis. Her secret hope was to catch a creature at the moment of becoming other, leaving his or her old cast behind forever. On her more optimistic days she believed there must be such a moment, measurable in time, and believed that she might witness it. She wanted to be there when a moth emerged from its chrysalis, though understanding that the change had already taken place inside, protected from her prying eyes. She wished to record that moment of deep cell change from *this* to *that,* satisfy herself that she had indeed observed it. That the camel fascinated her was related to this more general interest - a study you could call it - though she hesitated to glorify her watching by that name. And spoke only to herself of this, or any other matter. It was almost a year now since Camilla Renfrew had lost the power of speech.

She'd been watching the camel for some weeks when it came to that September twilight. Straddling the fence on the opposite side of the paddock, the one nearest the road, was a large brown saddle decorated with strips of red and orange leather. A golden fringe hung down along one side, rows of small hexagonal mirrors creating a border between it and the leather. They were decorations such as an Afghan woman might have added, sewing cross-legged on the ground, at a bazaar somewhere in the middle east, or on the outskirts of Alice Springs.

The skittish creature, with his hump half grown, was clearly too young to take the saddle. Was it there for show? Camilla knew nothing about training camels. Such an eye-catching saddle it was, so elaborately wrought. The youngster stopped in his circuit of the fence and stood looking down his nose at her. It was such a long nose for a generally undeveloped creature, and his attitude of looking along it, then turning his head slowly to the side, unexpectedly decisive and mature.

The trainer pulled on the rope impatiently, and scowled at Camilla. She called out suddenly - 'Riza!' - the name a kind of hiss.

Camilla chanced a smile, which was not returned. She thought it best to move off, though in no way trespassing, the sandy path through the Moonah, on her side of the fence, being public land.

It was then, as she began her climb through the sandhills, that Camilla remembered a woman coming towards her out of the fog. It had been a summer fog, unusual, and the woman's face had shone, white and somehow enlarged. But before she could take more than two steps, the woman was gone.

Then, the next day, or two days later - Camilla wasn't sure - she'd been on the cliff path again when she'd heard a scream. One scream. Cut off abruptly.

There'd been no one else on the path at the time. Camilla had walked to the lighthouse and back without seeing anyone. She'd wondered who she ought to tell now that she remembered. If she'd been able to speak, she would have gone to the police station. But the effort of explaining - how? - in writing? - was too much for her. The police would want to know why she'd waited so long. They would laugh at her, safe in the knowledge that their vocal cords were in perfect working order.

On the other side of the dunes, not far from the paddock which was home to an exotic creature, a man was scavenging along the tide line. It was his habit to do this, and most days at low tide found him walking slowly, head down, along one part of the shoreline or another. From a distance, he could be seen as no more than a shadow, thin and stooped. He wore a long coat of some dark material, buttoned tight against the wind, though, by his gait and demeanour, when a person came close enough to observe them, it was apparent that he was no stranger to cold winds. He was an old man, bearded, his long grey hair tucked underneath a beanie. Once he'd made his living as a sailor. Now he concentrated on what each flood tide happened to deposit at his feet.

Camilla Renfrew and Brian Laidlaw knew each other well by sight, yet not even in the days when Brian was an active seaman, and Camilla's tongue worked as well as anybody's, had they exchanged a word.

TWO

Anthea Merritt had been disappointed to be sent away from Melbourne, and in her first few weeks at Queenscliff police station had allowed this disappointment to show, getting off on the wrong foot with her boss. It wasn't so much that she objected to stray dogs and complaints about speeding fines as the highlights of her week's policing, with Friday night drunks thrown in - though she *did* object. It was a poor conclusion to two and a half years of training. Anthea knew she hadn't graduated with as good marks as she'd hoped, and that this was largely her own fault, which brought her to the real reason for her discontent, and that was separation from her boyfriend.

She couldn't phone Graeme again, at least not for a few days. She'd read a piece in the paper reminding women that men knew how to use the phone. If a man didn't return your messages or calls, it was because he didn't want to. Some women unfortunately just didn't get this, the writer of the piece had said. Anthea's ears had grown hot as she read his words. She'd hated his tone of infinite superiority.

Anthea was eating her morning tea in a park overlooking the bay, having told herself that she needed some fresh air. Her inability to appreciate the view only worsened her mood. She supposed that, in other circumstances, Chris Blackie might have become a kind of mentor. But if there were things that she could learn from him, he was keeping them well hidden. In a rut had been her instant summing up, and nothing had happened to make her change her mind.

Anthea was afraid of arguing with Graeme, afraid of the shutting down of her mind and body that a confrontation would produce. She forced patience on herself, knowing that Graeme was the kind of man for whom the present moment, and the people who occupied it, took up all of his attention. She must wait until it occurred to him to miss her.

There were women friends in Melbourne with whom she could have talked about this, found some comfort in airing her feelings. But increasingly these friends seemed far away, busy with their own lives. Negotiating traffic every day, getting from here to there, took up heaps of time; and there was always somewhere to go in the evenings. In Queenscliff, Anthea felt time as a physical burden, a weight that must be lifted, invisible, yet no less a force for that.

Her first impression of the station had stayed with her. The well-tended beds of lavender lining the path that led to the front door, next to it the sign with the royal crown and ER in a curly script, looked as prissy and ridiculous as they had the day she'd arrived. Lavender grew along the fence as well, while roses formed the centre piece, in circular beds in the middle of a lawn. The fence was divided by a white-painted wooden gate, offering no security whatsoever. It was a plain brick veneer house, built in the early 1960s. For its present purpose, the basics would have done - Anthea was sure there must be other country stations like it - but instead the building had been turned into a confection. A Hansel and Gretel house. Anthea felt so bored she wished that she could find a witch.

The first time she'd seen Chris Blackie bent over in the garden with his bum in the air, she'd had to turn away to hide her smile. Apparently the man thought it was normal to grunt and wave his gardening gloves in his junior constable's direction, not bothering to look up as he outlined her tasks for the morning. This was his daily exercise, Anthea soon found out, and he got to work early in order to accomplish it. He didn't run or swim, and played no team sport. She imagined his own garden, no leaf out of place.

Constable Blackie was one of those sleek, smooth men who look young, apart from thinning hair, through their forties and even past that; men who, when they age, age suddenly, shrinking and shrivelling, a thousand fine lines appearing all at once, their skin drying and flaking as though at the switching off of an internal sprinkler system. Anthea had known men like this, and immediately picked Chris for one of them, recognising also that the process was still some years away for him. She had seldom met a man who paid less attention to himself *as a man*. Not that he was dirty or untidy. His uniform was always pressed, his shirts changed every day. His fine, dark brown hair was short and neat underneath his cap. But this was the work of others - dry cleaners, laundries, barbers. He put armour on each morning, with no more thought than he gave to brushing his teeth.

This lack of definition in his masculinity, his maleness - when Anthea thought it over, she was unable to hit on the right word - made her conscious, along with her irritation that it should be so, of a vagueness, an amorphousness, in their dealings with each other. The image she came up with was walking on a waterbed, but this was inaccurate and irritated her as well. Again she was reminded that she would have laughed, and her cross mood would have faded, if she'd had a friend to share it with.

Anthea was fond of summing people up, and fancied she was good at it. She would have liked to dismiss Chris Blackie as an old fuddy-duddy, or a closet gay; but found she couldn't, quite. She was conscious of a quick defensiveness when it came to men, and was not above donning her own uniform as a suit of armour, an action - not that she could *choose* to leave it off when she was on duty - that sometimes provoked them further. She'd been trained to confront and handle aggression in many forms, and was proud of this training and acquired skill. She was sensible enough not to seek to provoke anyone, man or woman, in the course of her work; but there was something else, an innate timidity perhaps, or else simple inexperience, which she was scarcely aware of, and preferred not to acknowledge. It showed itself in her attraction to forceful men with definite ideas, men who knew what they were about as men.

That windy morning, sitting on her park bench, nursing her bad mood, Anthea was prepared to dismiss her boss, kneeling in his flower beds on a rubber mat, in his dark brown gardening gloves and track pants, old white shirt and heavy cotton hat. She dismissed the senior constable's hobby and his means of pursuing it. It embarrassed her to receive compliments about his roses, in the chemists or the greengrocers, delivered as though she could not be anything but grateful; almost as though she'd had a hand in growing the prize specimens herself.

She ached with embarrassment as she imagined accepting his offers of beans, carrots and tomatoes, as though there was no question that she'd stay on through the summer. She'd learnt from the woman in the sandwich bar where she bought her lunch that Chris lived in a fisherman's cottage next to the boat harbour, the same house he'd been born in, where he'd nursed his mother until her death from breast cancer. Anthea had nodded as though she already knew this, though the shrewd look the woman gave her indicated that she saw through the pretence. One point of the story was that the house was on a tiny block, front and back yards no more than pocket-sized.

'Of course he grows what he can,' the woman had said, as though to teach her a lesson.

Anthea's phone rang, startling her. She hoped, as always, for Graeme. But it was Chris, with some twaddle about a missing camel.

THREE

'The lock's broken!' cried Julie Beshervase. 'Who'd do such a thing?'

Chris Blackie, who'd brought Julie to the station and was questioning her while Anthea took notes, asked when she'd last seen Riza.

'Last night. Evening. Getting dark. Who's taken him? Where is he?'

'Calm down, Ms Beshervase, we'll get your camel back. He's too big to hide.'

'That paddock is deserted! No one ever goes there, except me and mad Camilla Renfrew. It must have been her!'

Frank Erwin met them at the paddock he rented to Julie, looking, Chris thought, as though he wished camels had never been invented.

Chris wore gloves to remove the broken lock and chain.

'They must have come in a horse float,' Frank said. 'See these tyre marks? Two together either side.'

'Right,' Chris said. 'I'll look into that.'

'Are you going to question that witch-woman?' Julie demanded.

'If you want to help, Ms Beshervase, start by asking round the village. If a horse float was used to steal your camel, someone will have seen it.'

From the look on Camilla's face she'd forgotten what a horse float was. Chris sighed. He might have known that it would be like this. He'd had to wait outside her house for twenty minutes before she appeared on the dunes path, wearing a ridiculous hat and looking like a scarecrow.

When he'd instructed Anthea to begin a door-to-door, she'd looked mutinous and pressed her lips together.

Chris sighed again. Camilla approached him with a desperate expression.

'How often do you go to the paddock, Mrs Renfrew?'

'At what times?'

'Who do you see there?'

Camilla shook her head from side to side. Spittle flew from her mouth and Chris, embarrassed, looked away.

'Mrs Renfrew, can you hear me? When did you last see Riza?'

Camilla held up her hand to indicate that he should wait. She disappeared inside the house and came back a moment later, carrying a notebook and pencil.

'What's happened?' she wrote, and underlined it twice.

'Riza's missing. Looks like he's been stolen.'

Chris continued asking questions while Camilla wrote. When she'd finished, she handed over her notebook.

1. I was at the paddock yesterday. 2. I saw Riza. 3. I heard a woman scream.

Aware that his own nervous tension was making her worse, Chris took a deep breath and said, 'When was that, Mrs Renfrew?'

Camilla took her notebook back and wrote, *in the summer.*

Chris thought it would be better to come back after she'd had a chance to calm down.

Of course, it didn't have to be a horse float, he reminded himself as he got into his car. The camel could have been led away. But then, where were its footprints? Once on the road, they wouldn't show. But the same damp earth that had recorded the tyre marks Frank had pointed out would surely have held prints of those large, gentle feet.

Chris felt sure that the thief was someone local and the motive personal. He made a mental note to ask Julie if Riza was insured, and how much he was worth. It couldn't have been easy to catch Riza and lead him into a horse float. The Erwin's farmhouse was on the other side of the hill. Lights might have frightened the young camel, unless of course he'd known the person and gone willingly.

Chris's reaction, as he approached Julie Beshervase's house, was that it was far too big for a woman on her own. The house looked deserted, curtains drawn and front garden neglected. Chris parked a short distance from the overgrown driveway and paused for a few moments, wondering how Julie occupied herself when she was not with Riza.

'Have you found him?'

It was clear that Julie had run to the door.

'I'm afraid not. May I come in, please?'

Chris followed Julie down a dark corridor. She didn't ask him to sit down, but he did so anyway, on a chair next to large windows facing west, overlooking the back yard. The windows were dirty, but at least the curtains were pulled back.

'I'm sorry about Riza, Ms Beshervase. Was he entirely yours?'

'You mean, did I own him, had I paid for him, do I have a receipt to prove it? Yes!'

Julie lowered herself onto the edge of a straight-backed chair. Chris thought it odd that she should be so tense and ready to run in her own house.

'Camilla Renfrew took him,' she said.

'Why?'

'Because she's nuts.'

Chris decided to ignore this. 'Renting the paddock from Frank Erwin - how did that come about?'

Julie said she'd heard that the farmer made a bit of money out of horse agistment. She'd rung up and inquired. The rent had not been impossible. The situation was good, and there was water.

'How did Riza get here?'

'In a horse trailer. The man who sold him lent it to me.'

Chris asked for contact details.

'You don't think *he* stole Riza, do you?'

'I'd rather keep an open mind at present. Did Riza settle in well?'

'Perfectly.'

'What about Mr Erwin? Were there any problems there?'

'Why should there be problems? I've always paid on time.'

'Did Mr Erwin ever help you out with transport? Did Riza ever need to be taken to the vet, for instance?'

'You mean in Frank's horse float? It's falling to bits.'

'So Riza's never needed to be taken anywhere?'

'Not since I got him. He's a perfectly healthy young camel.'

'Is he insured?'

'No,' said Julie. 'I couldn't afford insurance.'

Her voice caught and she bit her lip.

When Chris asked how much the camel had cost, Julie said, 'Five hundred dollars', and explained that, after his mother had rejected him, Riza had been sent to a horse stud up along the Murray, but that none amongst the small herd of camels there had wanted to have anything to do with him.

Chris wrote down the name of the stud, then asked Julie where she'd got the money

Julie bit her lip again and looked annoyed. 'My brother lent it to me. My older brother. And in case you're about to ask, no, I couldn't afford to rent this house on the open market. It belongs to friends of my brother's. They've gone to France and Italy.'

'Do you train camels for a living?'

'Not much of a living, obviously, but you could say that.'

Chris went on asking questions in a mild, uninflected voice; how Julie had found out about Riza in the first place, who had watched them together besides Camilla, whether she'd seen anyone suspicious hanging round the paddock. He left when he thought he'd got as much as he was going to get from her, for the time being at least.

Julie had begun that morning by eating a small bowl of cereal. She'd put an apple and banana in her backpack along with the water bottle that she always carried. She'd planned to introduce Riza to the halter. She'd found one on eBay, where she'd also bought the saddle with the mirrors and the fringes, now sitting on two chairs in front of her living-room windows. Sometimes she liked to take it to the paddock with her; it seemed to hold a kind of promise for the future, and it made her happy to watch the sunlight reflected off the mirrors. On these days she walked, carrying the saddle. But that morning was cloudy, and she'd decided to leave it behind.

She'd strapped the halter onto the back of her bike, turning her head, as she wheeled it down the driveway, for a last look at the house. Riding to the paddock, avoiding a patch of sand, she'd reminded herself that she ought to get a job. Her inquiries, since she arrived in Queenscliff, had drawn the response that there were waiting lists for the few casual jobs available. Disagreeable reflections on the state of her finances sank as she breasted the last rise. She had to puff up the rise; but liked forcing herself, liked the warmth flowing through her legs and back.

She had not been able to believe that the paddock was empty. She'd run round and round it, calling Riza's name.

When Julie thought of Camilla Renfrew, anger made sharp red points in front of her eyes. It was a ruse, a trick, that not speaking thing. It was like the child who covers her eyes with her hands and imagines herself to be invisible. The old witch had the locals wrapped around her little finger, but she'd done an evil thing.

Camilla wasn't considered mad because she was a local, having lived in the town all her life; whereas she, Julie, was a newcomer, and engaged in what she was well aware some of the locals described as mad behaviour. 'What on earth's she training a camel for?' 'We've got plenty of sand, but we don't need camels to get round on it.' 'Pretty beast. Maybe she'd going to sell him to a circus.' These were some of the comments that Julie half-heard, as she turned away with her litre of milk or half kilo of apples from the small supermarket.

'Bit eccentric, but she's harmless,' was how Frank had described Camilla, when Julie had asked if he might persuade the old woman to stay away. She hadn't liked Frank's smarminess when he'd rolled up in his ute, the excitement in his eyes when he'd been told that Riza was missing.

FOUR

Anthea discovered that, almost without exception, the inhabitants of Queenscliff had been indoors watching television the night before. The half dozen who'd ventured to the pub had been glued to the TV too. It seemed to Anthea that she was making inquiries on the flimsiest of evidence. She thought it most likely that Camilla Renfrew had taken the camel, and that it was a waste of her time and Chris's to be looking for it.

It didn't make Anthea feel any better that the people she questioned looked at her as though *she* was crazy. They kept peering over her shoulder, as though expecting Chris to turn up any second and rescue them from the embarrassment his offsider was causing.

The chemist laughed when she told him. 'Sounds like somebody's idea of a joke.'

Anthea wanted to agree, to justify herself. 'Just find out about the horse float,' Chris had said. Well, no one had seen a horse float, especially not one that had been used to make a camel disappear.

Anthea stood on the footpath while her sandwiches were being made, not wanting to talk to anybody else. She didn't want the smirking girl behind the counter asking if she'd found her camel yet.

The sandwiches were good and Anthea was hungry. She took them to the bench in the park she was beginning to think of as hers, and stared out across the channel. A container ship was slogging its way towards Melbourne, while the small orange pilot boat sat on the horizon waiting for another one. The sea was flat, the trees on the headland barely touched by wind.

Why couldn't Graeme phone? Now would be a perfect time.

Anthea considered going home for the afternoon, saying she was sick. But that would look pathetic. She guessed that Chris had little tolerance for falsehood or deception, white lies that other superiors might be prepared to overlook. Yet it was thoughts of home that drew her, as she rested her eyes on the grey-blue horizon, the bay calmer than it had been since she'd arrived in this poor excuse for a seaside resort.

Home, for the present, was a one-bedroom flat overlooking Swan Bay. She hadn't unpacked her books or CDs, and half her kitchen utensils sat in boxes alongside them - that was how temporary she'd been hoping this period in the wilderness to be.

Anthea admitted, scrunching up her sandwich wrapping, that her morale would improve if she unpacked. Her tiny living room, with a kitchen alcove at one end, wouldn't feel so cramped. Her bedroom was just big enough to hold a double bed, and she was sick of climbing over boxes.

Up till now, it had seemed to Anthea that the only good thing about her flat was the view over the bay. When her landlord told her how lucky she'd been - a tenant who'd already paid the bond having pulled out at the last minute - she'd tried to look and sound appreciative, instead of showing the disbelief she'd felt. People actually *wanted* to live here? They *competed* with each other to claim such an address? But today it was unpacking those boxes that attracted, rather than the prospect of going back to work, returning to Chris Blackie and his one-man show.

Chris filled in some background over mugs of tea which they drank sitting on cane chairs on the station's back veranda.

'I've known Camilla all my life,' he told Anthea, expecting to see a downturn of ill-concealed mockery around her mouth, yet disappointed when he did so. 'She brought her son up by herself after her husband died. Always kept him clean and well-dressed. And her house is a palace of cleanliness compared to the mess that Beshervase girl's living in.'

Anthea warmed her hands around her mug and made an effort. 'I wonder what the owners will say.'

'She'll clean it up. Or I should say she'll intend to. She'll leave it too long and then get in a panic.'

Anthea thought of Graeme and the lists he left for his cleaning lady who came every Tuesday. She felt a moment's sharp envy for this woman who could visit Graeme's flat, who could come and go.

'That trouble with Camilla's voice - ' Chris was saying - 'I couldn't tell you when it started. It's not as though I've been keeping tabs on her.'

'What about the son?'

'It'd be worth having a word to him. He's married, or at least he was. I've never met his wife.'

Chris noted the change in Anthea's expression. It occurred to him that she might be having an affair with a married man.

He breathed out heavily when she left the veranda, then went inside to his computer, where he busied himself looking up Wallington Park stud. He pictured the Murray River with its flood plain and rich, absorbent soil.

Camilla drank water standing at her kitchen sink, but it did nothing to ease the burning in her throat. Riza had been stolen. Perhaps he was dead.

She saw the white face and heard the scream again, then rushed to the lavatory.

Camilla gagged and clutched cold porcelain to stop herself from falling forward, re-living those minutes underneath the lighthouse.

She steadied herself, and returned to her living-room.

Camilla sat in a chair and waited for Chris Blackie to come back, thinking of old Brian Laidlaw scavenging along the tide line, and how it was too late to speak the simple words of greeting. She smelt the fear of nocturnal creatures who had no defence against feral cats and foxes. So quick and unmarked the change from life to death, the small animal swallowed in a morsel, or, mortally wounded, scurrying away to die.

She remembered picking grass and holding it out on the flat of her hand, Riza drawing back his thick lips, the feeling ticklish and delightful.

His trainer never used the gate, lifting her leg, instead, to slip between the fence wires. In the next paddock, a tree gave good shade, half way up a rise, beside a dam. Perhaps the lock on the gate had been faulty and no one had noticed. Riza might have opened it himself.

Camilla recalled the playground in the small country school where she'd been a teacher's aid the year Chris had started. He'd been a skinny boy, though tall for his age, a quiet boy who watched and listened, rather than filling up the space around him with his own noise, a boy whose scuffed black shoes, outgrown felty jumpers and unironed shirts heralded a neglect that marked him out for teasing.

Camilla's mother would never have sent her off to school without a freshly ironed ribbon in her hair. Her own opinion had been that ribbons made her look a fool. She'd watched the new kid from her position as playground supervisor, that first hot summer of his formal education. Several times she'd had to break up fights. Once, a sixth-grader had to be enlisted to take Chris home with a nose that refused to stop bleeding. By mid-autumn the fights had stopped and Chris was left alone.

What was the good of a weak and silent witness?

It began to rain. Camilla opened the curtains and looked out over her front garden. Rainwater filled the gutters and splashed down the tea-tree. She stood at her front door. After the closed-up air of inside, the trees smelt wonderfully fresh.

Memories tripped her up like tea-tree roots. She wondered if that woman had stumbled off the path. She'd been wearing a dark overcoat, unusual for summer, even in the fog. Camilla knew it was a trick of memory that shapes appeared just when you were about to put your foot down, and felt right then the immense gap between a person's raised shoe and the waiting earth.

It was her experience that a bad day generally got worse. Had she wished, she could have measured the progress of her affliction in mornings that began with boredom, or with indigestion.

The doorbell rang. Chris Blackie stood on the porch, his uniform covered in tiny drops of moisture.

Camilla invited him in. He sat on the very edge of a chair.

'Did you take the camel, Mrs Renfrew?'

Camilla shook her head, but a doubt crept back, the sensation of tree roots rising up to meet her.

'What time did you leave the paddock?'

'About six,' Camilla wrote in her notebook.

'And the camel was there then?'

Of course he was. She nodded.

Chris went on asking questions, keeping his voice and his expression level, and Camilla tried to answer them in writing.

Chris read patiently, then cleared his throat and said, 'Mrs Renfrew, I'd like you to do me a drawing. What if I leave you to it, and come back in half an hour?'

Chris thought he would spend the time walking through the sandhills - not that he believed Riza had taken himself up there, or that whoever had stolen him had let him go. If that had been the case, someone would have found him by now.

Still, he looked for hoof prints, glad there was nobody to laugh at him for doing so. He shaded his eyes and squinted at a dark object, half covered in sand, then began to walk towards it. He should have been wearing sunglasses to protect his eyes, but he never thought of things like that.

It was a woman's coat, black, or at least it had been. Chris started to shake the sand out, then gave up. He stood with his back to the wind, and asked himself if it was possible that whoever had stolen Riza had been wearing such a garment, at the same time telling himself not to be a fool. The coat had been exposed, out in the weather, for months. Anthea wrinkled her nose when Chris walked into the station with the coat. She listened to his account of finding it, wondering what role she'd be expected to play in tracking down the owner. If it had been left up to her, she would have thrown the filthy garment in the bin.

But she took another look as Chris was folding the coat into a plastic bag. It would once have been expensive.

Anthea surprised herself by holding out her hand for Chris to stop, while she looked for a label. It was faded but legible, and carried the name of a fashionable designer. She became aware that Chris was letting her take her time, and that he seemed quite comfortable waiting in silence.

She turned the label over, then took the coat to the window, the better to read the name on the other side.

'Margaret Benton. Isn't that the woman who went missing up along the Murray?'

Chris stared at his assistant, then gave a brief nod. He checked the label for himself, then rang Swan Hill police station.

They made tea together and took it out to the back veranda. The air between them felt lighter than it had since Anthea had come to Queenscliff.

An hour later the phone rang. It was Swan Hill ringing back, asking for the coat.

Chris hung up. His temples were throbbing and his face was flushed. For some reason, he didn't want Anthea to see this, but he knew she had.

Anthea went over to the window and stared out at the lavender and rose bushes.

'What about that camel?' she asked, swinging round to face her boss. 'Maybe he tromped all over it. Are you going to say in your report that we're investigating the theft of a dromedary?'

Chris caught the glitter in her eye. He laughed in spite of himself and said, 'Jesus love us.'

Anthea laughed too. 'Will I ring for the courier?'

'I will,' Chris said, reaching for the phone again.

When they'd told him they were sending him a woman, Chris had felt both pleased and nervous. It would make a change. His last junior constable, while they'd gotten along all right on the surface, underneath they'd never warmed to each other. The times they'd had a beer together after work Chris could number on the fingers of one hand.

He wouldn't have minded running the station solo. He knew practically everybody in the town, and they knew him. For two months of the summer, there was more than enough work for one man, most of it late at night when the drunks got belligerent. But the rest of the year, no. And Anthea had come looking for drama. He'd seen it in her eyes the minute she walked in. Both the anticipation and the almost instantaneous disappointment had been there. Trouble with the boyfriend. He'd guessed that too. Boring or not, Queenscliff was *his* backwater, and he wanted it to stay quiet. He wanted to go on managing the town his way.

Yet he was conscious of a sharp tug of excitement. What if the coat turned out to be important? He thought how Anthea had lifted it to the light. It hadn't occurred to him to turn the label over. He was aware of his assistant's grace and neatness, the clean lines of her silhouette, holding the mucky coat in her arms. Excitement caught him, a swell beneath the wave's head, unnoticed till it hit you hard.

He'd forgotten all about Camilla Renfrew; he'd told her he'd be back in half an hour.

FIVE

Dusk found Anthea by the boat harbour, vaguely embarrassed to be seen wandering about on her own. As the senior officer, it would have been a courtesy for Chris to have invited her over for a meal. There was propriety, of course; but she was sure that Chris did not think of her as a woman. As for herself, God help her when she became that desperate. He hadn't mentioned his address, but most likely assumed that she already knew it.

Anthea guessed that her superior's reserve had developed over many years, part of his armour - though it could easily have gone the other way. He could as easily have become loud, crude and aggressive, and have got away with it - a small fish in an even smaller pond. She saw Chris, at that moment, as a man who kept his own counsel, a man with private tastes and inclinations hidden behind an exterior developed to suit the job. She also sensed that there was some kind of war going on inside him, and knew it had to do with more than a black coat with the name of a missing woman underneath the label.

The house, when she found it, surprised her by its smallness. It was built right on the street, with no front yard at all. There were no lights on, at the front at least.

Anthea's embarrassment left her as she continued on to the harbour, breathing in the strong smells of fish and seaweed. No one was about and she walked up and down the jetty several times, reading the names on fishing boats and watching the ebb tide, swift, green and muscular, flowing with such strength it seemed to her that it would not stop until it reached Tasmania.

Anthea had never spent time around the Melbourne docks and regretted this now in a mild, nostalgic way, lacking precise memories in which to anchor her nostalgia. One study assignment had involved securing an area of dockland, another working with customs to track down a shipment of heroin in a container. She recalled how keen she'd been to get good marks in her first year, before she met Graeme, and how these assignments now seemed impractical and overly ambitious.

The harbour was attractive in its way. Anthea could imagine Graeme there, with herself as guide, showing him the sights. Graeme would take an interest in the rigging of the yachts. Perhaps she should learn the names of different pieces of equipment. Could these be the kinds of facts he would expect her to pick up? Graeme would ask confident questions of the fishermen, about the 'take' and what was 'running'. The conversation would put him in a good mood. They would buy the freshest whiting, which she would cook to perfection.

Anthea paused in her wandering, having come to a halt also in this imagined scene. Would she point out Chris's house? She'd noticed that the outside had recently been painted, and was sure that Chris would have done the job himself. She foresaw the precise way in which Graeme would turn up his nose, a delicate widening of the nostrils, and, in profile, a lifting of his chin away from what held no aesthetic interest. Through the open door of a tiny pale blue house, she glimpsed a gleaming dark wood passage. At the front was a carefully constructed arch for climbing roses, starting from a pocket-sized square of soil.

On the whole, she did not think she would walk Graeme past Chris Blackie's house. Enough that he would be sure to laugh at the lavender and roses, the sign with the big ER and royal crown next to the station door. Enough that it was already an occasion for behind-hand smiles that she'd chosen a career in the police force. 'My girlfriend's a copper.' How often had she forced a smile in return?

Anthea rounded a corner and came upon another section of the harbour, with huge, hangar-like buildings right on the edge of the water. Two orange boats were moored side by side, bucking against the tide. They were long-prowed, small for the task she'd seen them performing, carrying pilots in and out through the Rip, pilots whose job it was to guide container ships and ocean liners through the narrow channel.

Anthea walked on, Graeme and his jokes forgotten. Serious work was done here, by these modest orange arrows and their crews, work without which trading in and out of Melbourne could not function. She felt glad that the headquarters was situated in Queenscliff. She wondered when, and under what circumstances, the pilot service called on the police. She thought of Chris labouring away in the station garden, head down and back to the ocean, a deliberate turning away. She recalled his expression when she'd mentioned her walks along the cliff top, how his reaction, a swift closing down and turning inward, had seemed a barely conscious act of self-protection. She wondered if there'd been something offensive in what she'd said, and remembered how her one question about swimming had been met with a moment's silence, then the quiet reply that nowhere was completely safe. At the time, she'd passed this off as further evidence that he was a fussy old maid.

Gradually, as Camilla waited, her drawing took shape and filled out. There was the paddock with the fence around it, the Moonah, seaward side, where a fat lip of dune gave shelter from the southerlies. Camilla did not attempt to draw herself, only to pencil in an arrow at the place where she'd often stood and watched.

She drew the young camel as well as she could, sending out a silent apology for the clumsy figure; then tackled other, human ones. Her fingers worked the pencil, strove to make the lines true. She stuck her tongue out, as a child might, that useless tongue whose ordinary work was forfeit.

Camilla decided to include all the people she'd seen at the paddock since Riza had made his home there: Julie, then Frank Erwin and his wife Cynthia; Frank's son Jim, who'd stayed for a week with his wife and their baby; Brian Laidlaw riding past on his bike.

Cars passed, but mostly at a distance, on the main road. Few ventured along the dirt road, for the simple reason that it led nowhere except to a walking track through the sandhills. From time to time cars did come down it, though the sign said clearly, No Through Road.

They turned at the end, where there was just enough room to do so. Of course, the driver and passengers couldn't always be seen clearly; sometimes not at all.

Then there were kids - kids used the dirt road and the dunes in ways that adults never did. They kicked up dust with their bikes. They made cubby holes and hideaways. Four boys in high school uniform had propped their bikes against the fence one afternoon and stared at Riza as though they'd never seen a camel. They'd been back next day, whooping and laughing, kidding one another.

Camilla completed her drawing and leant back in her chair, thinking of the dunes whose movement was governed by the wind and their own weight. As a child, she'd believed they crept forward in the night, on feet the size of football fields. She enjoyed the steep incline, wind that met her headlong, catch of moon and starlight at the tops of waves. She enjoyed walking at night. She wondered if she went that way now, in the darkness, she would hear the scream again.

Camilla missed Riza terribly, the beauty that was in his every step. No drawing of hers could come close to expressing that. The fact that an old woman of no account, whom children taunted and adults dismissed as mad, had been able to feast each day on beauty - now that had been something. She pictured the baby fluff and softness, those legs of a sweet, comical length. She almost tore up her drawing in frustration. Where was Chris Blackie? What was keeping him?

She decided to get out of the house, to calm herself by walking.

It seemed important to choose the right hat.

Camilla fetched one from the hall cupboard. She supposed it was the kind once worn for tennis, though she'd never enjoyed the game. Proficiency at sports had eluded her, like so much else. But youthful losses were vague now, and that was a blessing. The memory of missed opportunities had become so slippery that she no longer felt the need to grapple with it, to ask again whether such-and-such a skill had ever been within her grasp. Still, she stared at the old white hat with its rust-coloured brim and put it on with a sense of reliving some kind of athletic occasion.

The phone rang. It was Simon.

'Is that you, Mum?'

Camilla wondered who else it could be, and why her son insisted on phoning when he knew she hated it.

'How are you, Mum? Is everything okay?'

Camilla nodded at the phone. She put a hand up to adjust her hat and realised with shame that she was crying.

Simon said she shouldn't live alone. It was not the first time he had said this. He told her he was sending her some brochures in a querulous, insistent voice.

Camilla put the phone down, asking herself when things had begun to go wrong between herself and her son, if she could mark the point where a hostile young man had emerged from the chrysalis of childhood. She knew that Simon blamed her for his father's death, still blamed her, with the unforgiving grief of a ten-year-old boy. And wasn't this the point, that blame and grief had remained locked in him, unchanged? Any attempt to talk about it while he was growing up had been met with hostility.

Alan Renfrew had died of a heart attack at the age of thirty-eight. His heart had been weak, but nobody had known that until it was too late. The day before the heart attack, they'd argued. Alan had been a cold, punitive and jealous husband, and had punished her for failing to produce more sons. After eleven years of marriage, she had hated him. Simon had loved his father. Father and son had loved one another.

Camilla shrank from the idea of selling the house she'd been born in; but perhaps she should. Perhaps she should give in.

She jammed her hat firmly on her head and closed the door behind her. Already she felt guilty for hanging up on Simon. Nervous of giving offence, she had always shied away from the question of why Simon's wife had left him after they'd been married for only two years. Now any matter between mother and son was best broached in writing. The failure of Simon's marriage was a subject that remained firmly closed.

SIX

One photograph of Margaret Benton showed a dark-haired woman in her middle forties staring into the wind and clutching the collar of a black coat with her left hand. Wedding and engagement rings caught the light, but she wasn't smiling, and the mood of the picture was sombre.

Anthea stood beside Chris in the clear morning light. He felt her involuntary shiver. She'd downloaded photographs of the missing woman from the internet, and they'd pinned them up. They'd photographed the coat Chris had found before delivering it to the courier and were sure that it was the same.

Margaret Benton had been missing for eight months. Until her disappearance, she'd lived with her husband, Jack, on an orchard on the outskirts of Swan Hill, within walking distance of the Murray.

'Have you found him?' Julie Beshervase demanded.

'We're working on it,' Chris said mildly.

He took out Camilla's drawing and handed it across. Julie threw it on the floor. 'I don't believe this!'

Chris picked the drawing up and pointed. 'These boys, do you recognise them?'

Julie made a noise in her throat that was somewhere between a growl and a sob, but she did condescend to look.

'I think this one's parents run the caravan park,' she said.

After Chris left, Julie rang her brother, Clive, to tell him about Riza's disappearance. She'd left messages the day before, which he had not returned.

'You'll find him, Sis, don't worry. He can't have gone far.'

Julie began to explain about the fences and the gate, how Riza wasn't all that big. She could tell her brother was only pretending to listen. She'd cried on his shoulder too often, and this was the result -

he made what to him were appropriately sympathetic noises, while his attention was elsewhere. He said the Talbots were having a good time, and that he'd had a postcard from Montpellier. He told her about a soccer match his son had starred in. When Julie felt a scream rising in her throat, she said a quick goodbye.

When Chris spoke to Clive on the phone, he confirmed what Julie had told him, that it was friends of his who owned the house.

'They must be well off.'

Clive said he'd lent his sister the money to buy Riza and that she would pay him back when she could.

'What does Julie live on?'

The answer was a disability pension. She'd had some 'troubles in the past'.

'So your sister is in considerable debt.'

'It doesn't bother her. She's never had much money.'

'Or a proper job?'

'Look, when Julie found Riza and decided to buy him, she was living in a horrible boarding house in Melbourne, with other, other - '

'Troubled young people?'

'I was happy to help out.'

Chris told himself that he could check with Centrelink, but he believed that Clive was telling the truth. He wondered if Julie had ever lifted a finger to help her brother, and surprised himself by the bitterness of this reaction

Still, he suggested that Julie could do with a visit. There was a short silence before Clive said that he would see about it, but he had a young family, he lived in Albury and worked long hours.

Chris decided to wait until after school before tackling Ben McIntyre and his friends.

He needed time to think. Normally, he'd do a bit of gardening as an aid to thought, get the old blood circulating. Now he felt embarrassed, knowing what his assistant thought of his hobby, though he disliked the word, and would not, himself, have used it. More than once she'd come across him on his hands and knees and stood there like some princess waiting for him to stand up and address her respectfully. Now he was working himself up into a lather, all because he felt self-conscious getting out his gardening gloves and trowel. And there was that untidy area up the back that he'd been meaning to get to for weeks.

Anthea came upon Chris with his wheelbarrow full of weeds, and the sweat of a warmer than expected morning slipping along his hairline into his cotton hat.

She'd taken photographs of Margaret Benton up and down the main street, but nobody recognised her, or admitted to it if they did. He knew he should have taken the photographs himself, but he wanted to involve his assistant, who after all had been the one to find the name.

Experience had taught Chris that people noticed more than they thought they did; but that while news of a certain kind might travel like lightning round the village, other kinds needed more time to reach him. Especially this was the case if one of the locals looked like getting into trouble. Chris - otherwise a local himself, otherwise perfectly trustworthy and acceptable - might find himself suddenly dropped from the grapevine, swinging free of the gossip he relied on to anticipate trouble.

It was possible that something of the kind was happening with regard to Margaret Benton. On the other hand, it was possible that she'd never been near Queenscliff, that her coat had got into the sandhills by some other means. Chris had already rung Swan Hill that morning and been told that they were handling it. There was no further news.

There was that scream too, that Camilla had heard. When he'd tried to ask her about it, she'd become so agitated that he'd let it go.

Anthea was standing with her arms crossed, staring at the wheelbarrow and frowning, waiting for him to take the initiative, tell her what their next move should be.

Chris would have scoffed at the idea that a young snip of a thing could embarrass him, that he'd be knotting inside himself with the desire to keep up an appearance of authority.

He indicated that she should follow him and stomped inside.

Anthea stared at her boss's departing back, conscious that he was heading for some kind of humiliation. The thought made her angry and frustrated. She suspected at least one of the shopkeepers of lying to her, and had been on the point of losing her patience back there, in the main street.

Chris's attitude to women bordered on the fearful. He was reluctant to inflame Julie Beshervase and he pussy-footed round Camilla Renfrew. Anthea wondered where that left her. Pursuing a conversation with a khaki backside?

Chris made a list of everyone in the town and surrounding farms who owned a horse trailer. There were seventeen, and he began interviewing them systematically. He took it for granted that all of them knew about Riza and Frank Erwin's rental arrangement. Not for the first time, it occurred to him that the target of the theft might have been Erwin, not Julie Beshervase. He could spend time pondering who might want to embarrass or get back at Erwin once he'd made a short list.

He didn't want to judge his assistant prematurely, and was aware that he might have done a lot worse. If and when Anthea left - it was surely a matter of when, not if - they'd probably send him a young man.

Chris was grateful that Anthea didn't expect him to entertain her after work. But she'd grown up in a city, and was used to working at a city's pace. On top of that, she made the mistake of assuming that the surface of a person, or a thing for that matter, told you what they were like inside.

Chris listened to what was, and wasn't, being said, crossed some names off his list and put question marks alongside others, wrote notes between them and in the margins of his notebook.

He took a mug of tea out to the back veranda, avoiding the tiny triangle of sea just visible between the trees, while he mulled over what this or that one of his horse-owning acquaintances had been doing on the night Riza disappeared. He didn't rule out any of them. His crosses and question marks had been made in pencil, and he kept his rubber handy.

He went back indoors, phoned Frank Erwin, and told him he was coming over.

Though Chris greeted the farmer politely, Frank made it clear that he was affronted. His daughter's horse had long since been sold, but Chris knew the trailer would sit there until either it fell apart, or Frank pulled it apart and used the bits for something that was even further gone.

'I pointed out the bloody tyre tracks. And I'm renting my paddock to that hippy, aren't I? She's paying cash in hand.'

'It's routine, Frank. I have to cross you off my list.'

'But - '

'Come on now. Let's get it over with.'

The horse float looked as though it hadn't left the shed in years. The paint was practically all gone. The aluminium was coming away from its seams. Frank stood just behind Chris while he examined it, making noises of disgust when Chris measured the width of the tyres, two close together on each side. The tension emanating from the farmer might have been caused by guilt, but might equally have been the result of this unexpected intrusion, these suspicions voiced by a policeman whom he'd thought of as a friend.

Dirt embedded in the tyre treads ought to have been old and dry. It wasn't.

Chris noticed a new padlock on the door. 'I'll need to see inside,' he said.

'Why, in God's name?'

'Just get me the key, Frank. Please.'

There was nothing to show that the float had recently been used to transport any animal, let alone a stolen camel. But the hackles were up on Chris's neck as he peered around an empty and dilapidated interior. The corners were thick with dust and old brown horse hairs, a few amongst them of the palest yellow-white.

Chris pulled some latex gloves out of his pocket and a small plastic bag, while Frank snorted behind him. He teased out the hairs and bagged them.

SEVEN

Anthea held up the small bag and studied the hairs inside it, while Chris typed a report. Typing was not his strong suit, but it would have embarrassed him to ask Anthea to do all his typing for him. He told himself that the report could be a short one, simply stating where he'd found the hairs and asking what species of animal they'd come from.

When Anthea asked what Frank Erwin had said, Chris paused with his hands above the keyboard and looked at her along his shoulder.

'If we found the beast in Frank's living-room, he'd deny knowing how it got there.'

'But why?'

'Why would he deny it, or why would he pinch Julie Beshervase's camel?'

'Both,' said Anthea, raising a neat eyebrow, 'but the first one first.'

'Actually, I think the second answer does for both. The Erwins have owned and farmed that land for three generations. Frank may have rented out the paddock, but in every way he regards it as his. If the Beshervase girl did something to annoy him - '

'Did she?'

'I don't know.' Chris was heartened when he paused again, and felt that Anthea was listening. 'And Julie won't admit it either,' he continued, 'not if it was something she's ashamed of. It'll need looking into once we've got these confirmed.'

He flicked a finger at the plastic bag.

'Julie Beshervase doesn't seem the type - ' Anthea ventured.

'To hold back? I agree.'

Chris noted the way his assistant's mouth pulled in when she wasn't speaking, as though there was too much that she needed and was reluctant to say

'I'd like you to talk to Julie. Don't mention the hairs or the trailer.

Just ask her what she thinks of Frank, how they've been getting on, that kind of thing.'

Anthea felt a twinge of self-importance as she talked to the courier and arranged for the pick-up, imagining, as she put the phone down, that she was the one making the trip to Melbourne, that things between her and Graeme were so good he'd rearrange his morning's schedule to meet her for coffee, plan the weekend they would spend together. Melbourne was so close, only a couple of hours away. She thought that Graeme's rejection would have been easier to bear if she'd been sent to the opposite end of the state.

Anthea began by asking Julie about herself, where she'd grown up, where she'd learnt about camel training. She discovered that Julie was twenty-three and that she'd been born in the Northern Territory.

'My parents used to train animals for use in films. Once they had, rescued actually, a baby Bactrian. They gave her to me. I was fifteen, and so rebellious I ran away every second weekend.'

Julie's parents had died in a car crash, her younger brother too. 'They were hit by a road train. I should have been with them, but that was one of the weekends I was busy running away.'

Anthea said that she was sorry. Julie refused to meet her eye.

'That camel - her name was Greta, after Greta Garbo. She was my mother's favourite actress - I trained her myself. And she *did* work in the movies. She lived up to her namesake.'

'And your older brother?'

'He keeps an eye on me. Tell me this!' Julie turned on Anthea, pulling at her spiky hair. 'Riza was mine and now I've lost him. *Why do I feel so guilty?*'

Anthea boiled water and found tea bags, trying to ignore the cockroach droppings on the kitchen bench. She did not know the answer to Julie's question, but the fact that she wanted to find one, that she was thinking about it, surprised her. She'd marked Julie as a drama queen whose rhetorical questions weren't to be taken seriously.

She made the tea black and sweet, not wanting to think about the state of whatever milk might be in the fridge.

The two women sat facing one another, not directly, but at an angle which made all their glances sidelong.

'Frank's okay,' Julie said. 'It's not him who's been perving on Riza and me.'

'Who has?'

'You mean, apart from the witch? No one.'

When Anthea asked about the boys, Julie shrugged and said, 'Just kids mucking about after school.'

'Cynthia Erwin?'

'She hardly ever comes down to the paddock. She seems nice enough.'

They went on talking about the farmer, Julie rounding out her opinion that he was friendly without being interfering. Most men, she said, would have assumed they knew more about training camels than she did, even if they'd only ever seen them giving rides to kids. Which, by the way, was how she planned to earn a bit of money, once Riza was old enough.

Julie swallowed and dragged at her hair again. Anthea steered her back to Frank, who was proud of his son and daughter, and seemed especially proud of Jim, who lived along the Ocean Road and had just given him and Cynthia their first grandchild.

Anthea thought of the pale hairs, but decided not to mention them. She thought it would be nice to have a father figure, and wondered briefly why, since the death of her own parents, no candidate for this role had ever appeared on her horizon. She asked Julie what it was about Camilla that got under her skin.

'If it was an old man in a raincoat, he wouldn't be allowed to get away with it - but it's an old woman who's lived here all her life, so people say she's harmless. I bet she's rich as well. She could have taken Riza and hidden him somewhere, or paid someone to do it. Do you know how many properties she owns?'

Anthea did not want to admit that the answer to this was no.

'Do you have any enemies, Julie? Is there someone who wants to hurt you, or get back at you?'

'What, down here?'

Anthea reached in her pocket for the photograph of Margaret Benton.

'Anywhere,' she said.

EIGHT

Chris was waiting outside the high school when the bell went. Ben McIntyre did not seem surprised to find a policeman waiting for him, but Chris reflected that fourteen-year-old boys were better at hiding surprise than other reactions - fear, for instance, or excitement - which you could smell on them.

'A few quick questions, Ben. My car's over here.'

'I had nothin' to do with that stupid camel!'

'When were you last at the paddock?'

Ben looked as though he was about to make a run for it. 'It was nothin'!'

Chris took the sullen and monosyllabic teenager through each step, how someone - he couldn't recall who - suggested that they ride over and see if the camel lady was there. When she hadn't been, they'd tried to get Riza to come to the fence. Ian Lawrey had picked some grass and Zorba had some butterscotch in his pocket and he'd tried to give him that.

'What happened then?'

Ben sighed and looked down at his hands. 'Zorba wanted to ride him. Ian bet him fifty bucks he couldn't stay on for five minutes, but - '

'One of you *rode* the camel?'

'Zorba was gunna. I mean he was game. But then that old bat showed up.'

'Mrs Renfrew? What did you do then?'

'We left.'

'All together?'

'Yeah.'

'And never went back to give Zorba a chance to win his bet?'

'The camel got nicked, didn't it?'

'And you swear you had nothing to do with that?'

'I swear to God,' Ben said, and clasped his hands.

Chris let the boy's last word hang in the air for a few seconds before remarking, 'Fifty dollars is a lot of money.'

'Not for Zorb. His parents are rolling in it.'

'What about Ian? Where would he have got the cash if he'd lost the bet?'

Ben shrugged.

'Who was the fourth boy?'

'Rasch,' Ben said reluctantly.

'Raschid Abouzeid?'

'Yeah.'

'The others gave him grass and butterscotch, and Zorba was prepared to ride him. What did you do?'

'I've gotta go now. Really.'

'All right, Ben. I'll have to talk to your friends, but I won't say I've spoken to you. I'll say I worked it out from the descriptions Mrs Renfrew gave me.'

'She can't talk!'

'You're right about that, but she draws a mean picture.'

Chris gave the boy half an hour's breathing space, during which time he made notes while the conversation was fresh in his mind.

He paused in the doorway of the caravan park office, nodding hello to Penny McIntyre, seeing that she was expecting him, and that she would take her son's side if and when sides needed to be taken. Chris respected Penny for this. He would have thought less of her if it had been otherwise.

'Come in, Chris,' she said. 'Ben's told me about your little chat.'

If there was a sting in the end of this, Chris chose to ignore it. He pulled a chair out from the wall and sat down.

Penny offered tea, returning with a tray covered with a small white cloth, and delivering what were clearly rehearsed lines. 'I imagine it's thirsty work, bailing up young lads on their way home from school.'

'I didn't bail him up, Penny.'

'Ben wouldn't hurt a fly.'

'I'm not saying he did.'

'What then?'

'It was most likely a bit of harmless mischief, up there at the paddock. But the timing - a group of boys messing around with the camel, then he disappears.'

'That's a coincidence.'

'What did Ben tell you about it?'

'Nothing. I mean nothing till today. He said they went to watch that girl trainer, but she wasn't there.'

'Did he tell you Ian Lawrey bet Zorba Kostandis fifty dollars that he couldn't stay on for five minutes?'

Penny chose not to answer straight away. After a few moments, she said carefully, 'Nobody rode the camel. If you had kids yourself, you'd understand.'

'If Zorba had won the bet, where do you think Ian would have got the money to pay him?'

Penny frowned. She knew the Lawreys as well as he did, how the mother's health was poor, how strict the father was, how their struggle to bring up four kids on a labourer's wage had been made immeasurably more difficult by Phil Lawrey's accident.

It was Chris's opinion that Ian would have stolen the money, and he knew that Penny thought so too.

He thanked her for the tea and said goodbye. He did not want to front up to Ian Lawrey's parents, much less Zorba's and Raschid's. The Greek family he knew: they'd lived in the town for longer than his own, arriving as fishermen in the mid 1800s, with branches quickly becoming established in local businesses. Zorba's grandfather had started a hardware chain. Many of the Kostandises had married Greeks and every New Year they had a big party in the park above the bay.

Raschid's family were recently arrived. Chris had been surprised when Ben had named him as one of the four. He hoped the other boys wouldn't take their punishment of Ben too far. But it wasn't to be helped. He had to talk to them.

The Kostandises lived in one of the town's most expensive streets, in a two-storey bluestone house overlooking the sea. It had been one of his mother's favourites. She'd often told him how she used to take him for walks in his pusher along that street, to look at the houses and gardens. These stories had embarrassed him, but during the year before she died, he'd often taken her back there; it was still her favourite walk. When she'd grown too weak for walking, he'd driven her in his car, and sat with his eyes half closed while she kept up a kind of monologue; listing plants, noting renovations.

No one answered his knock on the door and there were no cars in the driveway.

Ian Lawrey was out the front of his house, playing cricket with his younger brothers. He stopped as soon as he saw Chris pull up, and began to walk away, his red-gold hair sticking out at odd angles.

Three small boys watched while Chris caught up with Ian, who half turned and glanced back nervously. Chris understood that he was worried because his father was inside. Phil Lawrey had been off work since he fell off some scaffolding on a building site. A man with three broken ribs and a broken ankle must be getting pretty bored by now; and the man had a temper.

'We'll stay out here,' Chris said. 'Keep going with your game.'

Ian took the cricket ball from his smallest brother, who'd been holding it with both hands, as though entrusted with a treasure.

Once Ian had bowled, and a kaleidoscope of small legs had followed the ball, Chris asked, 'So whose idea was it to go to the camel paddock?'

'We never - '

'Now Ian, that won't do.'

Ian frowned, but had command of himself. 'It was mine,' he said.

'I must say I think the bet was a dumb idea.'

Ian pursed his lips together, getting ready for another denial.

'Where were you going to get the money if Zorba won?'

'From my savings.'

They caught each other's eyes, then Ian looked away.

'I'm going to find out what happened. You'll make it easier for yourself if you tell me now.'

Having delivered his warning, Chris gave Ian time to think, standing back while each of his brothers took a turn to bat. He noted how Ian placed the ball within their reach, and praised them when they hit it.

'Who went back to the paddock?' he asked when Ian took a break from bowling.

The boy couldn't keep his fingers still. Empty of the ball, they made for tufts of bronze hair.

'Zorb wanted his fifty bucks.'

'So you and Zorba went back to the paddock. When?'

'The next day. After school.'

'Did Zorba ride the camel?'

'That lady who owns him, she was there talking to Mr Erwin. As soon as we saw 'em, we got off our bikes. Zorb wanted to wait, but I said I couldn't. I didn't know how long they'd be. Mum expects me to mind my brothers after school.'

'So when was the next time?'

'What?'

'I don't expect Zorba gave up that easily.'

'The next day he couldn't go because of soccer training. The day after that we went, but the camel was gone.'

'Did you see anybody else at the paddock?'

'Only Mrs Renfrew the first time and the other lady and Mr Erwin the second.'

'Anybody else? Please think.'

Ian made a face as if to protest that he was doing that. One of his brothers ran up and asked him to bowl again.

'In a minute,' Chris said. He watched Ian carefully while he pulled out a photograph of Margaret Benton

'Have you ever seen this woman?'

'No! No, I never!' Ian cried, suddenly going pale.

His brothers stared with undisguised alarm.

'It's all right. Calm down. Think about it. I'll be along to talk to you again.'

Chris checked his watch. Not much past five. He felt as though he'd been at the Lawreys for much longer than a quarter of an hour. They'd set up the sunroom at the back for Phil, but Eileen Lawrey had a dozen eyes and ears - with that brood she had to - and he doubted very much if his visit had gone unremarked. Then there were the small boys, who might be bribed to keep their mouths shut, but could still forget.

Chris knew he should go back to the Kostandises' place. To stall for a few more minutes, he got out his notebook and wrote down Ian's denial about having seen Margaret Benton, wondering why the boy had lied.

Maria Kostandis called Ian Lawrey names he wouldn't have expected her to get her tongue around. Her son ride a camel? Ridiculous! Taking bets? It was all malicious invention. She didn't let Chris get anywhere near Zorba, though he knew the boy was at home. He'd watched them going inside together as he was pulling up. He could wait for Zorba after school, but the boy would echo his mother's denials, then go home and complain.

Chris walked fast along the street, turning his back on the southwesterly, walking off his annoyance. He recalled his mother's admiration, and felt annoyed with her as well, and then surprised, because annoyance with his mother was something he seldom allowed himself to feel. It quickly gave way to shame, as he remembered how white and paper-thin she'd been the last few times he'd driven her to the house belonging to the wealthy Greeks; the expression of contentment - never envy - on her face.

The same oblique sun that struck those huge, hewn stones had been touching her; but there it was absorbed by a dark mass, a shelter announcing itself as impenetrable. Light had passed through his mother's skin as through the window of a car, as through cobwebs, or air. She'd thanked him for the outings as he helped her back inside, in her voice the acknowledgement each time that it might be the last. Her voice was paper-thin as well, though never maudlin or self-pitying. He always said that it was fine, don't mention it, while he felt his insides crumbling; and hoped, and felt ashamed of the hope, that he wouldn't have to go through the ordeal again.

Sometimes he added that he would drive her anywhere she wanted, and understood, by the silence that followed, that she saw through this offer. He hated himself then.

Even after she became too ill to leave the house, his mother used to ask him if he'd been by there, and what was out, or budding, in the garden. He wished it hadn't been Zorba's mother who'd been obstructive and belligerent, and he wished he hadn't had to endure her tongue-lashing while standing on her expensive Turkish rugs.

Raschid had nothing to add to Ben's and Ian's stories. He confirmed the bet, and the way that Camilla had interrupted them. Chris wasn't sure whether Raschid was telling the truth when he said he didn't know that Ian and Zorba had gone back to the paddock on their own. He thought that, on balance, the boy was most probably lying.

Raschid's mother stood anxiously in the doorway while Chris questioned her son, but she didn't interrupt. Chris felt her anxiety as something he could touch, and understood that it was caused, not by anything Raschid had, or had not done, but by the possibility that her husband might come home to find a policeman in his living room. For her sake, he got through the interview as quickly as possible.

NINE

A gentle hopping glow attracted Camilla from the doorway of her bedroom. She paused in the act of switching on a light, wondering who could be out there at this time of night. A burglar would hardly attract attention with a torch. She wondered if the police had come back to search. But why the need for subterfuge?

Camilla made her way silently down the corridor to the back of the house, thinking of the drawing she had made, the speed with which news travelled around Queenscliff. If Riza's abductor had come to silence her - she paused a moment for the irony in that - then the best thing would be to run away.

But Camilla braced herself against the temptation of a cowardly escape. If the thief were really out there, she was being given a chance to prove that she wasn't a coward after all. She stood in deep shadow by the kitchen window and watched the dim, bobbing light pass across the back yard and stop outside her garden shed. She watched the light disappear as whoever was carrying it went behind the shed. Camilla guessed who it was then, and what she was doing. She smiled to herself in the darkness, as, just in case she was wrong, she bent to take a rolling pin out of a drawer. She stared down at her tense and whitened knuckles grasping the makeshift weapon, catching her breath at the ease with which a violent impulse could rise up without warning.

The light was lowered and became even dimmer. The torch had been placed on the ground, revealing the shed window from below, and Julie Beshervase peering into it. Camilla watched as Julie tried the catch, then cupped her hands around her face. She wore dark clothes and a scarf around her head, but it was Julie's figure all right, Julie's long-legged stance.

Camilla loosened her grip on the rolling pin and smiled again, thinking of the contents of her garden shed. She watched until Julie picked up her torch and returned the way she'd come.

No building in Camilla's vicinity had such solidity and stature as the lighthouse. When she woke to a foggy morning, she got up and headed for the cliff path.

The fog horn filled every cranny in the rocks; even the rests between each blast were sucked up by the echo. Camilla was fascinated by the thick white stalk of the lighthouse, appearing and disappearing through the fog. Behind her, the pier squatted as a vague horizontal line, a grey denser than the sky. Its verticals were lines of shadow legs, a giant centipede.

On occasions like this - and it was far from the first one - Camilla stood spellbound by the spectral pillar and the deafening noise. She grimaced, hands clamped to her ears, thinking that it might be a relief to change her loss of speech for loss of hearing, and then frightened that this wish might be taken as ingratitude for what she still possessed. No one had told her to stand under the lighthouse in a fog. In fact, there were signs that expressly forbade it.

Camilla proceeded along the cliff path, grateful that she knew where to put her feet. She stopped, recalling the white-faced woman. When Chris Blackie had shown her a photograph, she'd hesitated and then shaken her head. She could not be sure. But the woman had been wearing dark clothes and she'd indicated this to Chris. She wondered if she should make another drawing.

When, exactly, had she heard the scream? Chris had asked her this, but again, she couldn't be sure. Her thoughts were muddled and she was afraid of being misunderstood. Chris had not been unkind, or hasty, but still, Camilla knew she was suspected of taking Riza, and that she must be careful.

Thinking of the woman, she felt the membrane between her being and another's to be stretched so thinly that she might pass through it unseen. She longed for a voice to shout with, to shout a warning that she feared was too late.

The phone was Camilla's enemy. When it rang, she fumbled the receiver, hot of hand and face, lifting it with shaking hands, straining towards the voice on the other end. It was usually somebody selling something, or her son. If the former, she felt relieved. If the latter, she tried hard to indicate, by the quality of her listening, answers to his questions about her health, about what she'd been 'up to'. She knew the questions were a test that she was bound to fail. Success would be recorded when she could reply in a normal voice. She marvelled that this person to whom she'd given birth could be so cruel.

But now, when Camilla passed the telephone on its stand in the hallway, she thought of Chris Blackie and wondered what progress he was making. She thought of writing him a note about Julie Beshervase coming to her place at night, but decided not to. She didn't want to get Julie into trouble.

TEN

Anthea woke to the sounds of water birds and opened her curtains to the slow movements of swans across the bay. She felt she would never get used to the sheer number of birds. There were thousands out there feeding when the tide was right.

The light was pearly over the water as the fog began to lift, sun strengthening every second, turning the sea and sky into a soft blue-grey. In the distance, on the opposite shore, a line of light hit the tree-tops. Round the corner, hidden from her view, the town was beginning to stir.

Before plugging in the kettle, Anthea switched her phone on and checked for missed calls. It was her habit to do this each morning, though she'd given up hoping that Graeme would ring or text her late at night. At least she turned her phone off when she went to bed. The first two weeks she'd left it on, sleeping fitfully; at every creak the wind made she'd grabbed the small rectangle from her bedside table, as though it was the weather's fault that it refused to ring.

She'd grown used to the night sounds. There was so little traffic on her narrow street that every car announced itself as individual. It would be easy, she thought as she ate her solitary evening meals, to amuse herself by spying on her neighbours. Sometimes she went outside at night, just to feel the cool dark air all around her, taste its briny texture, smell the strong weedy smell coming off the bay at low tide. A footpath wound its way along the top of a low cliff. After dinner the night before, she'd taken her torch and set off along the path.

After a while, she'd turned the torch off. The moon had been up and she'd seen quite well without it. She'd thought of her phone not ringing on the bedside table, how the air of expectation in her flat was squeezed and squeezed until she couldn't bear it any more. She'd stood still and traced the outline of Swan Island, where there was an army training camp, imagining all those waterbirds roosting in military lines.

She'd pictured herself getting in the car, not stopping till she reached Graeme's suburb, and the house he shared with another architect. She would confront him, forcing answers to her questions. Hadn't she been trained to do just that?

Anthea had kept walking, tiring herself out. Back at the flat, she'd had a shower and fallen into bed, slept well for the first time in weeks, woken to a different question, or the same one differently put. Did it require more courage to wait, or to have it out with Graeme?

Anthea had never been a patient person. She forced herself to be patient when dealing with members of the public, but it did not come naturally. She expected others to come up with answers as quickly as she put the questions. She was inclined to interpret hesitation either as evasion sliding into lies; the wish to prevaricate while thinking up a lie; or a sign of cowardice. After all this time, she asked herself, what did she want from Graeme? Did she want him back, or did she want to shout at him and tell him to go to hell? Did she want him back if it meant pretending that these miserable weeks had never been?

Before leaving for work, Anthea made a start unpacking her boxes, stacking her books by subject and alphabetically on the built-in bookshelves along one wall of the living-room. Then she made a shopping list, wondering if it was a cause for congratulation that her needs were so modest.

Anthea guessed that there was no love lost between Frank Erwin and her boss, and that perhaps some old rivalry or mistrust had led Chris to focus on Erwin's trailer.

Chris knew everybody's property - how many sheds, what kind of garage the townsfolk and surrounding farmers owned. He hadn't examined every single one, but he'd been over Frank's and Camilla's with a fine tooth comb.

Chris and Anthea sat over an early morning cup of tea on the station's back veranda, while Chris outlined their tasks for the morning. He wanted Anthea to check on Julie Beshervase's insurance.

'She said she couldn't afford it, but she might be lying. Then I want you to go and talk to her again.'

Anthea was quick to read the challenge, and wondered why Chris was palming Julie off on her. He seemed prickly and disagreeable, as though he'd got out of the wrong side of the bed.

Julie shook her head in disbelief. 'I ought to throw you off the premises for that. I know my rights, even if I can't afford a lawyer.'

'I'd go as soon as you asked me,' Anthea replied, 'but it's better if we clear this point up without wasting any more time.'

'Why would I lock my own camel in a garage when I've got a perfectly good paddock to keep him in?'

Julie shot this over her shoulder as she took down a bunch of keys from a hook behind the kitchen door.

Anthea observed that the room was in an even worse state than the last time she'd been there. Some people didn't notice dirt. She'd come across a number of blokes who were literally blind to it. Though not Graeme: Graeme was fastidious.

She realised that Julie was waiting for her to say something, and asked, 'Where's the Talbots' car?'

'They've lent it to their daughter while they're overseas.'

'I'd like her contact details, please.'

Julie pressed her lips together and shook her head as though in disbelief.

She stayed outside the garage, leaving Anthea to walk around it by herself. There was a work bench at one end, an old fridge, various tools and boxes.

Anthea opened the fridge door, wondering if she was missing something obvious. She could search the garage properly, and felt confident of her ability to ride down Julie's objections while she did so. But she did not believe that Riza had ever been hidden there. And the camel hadn't been insured; Julie had been telling the truth about that.

Dangling the keys by a forefinger, Julie strode back into the house.

But once inside, she did not ask Anthea to leave. Instead, surprisingly, she offered tea. Anthea made herself look and sound appreciative, trying not to think about the grimy rings around the mugs.

'Have you given any more thought to what we were talking about the other day, about people who might have a grudge against you?'

Anthea waited for another complaint about Camilla.

She wanted to tell Julie about the bet to ride Riza, see how she reacted; but Chris had warned her not to. He'd said he wanted to investigate further before presenting Julie with the story.

'What about the shops - the newsagents, the supermarket?'

'You mean, have I made enemies of checkout chicks? Why would I *bother*?' Julie shook her head again, impatiently this time. 'I'm still paying rent, you know.'

Anthea reflected that, if she'd been asked six months, or even six weeks ago, how long it would take to find a camel that had disappeared from a paddock on the outskirts of a small town, she would have laughed and said a morning max. Yet when faced with the actual problem, her skills and training seemed to be of little use. If she'd been asked whether she would have cared about a missing camel, her answer would have been a disdainful no. She shook her shoulders irritably. Her thoughts returned to Graeme once again, and how, if she'd been expecting him that weekend, she'd be buying the best coffee and fresh croissants from the bakery.

'Would you like to see Riza's saddle?'

Anthea nodded, surprised at the question.

Sitting on some sheets of newspaper, on a dusty floor, in an empty room, the saddle looked like a throne. Anthea understood that Julie had put it in an unused room because she couldn't bear to look at it. Then why the invitation?

She bent down and ran her fingers gently over the tassels and the mirrors. In each one was a view.

Behind her, Julie was speaking softly, describing how she'd loved to turn from her training sessions and see her face reflected in them, to bring Riza up close and see his reflection too.

She talked about the Afghan women sitting in their camp circle outside Alice Springs, camels hobbled a little way behind them, her childhood in the Territory and how it returned to her in nightmares whose precise details she could not, awake, recall, but whose mood she always could.

Anthea stood up and breathed in deeply. 'You said no when I showed you that photograph of Margaret Benton, but you recognised her, didn't you?'

A woman had been standing at the gates of Wallington stud, back in December last year, when Julie had driven out with Riza, full of unbelieving joy that he was really hers. The woman's fearful attitude, when she slowed down and pulled over, had pierced Julie's happiness. When Julie had asked if she needed a lift anywhere, the woman had stared at her and shaken her head. Then a Landcruiser had come tearing down the driveway, kicking up the gravel. The door had swung open, and the woman had stood absolutely frozen for a few seconds before getting in.

Had she noticed who was driving the vehicle?

It had been a man, that's all Julie could say.

Without intending to, Anthea parked in the main street and went into the supermarket. She chose the most expensive coffee, ingredients for a tasty sauce to serve with fresh pasta, a bottle of chardonnay. Then she had to drop them at her flat before she could return to work, all the while mulling over Julie's story.

Pulling up outside the white fence, the lavender and rose bushes, Anthea surprised herself by feeling what amounted to a physical longing for the hard anonymity of a metropolitan police station, where hierarchies were clear. Perhaps she should have stayed on and done her detective training. But she'd wanted to work; she'd wanted to be out there *doing* something.

If she'd stayed in Melbourne, Anthea told herself, the breach with Graeme would not have occurred. But she couldn't go back now. She couldn't go back to the way things had been. And she knew she was simplifying matters too. It had been partly as a result of Graeme's teasing that she hadn't continued with her training. Her marks had been borderline, certainly not brilliant. She'd spent every free minute with Graeme, and the limits had been mostly ones he'd fixed - limits set by his work and what he liked to call his 'other commitments'.

Anthea asked herself what career would have found favour with her boyfriend. A profession? Not architecture, since that was his field. A lesser profession then - teaching, perhaps, or accountancy. She admitted something else about her departure from Melbourne; she had wanted financial independence.

But she hadn't realised that living in a small community would feel like drinking water that was always tepid, never hot or cold.

What was it she really wanted? Drama she could fling herself into, as others flung themselves into the surf? Was that what Julie wanted too? Was that what she sometimes saw in Julie's eyes?

Anthea got out, locked her car and stood staring at the park and park bench, and, beyond them, the bay and shipping channel.

At least she could wish for some absolute division between work and recreation, and that each should have a taste that was distinct. Anthea felt she would have preferred harshness or censure, rather than being left to find her own line through to what was important.

ELEVEN

Anthea found Chris sitting at his desk, which was covered with notes on bits of paper in his small, backsloping handwriting.

He looked up, flushed with excitement.

'Margaret Benton was definitely here in Queenscliff. She and her husband rented a cabin at the van park.'

While Anthea had been with Julie, Chris had started at the top end of the main street and called in at each of the businesses and shops. Most of the shopkeepers thought he was back to ask about the camel, and a few teased him for not having found it yet.

'Maybe the little fella's run away to the circus,' one suggested, and another, 'Maybe those greenies've got him, on account of being feral and a pest.'

Chris had laughed and replied, 'That's in the Northern Territory, you oaf. What you've got to worry about is cats like Snowy here.'

When he'd stopped by the caravan park, he'd found the office unlocked, but empty.

Ben came when he rang the bell, looking sullen and wary.

'Mum and Dad've gone into Geelong. I've got the day off cos I'm sick.'

'I'm sorry to hear that, Ben. This'll only take a moment. I just want you to tell me where you've seen this woman before.'

'I never - ' Ben began, turning white like Ian Lawrey had.

'It was here, wasn't it? When was Margaret Benton here?'

Ben's face was blank, the practised blank of adolescents. Chris waited for what might be going on beneath this.

He said finally, 'We were full up all of January.'

'I can appreciate that. And I can understand how faces must start to look alike.' He didn't add, especially the faces of middle-aged women. 'But you do recognise this lady, don't you?'

'I might.'

'Could you tell your father I'd like to ask him a few questions? I'll be back in an hour.'

Anthea told Chris her news. Chris rang Swan Hill police station again. Margaret's husband, Jack Benton, had been questioned about the coat, but claimed to have no idea how it had got into the sandhills. He said his wife had left him for another man.

'What do you think?' Chris asked his assistant.

Anthea said, 'If the coat's been lying there since January, why didn't someone pick it up?'

'Maybe it was buried. Maybe kids or a dog dug it up.'

Chris was thinking that he should have looked for signs of this.

He returned to the caravan park just as Penny and Alex McIntyre were getting out of their car. From the look of them, their trip to Geelong had not gone well. Penny's make-up was smudged. Alex was scowling and his lips were pulled in, as though to stop himself from saying something he'd regret.

Chris hitched up his uniform and approached them, holding out his hand.

'Alex. Penny. Just a few questions. Shouldn't take long.'

When Penny took his hand, Chris felt the tension in it, how it was hot and dry. 'I have to see about lunch,' she said.

Alex watched his wife's departing back, still frowning, then led the way to the office. He pulled two chairs out from the wall and let himself fall onto one.

Chris reached in his pocket for a photograph. Instead of looking at it, Alex went round behind the counter and opened his bar fridge.

'A beer, Blackie? Come on, mate. You can't stay on duty all the frigging time.'

'Okay then, a small one. Thanks.'

Alex smiled a private smile, drank deeply, then wiped his face with a tissue.

'That's better.'

His big frame relaxed as though someone pulled a peg that was holding complicated scaffolding in place. He wiped his face again, then aimed the tissue at a small metal bin, moving slowly to take the photo Chris held out.

Alex didn't speak for a long time. When he did, his voice was tired and full of what seemed to Chris like old and useless anger.

'The bloke gave me a bad feeling from the moment they pulled in. You know how it is sometimes. There'll be a hundred, and one will make your skin crawl.'

Chris nodded. He'd felt that often enough, going into a pub on a hot summer night, when one word out of place would start a fight. Almost straight away, he could pick the man who'd say that word, loudly, in his presence and in defiance of it. It was his job to stop that happening. It was Alex's job too. People wouldn't return to a van park where fights broke out, not people with young families, and fishermen who just wanted to sit on the beach with a rod and reel and cook their catch in the twilight

'Tell me about it.'

'The barbecues were full. This one's old man claimed he got there first.'

Alex lifted his chin and Chris understood that, rather than seeing Margaret Benton, it was her husband's outline that was before his eyes.

'Another camper claimed he got there first as well. He had friends to back him up, but he was willing to accept my ruling on the matter. It could have come to blows, would have, I think, except that Jack - oh, yes, I remember his name - took stock of his opponents and decided he could take on one man, but not four.'

'Benton was drunk?'

'Not so you'd notice. A nasty piece of work drunk or sober, and looking for a fight.' Alex indicated the photograph again. 'This lady tried to hose him down, but I don't think she expected to succeed.'

'What did you make of her?'

'I never thought about it, to be honest. Penny might have more to say on that score. She saw it on the news, that she'd gone missing.'

And never phoned to tell me, Chris thought but didn't say.

'How long were they here?'

'Less than the week they'd booked for. I told Benton he'd have to leave.'

'Could you dig out the registration details?'

'Now?'

'If you wouldn't mind.'

Chris sipped his beer while Alex took down a folder from a shelf behind the counter and began thumbing through it.

He found the page he was looking for, and Chris copied the information.

'Was Ben around when the argument broke out over the barbecues?'

Alex nodded. 'It was Ben who came running to tell me.'

They talked for a few more minutes. Chris thanked him for the beer and the information, and said he had to go.

TWELVE

A week of heavy rain washed Margaret Benton's body out from a bank of the Murray River. She'd been buried less than a kilometre from where she'd lived in Swan Hill.

Chris realised he'd known that she was dead; he hadn't had a moment's doubt. From Anthea's expression as she listened to the news, it seemed that she'd believed this too.

'The body was right on the bank.'

'What about ID?'

'None on her. Identified from dental records.'

'They'll send somebody down here now,' Chris said.

A river bank had disgorged a body. Chris replayed the scene in his mind, as though it was one he'd witnessed personally; not just any river, but the Murray in flood, the body spinning in the water, jostling those of sheep and luckless cattle, yet not rolling far. What if the dead woman's remains had not been caught in branches, stopped by a fallen tree? What if Margaret Benton had gone on rolling, kilometre after kilometre? What if she had never been found at all?

That was, of course, what her killer must have hoped for.

Anthea showed Chris her computer screen. On it was a photograph of a good-looking middle-aged man, with wavy dark hair and thick lips.

'It's him.'

'Good work.' Chris pulled up a chair. The name under the photo was in a tiny point size. Anthea zoomed in and the man's face went fuzzy.

'Does he have a record?'

'Stealing cars.'

'Looks a bit old for that.'

'Some men never grow up.'

Chris shot a glance at Anthea, but her eyes were firmly on the screen.

'I'll print this off, will I? It's something to go round with.'

'Good,' Chris said again. 'Print out the convictions too. I don't suppose there's a horse float among them?'

Anthea laughed and said, 'No such luck.'

'Don't play silly buggers with me, Frank. Where's your trailer?'

'You know what, Blackie? You've turned into an aggressive little shit since you acquired that lass with the pretty arse. I might have to get my solicitor to remind you of my rights.'

Chris rubbed his eyes and shook his head to clear it. 'Go ahead, Frank. But I'll be round here every day until I get an answer, so you might as well co-operate and save yourself the trouble.'

The farmer scowled, then said gruffly, 'My son's got it.'

'Jim?'

'Some of us do have families, you know.'

'What's Jim doing with your clapped-out trailer?'

'Moving a horse.'

'Where is he?'

'Well, I couldn't say for certain, not to the nearest metre.' Frank made an exaggerated show of checking his watch. 'Somewhere between Lorne and Apollo Bay would be a rough estimate.'

'I'll need it back. Today.'

'Don't know about that. Mightn't be possible.'

'Tomorrow, or I'll charge you with obstructing a police investigation.'

Chris knew Frank was laughing at him. But whether it was guilty laughter, or pleasure at having got the better of the local law enforcement, this he couldn't say. He was annoyed with himself for over-reacting.

If the grapevine had done its usual work, Chris was sure Frank Erwin knew all about the Bentons' stay at the McIntyre's van park, and what had brought it to a premature end. The whole town would know that the murdered woman had been in Queenscliff last summer; they'd be watching with curiosity to see what happened next.

Chris told himself that he could chase Jim up, go back to Frank and find out what he was driving, get the rego details. He could ring the stations at Lorne and Apollo Bay and ask them to keep a look out. There couldn't be that many horse trailers on the Ocean Road today. But he felt in his bones that it was too late.

He wasn't surprised when he picked up the phone an hour later and there was Frank on the other end, a Frank much chastened and apologetic. He was terribly sorry, but there'd been an accident. His trailer had gone over the side of a cliff, around a nasty bend.

'You know that really bad stretch just before you get to Wye River. And it's blowing a gale down there today.'

'So the trailer came loose. Where is it now?'

'Over the side, like I said.' Frank sounded aggrieved. 'And thanks for asking after Jimmy. He wasn't hurt, by the way.'

'I'm glad to hear it.'

Chris had no authority to order any kind of salvage operation, and James Erwin would have made sure that pieces of the trailer were scattered far and wide. He began typing another report, outlining a connection between the missing camel and Margaret Benton, but stopped when he realised that he wasn't even convincing himself. He knew that the trailer would remain at the bottom of whatever cliff it had conveniently fallen over, until it was washed away by the spectacular high tides that were famous along that stretch of coastline.

He put the half-written report aside and rang to ask about the lab results on the hairs. After being put on hold for what seemed like forever, he was told they'd once belonged to a palomino pony.

When Anthea came in, flushed from her door-to-door, Chris didn't want to tell her about the debacle over the trailer, but he made himself get it over with.

Anthea listened in silence. When Chris had finished, she bit the inside of her cheek and frowned.

'But if Frank knew he was innocent, why go to all that trouble?'

The same question had been in Chris's mind too, as he pictured shards of wood floating out to sea

'Frank told me the hairs weren't Riza's. He was angry when I didn't believe him.'

Anthea said, 'Everyone's speculating about who killed Margaret Benton. You should hear the theories.'

Chris put his head in his hands and muttered between them, 'Spare me.'

The spaghetti sauce smelt good. Once Anthea had got over her surprise at asking Chris to share it, it seemed a lucky chance, a pleasant kind of omen, that she'd bought enough ingredients for two.

Anthea poured wine, glad she'd had the foresight to put a bottle in the fridge.

'Cheers,' she said, serving with a small show of ceremony, wondering if Chris would notice that she had two of everything - two good glasses, deep bowls for the fettuccini, salad plates, linen serviettes she'd only just unpacked.

Chris fell on his dinner and began shovelling it in.

He looked up at Anthea's quizzical expression.

'Sorry,' he said, wiping his mouth. 'I - it's good.'

'I'm glad you like it. And don't be.'

They ate without speaking for a while, Anthea finding the silence restful rather than a gap needing to be filled. She reflected that Graeme would have expected her to entertain him - while she was cooking, while they were eating, and after the meal. She would have prepared jokes, amusing anecdotes about the town and its inhabitants. She would have rehearsed them, and been anxious that they should go down well. Suddenly, she missed Graeme dreadfully. It was impossible that they'd come to this lack of contact, this nothing.

Chris leant back in his chair. Anthea noticed that he'd hardly touched his wine. She refilled the carafe of water she'd put on the table and he drank some of that.

She was aware of every move Chris made, aware for the first time of the masculine weight and heft of him, the growl his chair made as he scraped it back, sounds she was sure he scarcely heard himself.

They washed up together, Anthea absorbed by a new sensitivity towards her boss as a man. She felt certain that any change in her behaviour towards him would cause them both discomfort. Not that she intended to behave differently; but signals were given and received whether or not the exchange was intentional.

Chris was an odd mixture, which Anthea hadn't come across before, of sensitivity and ignorance where women were concerned. She found herself revising her initial impression, which was that for her boss never to have married, or even to have had a long-term relationship - she suspected this was so, without really knowing - meant that there was something wrong with him. Weeks of having kept her ears open for gossip about past girlfriends had not netted her a single name.

Anthea stared intently, over the automatic movements of her fingers, at neutral or grey areas she had not previously thought it worth her while to contemplate.

She thought that Chris was too close to the townspeople, and that was why he felt inadequate and anxious now. He'd grown used to behaving like a mother hen, shepherding his flock and keeping them out of danger, when even fools knew that danger had a habit of rearing up and clobbering you, even in a boring country town.

After Chris had left, Anthea grabbed her torch, glad he hadn't overstayed his welcome. She climbed the cliff path with a greedy sense of anticipation, as though the pleasures to be gained there - salt wind in her hair, calls of the night birds - answered a need as physical as hunger. She was getting to know the path, where bulbous tree roots rose to trip a person, with their look of nocturnal animals frozen in the act.

She recalled her loneliness, now that it was diminishing, in the first few weeks of what she'd thought of as her banishment. Nothing in the night had answered it; nothing human, or made by humans, such as a café or a bar where she might have found someone to have a drink with. She shrank from going into a pub alone here, being recognised and talked about.

Of course, if she'd been in Melbourne, not wandering around asking for her ankle to be broken, then Graeme would have been there too, looking at the same lights, breathing the same air. It was the absolute contrast of night down here that got to you. Back there, even if she'd been alone, the city lights would have touched her with a human touch. Here there was nothing to answer, though it was not a wilderness she lived in, but a seaside town. She thought of the two single women she'd come across - Camilla Renfrew, Julie Beshervase. Out there, on the cliff top, the idea of walking Riza to his hiding place seemed more than plausible, the idea that Camilla might have taken him, out of love and loneliness, a distinct possibility.

Anthea had been in such a hurry to begin her walk that she hadn't remembered to leave her phone behind. It was still in her jacket pocket. She was as startled when it rang as if she'd never heard a mobile phone before.

It was Graeme. What was she doing at the weekend? If the offer was still open, could he visit? See the local sights? He fancied a boat trip. What passed for entertainment down there on the Bellarine Peninsula?

THIRTEEN

Anthea held her phone to her ear, took a deep breath and glanced across at Graeme, who did not look up from the travel section of the *Age*.

'I see,' she said. But she didn't see. How she could have been so stupid as not to tell Chris that Graeme was coming down? She couldn't tell him now, with Graeme sitting opposite her, waiting for her to get rid of whoever was interrupting their breakfast.

Julie's waiting for you at the station was not a request: it was an instruction; and from the way Chris spoke, he wasn't sorry for ruining her Saturday. But she'd never given him any cause for thinking this particular Saturday might be open to ruin.

Still not looking up, Graeme said in a mild voice, prepared to be mollified, 'Got it sorted then?'

'I have to go in to work.'

Graeme raised his dark blue eyes with an expression which asked what kind of emergency could possibly justify leaving him alone. Instead of replying immediately, he took his time to fold the paper, then pressed the long fingers of his right hand to his lips. Anthea imagined holding them. She took a gulp of air.

'An old lady's had an accident. She's broken her leg. That was Constable - that was Chris - ringing from the hospital. I'm sorry. I'll be as quick as I can.'

'What's that supposed to mean?'

Graeme could keep her there explaining for ten minutes. But the explanation would mean nothing to him, and would end in acrimony.

'Take the spare key.' Anthea was suddenly all energy, rummaging in a kitchen drawer. 'Go for a walk. Just across the road, there's a path that winds along the cliff.'

She put the key in front of him, fearing what she would see if she raised her eyes. But then she did raise them. Graeme was smiling, it did not seem unkindly.

'Hurry back,' he said.

Anthea fumbled with the car door and then the ignition. One of the traitorous thoughts that followed her along the narrow road was, why did Graeme pick this weekend, and why at such short notice? Perhaps his other plans had gone awry. She recalled his smile, pressed it to her eyelids. How ridiculous to assume he was incapable of amusing himself without her for an hour or two, or that she could be blamed for failing to amuse him. She told herself not to be so pessimistic.

When Anthea pulled up in front of the station, Julie's bike was outside, but there was no sign of Julie herself. Anthea inserted her key in the lock. She listened to her even footfalls, the creaking of the wooden floor, noticed the way Saturday morning light shone through the closed slats of Venetian blinds, the small solitary warmth that had collected behind them. She wondered how many police stations around the country were like this at the weekends - too small, too unimportant to be staffed.

The phone startled her, then stopped ringing as she moved to answer it. Another sound, one she couldn't immediately identify, was coming from the back. After checking to make sure she'd locked the front door behind her, Anthea walked at a normal pace along the corridor. Both office doors were shut and she did not stop to look into them. She opened the back door, but did not immediately step out onto the veranda. Instead, she let her eyes graze the backyard. Noticing a movement in the grass, right down near the fence, she thought of the neighbour's cat, who spent long hours following the sun around, and sometimes left offerings of dismembered creatures on the steps. But the movements were too large for a cat.

'Julie?' she called.

There was no answer, but the movements in the grass stopped. Anthea called again. Julie's head emerged from the green tangle, against grey-brown slats of fence. Anthea had the illusion that the head was somehow growing out between them. It wasn't until she had helped Julie inside, and made her strong, sweet tea, sitting close to her while she drank it, that the illusion disappeared, or that either of them spoke.

Julie hunched forward, then looked up at Anthea. Grimy streaks on either side of her mouth were dirt mixed with saliva. Broken capillaries in her cheeks were those of a much older woman.

Anthea put her arm around Julie's shoulders, willing herself to stay calm, and to find the means to calm Julie down as well.

Julie had found Camilla Renfrew on the track to Riza's paddock, or claimed she had.

'Had Mrs Renfrew been attacked?' Anthea wished she'd asked Chris, but her mind had not been on Camilla and what had happened to her.

Julie shrugged as if to say, are you accusing me? But it was an exhausted shrug, as though she had no energy left for anger or self-defence.

She'd gone for a walk to watch the sunrise and had found Camilla on the path. Camilla had been conscious, but disoriented.

'I didn't expect her to speak. I mean, I know she can't, but it seemed like she couldn't hear me either. And she was so cold! I rang here. I had the number in my phone. I got a machine, but it had Constable Blackie's number. When he got there, Camilla tried to talk, but nothing came out. The ambulance guys carried a stretcher up the path. If she wasn't crazy before, she sure as hell is now.'

'The pain - '

'Yeah, well, like, if it was you or me - can you imagine lying there all night?'

A familiar stubbornness came back into Julie's face. 'What if she's got Riza hidden somewhere? And now she's in hospital. She won't tell anybody where he is. He'll die of thirst! He'll starve to death!'

'What were you doing on the path so early?'

'I told you! I wanted to see the sunrise. There's no law against it, is there? I couldn't sleep, so I got up early.'

Anthea thought of Graeme and wondered where he was. She made herself focus on Julie's sunken features, on the smell, insinuating itself into her nostrils, of human flesh that had not been washed for days.

'She's dead!' Julie cried. 'That woman I saw. *The river sicked her up!*'

Anthea reached for Julie's hand. 'It'll be okay. Calm down. Show me where you found Camilla Renfrew.'

The corner where Camilla had fallen was marked by broken twigs and churned up sand. Rocks and a huge tree root made the path much narrower. There was something foolishly wilful about venturing alone there in the dark. Anthea recalled her own night wanderings and stopped herself from checking her watch.

Graeme hadn't rung or sent a text.

Julie stopped on the other side of the tree root, where the path curved sharply to the left.

Anthea thought about the young woman's temptation, out there on the track at dawn - Julie, who hated Camilla, with Camilla in her power. Julie was disturbed, mentally and emotionally, and there was only her word for the fact that she'd found Camilla lying injured. Presumably, when Camilla had recovered sufficiently, she would provide her own account of what had happened, in writing.

At every gateway - country, town, and city - Anthea could imagine, if she wished, a woman desperate to escape.

The flat was empty. Anthea's breath caught as she went from room to room. She picked up the spare key from the kitchen bench, then began looking for a note. She found it pinned to her pillow, a cruel gesture she would not have believed Graeme capable of, and that made her breathing so strained she had to sit down before she could read it. She didn't want to sit on the bed, whose covers had been pulled up without it being properly made.

'Hey Ant,' the note began - Graeme's nickname for her in childishly carefree days. 'Couldn't wait around I'm afraid. Call you later in the week.' He'd simply signed it 'G'.

Anthea wanted to get into her car and follow him. It was as though the notion of compulsion had been introduced into the human repertoire for just such an event, and, with this leap into the future, she thought that perhaps she would never again owe allegiance to restraint. She imagined chasing Graeme up the highway in a police car, lights and siren daring other motorists to get in the way. She pictured herself arriving at his house. There wouldn't be much time lag because of his laid-back approach to treachery, her unnatural speed.

She was armed. She would confront him. The scene had such elemental power and rightness that the actions she willed herself towards left no room for doubt.

Gradually, Anthea's vision cleared. She told herself she could not spend the rest of the day alone in her flat. The cliff walk did not appeal because she'd suggested it to Graeme. Perhaps he'd taken her up on her suggestion. What if the walk that she'd begun to cherish had given a sufficient edge to Graeme's boredom with her, sufficient, that is, for him to scribble off that note and leave?

Characteristically, the break had not been expressed in clear terms. He should just have said 'Goodbye.'

Anthea's car followed the by now familiar turns and ended up back at the station. Graeme's betrayal felt like a stone in her stomach, replacing the food she'd gone without, taking up too much space. She felt sure that Chris, when he walked in, must see this.

But Chris was full of the accident, the hospital, Camilla's son Simon, who'd reacted with an irritation he hadn't bothered to conceal to the news that his mother had broken her leg.

'A piece of work,' Chris called him, putting on a plummy voice. 'My mother shouldn't be living on her own. I've been trying to get her into a retirement home for years.'

Anthea said, 'Does he want her house?'

'The money from it, possibly. I can't see a man like that burying himself down here.' Chris glanced at his assistant quickly, then away.

He thought that she was looking pale and tired. 'Of course, if he was rich enough he could keep it as a weekender, but I got the sense that Camilla's son has a real aversion to Queenscliff.'

Anthea was careful not to catch her boss's eye. She made a pot of tea and he accepted a mug gratefully.

'Oh, that's the other thing. Simon took his mother to a specialist in Melbourne. Her lack of speech - it's a medical mystery apparently.'

'Could it be psychological? Perhaps she doesn't want to talk.'

'It's possible. But when you see her struggling for words - well, what do you think?'

Anthea took a few moments to answer. 'I think Camilla wants to speak, but I don't think she wants to be bullied into it.'

Chris nodded, frowning, perhaps, at the recollection of a greedy son.

Anthea related what Julie had told her about finding Camilla on the path.

Chris listened, looking thoughtful. 'Are you okay?' he asked.

'Yes,' said Anthea, surprised that her voice sounded normal. 'Hungry. I missed lunch.'

Chris did not ask what her plans had been for the day, and she felt relieved, certain that he'd recognise a lie.

Anthea used the toilet, washed her hands and face, then stood leaning against the sink in the station's small kitchen. The mug Julie had used was sitting on the draining board, but it seemed days, rather than hours, since she'd been there.

She stood staring, bug-eyed, at the crockery. When she came back to the present, it was with the relatively harmless observation that her boss had never cultivated charm. But he was sensitive enough not to want to give offence, and to try and guess, in advance, what might cause it. Up until now, he'd never asked her a personal question.

In Graeme, charm had replaced other qualities, like a coloniser squashing previous inhabitants.

'It's too late for lunch and too early for dinner.'

Anthea turned around and smiled.

'There should be an equivalent of brunch,' she said. 'A mid-afternoon meal that's more substantial than tea and cakes.'

'Right,' Chris said, and then, 'That Chinese along the Geelong Road's open all day.' He smiled back, patting his pockets. 'After you.'

FOURTEEN

They were the only customers. 'Diners,' Anthea said solemnly. 'We're the only diners.'

Egging one another on, they ordered enough for four people. The waiter showed no surprise at this, but the glances he gave them were wary, though neither was wearing a uniform.

They voiced their fears for and about Julie Beshervase. It was Chris's opinion that Julie was less reliable than Camilla, more inclined to lie if she thought she had anything to gain by it.

'You don't think she *broke* Camilla's leg, do you?'

No, Chris didn't think so. But there was really no telling, with a wild one like that.

Anthea put down her chopsticks. She liked eating with chopsticks and, when their food arrived, had decided not to be put off by the wince of embarrassment Chris offered her before taking up his knife and fork.

'Do you think Riza's dead?' she asked.

'I think he might be.'

'Do you believe his death is related to Margaret Benton's?'

'I said I thought he might be dead, that's all. But yes, in answer to your question, I believe it is.'

When Anthea had collected her car from the station and gone home, Chris made himself another cup of tea and drank it on the back veranda. A big meal like that should have made him feel sleepy, but he wasn't sleepy. His senses were alert and his mind flicked from one set of problems to another. He wondered if he should have found out what was bothering Anthea, but she'd made it clear she didn't want him to pry. She'd looked so white and strained; her small face had been pulled tight, to hold together whatever was going on behind it.

Chris's thoughts returned to Simon Renfrew and the interview he knew he'd handled badly. He reflected that, of all the circumstances under which he could have arranged to question Camilla's son, the way it turned out had been the least likely to produce a satisfactory result. He was annoyed with himself for not having spoken to Simon earlier, for having put it off till now, when his mother's broken leg was an added complication.

Chris had seen immediately that Simon was the sort of man used to dominating any gathering he happened to find himself in, even a gathering of two when the other individual was a policeman. First, there was his size. He was a good seven centimetres taller than Chris, who marvelled that a small, slight woman could have produced such a thumper. He understood that Simon was the kind of man who, having reached a peak of sporting prowess by the end of high school, too young to have learnt the relativity of any success, and no doubt confident that his would go on forever, had blamed the world when this turned out not to be the case. A sulky dissatisfaction in his eyes and around his heavy shoulders looked to be habitual, hinting at people and situations that went on letting him down.

Simon's features had taken on an attitude of boredom when Chris asked him how often he thought he'd be able to get down to see his mother. Then Chris had asked about the possibility of transferring Camilla to a Melbourne hospital, to make it easier for her son to visit, and had the satisfaction of watching an expression of alarm take over.

Simon's face would resist ageing; every muscle would resist it; but that challenge was still some years away. His straight fair hair was the type that thinned early. This realisation gave Chris a small, uncharitable satisfaction, till it occurred to him that his own hair was of a similar type. He recalled the café where they'd talked, how tense Simon had been inside the hospital and how his muscles had visibly relaxed after they'd walked through the main section to an outdoor eating area, decorated with plants in raised, brick-surrounded beds.

The sun had shone down warmly on the paving stones, and on the children's corner with its moulded plastic blocks and climbing frame. Chris had bought coffee for them both. They'd sat facing the You Yangs, and an oil tanker making its way across to the refinery. Chris had liked being on a level with the treetops. He could have gone on quite happily drinking his coffee, but he wished he'd been more adept at handling Simon.

FIFTEEN

Swan Bay caravan park was on the Geelong-Queenscliff road, well placed to attract visitors to the Bellarine Peninsula. The McIntyres had left most of the trees in front to provide a screen from the dust and noise of traffic. The cabins and van sites weren't cramped close together; between them trees and bushes had been used to good effect as well. It occurred to Chris that noise within the cabins - noise of an argument, for instance - would be muted. The place was clean and well maintained. He knew Penny was worried about the lack of custom, and he didn't want to add to her worries; but that couldn't be helped.

When Chris knocked on the office door and asked if he could have another word with Ben, Penny said he'd taken the dog for a walk around Swan Bay.

Chris hurried away before she could insist on being present when he questioned her son.

Once out the gates, he forced himself to face his fear. He was about to make himself do something he hated, all because he wanted to catch Ben on his own.

Chris was of an age and class of man who did not believe in therapy. He believed in getting on with it. This belief, or lack of belief, had been a source of corrosive disagreement with his mother, never openly expressed. Born in the Otways, never having learnt to swim as a child, Fiona Blackie had been, for all of Chris's life, and certainly before it too, frightened of the water. To give his mother her due, she'd tried hard not to pass on this fear to her only son. He'd had swimming lessons. He'd been encouraged, even forced against his will at times, to do what other boys did. It hadn't worked. He'd endured the lessons, and absorbed the emotions that lay beneath his mother's strained encouragement.

He'd been in Melbourne for five years when his father drowned. He'd had no intention of returning to Queenscliff and his mother hadn't asked him to, at least not in words. When it became clear that she wasn't coping, he'd told himself that he need only come back for a few months, to see her on her feet again.

'The sea took him,' his mother used to say. She never said drowned; always 'the sea took him'. She lived with her back resolutely turned towards it, but refused to sell the house and move. Chris hatched plans, applied for country stations, cajoled, persuaded and demanded, all to no avail. Fiona Blackie had possessed the intense stubbornness of the weak.

No body had been found; no grave to tend. Instead, this huge and terrifying ocean. His mother had not been religious, not in any way that Chris considered normal. Yet her duty of keeping vigil had been carried out with a dedication that was almost mystical.

All of which brought him more or less here, to his own avoidances and fears, to the flat, marshy expanse of Swan Bay, weeds that could hold a body down, if, that is, a body happened to be silly enough to venture into it.

Chris knew he never would. He'd never had that kind of recklessness, even as a child. When he'd fought with other boys it had been because he had no choice. Yet here he was, contemplating the ignominy of such an end, compared to that of his father, who'd died a hero's death.

Chris followed the shoreline, keeping his eyes down. At low tide, mud and rotting seagrass formed a kind of path. Water birds were feeding way out on the horizon. If he kept going, he would pass below Anthea's flat, where the land rose creating a mix between a sand dune and a crumbling cliff. He thought of that other cliff, on the ocean side, bordered by sandhills where he'd found Margaret Benton's coat, and the path to the lighthouse, where Camilla had seen the murdered woman, and had heard her scream.

As a boy, long, solitary after-school explorations had taken Chris to the town's boundaries and around them time and time again.

Once he'd found a tiger snake's skin and taken it home. His mother had refused to let him keep it in the house. Only hunger dragged him back from these expeditions, knowing the exact form of his mother's reproach, reciting the words now with a bitterness that made him shake.

His father's shift work had meant that he was often out in the evenings. Chris walked on, the exact taste in his mouth of how he'd dreaded going home, and how his hunger always got the better of him.

He kept on walking, overcoming a hurdle, notching up a success that no one would ever know about besides himself. The flat bay, the stink of rotting weeds, made his stomach turn. He could see no beauty in it anywhere.

He rounded a pile of broken rocks and came face to face with Ben, wearing a parka with the hood pulled up. As soon as the boy spotted Chris, he whistled loudly. A collie came running, and Ben put him on the lead.

'About that fight over the barbecues, Ben,' Chris said without preamble, 'was anybody else involved?'

Ben fiddled with his collie's lead in order to avoid looking up. 'You mean, like other campers?' he asked in a voice that was barely audible.

'Anyone at all.'

'Well, like, there were these guys and they both reckoned they got there first.'

Chris nodded, and took Ben quietly through the details before repeating his question. 'Anybody else?'

'The others just wanted to stay out of it.'

'What about Mrs Benton? What was she doing at the time?'

'Mrs - ?' Ben repeated, but seemed unable to get his tongue around the name. He scratched his head. Chris waited. Finally, the boy said, 'She tried to stop her husband from losing his temper. But it was too late.'

'Did you see where Mrs Benton went after your father sorted out the argument?'

'She left. With her husband.'

'Straight away? They'd have to pack. And what about their evening meal?'

'I dunno. I - I did see her talking to someone later on that night.'

'Another woman? Do you know her name?'

Ben shook his head.

'Do you have any idea what they were talking about?'

'You mean like, was I listening?'

'I thought, if Mrs Benton was upset, she might have - '

'I don't reckon she was *that* upset. She didn't show it anyway.'

'Where were the two women when you saw them talking?'

'Mrs Benton went back to her cabin, then later on I saw this other lady going in.'

'Thanks Ben,' Chris said. 'You've been helpful.'

'Is that all?'

'For the time being.'

'You haven't found that camel?'

'No.'

Penny invited Chris to take a seat in the office. In answer to his inquiry, she looked annoyed, but did as he asked and took down the big reservations folder

The argument over the barbecues had taken place on a Wednesday. The Bentons had booked till the following Saturday, but had left on the Thursday morning.

'How did they pay?' Chris asked.

'By credit card.'

'In advance?'

'Yes. Everyone has to pay in advance at that time of year.'

'Did they ask for a refund?'

'I don't think I was in the office when they dropped their key off. They may have asked Alex. There's nothing written here. I'm sure he wouldn't have given it to them.'

'Ben told me he saw Margaret Benton talking to another guest the night her husband got into a row. Do you know who that might have been?'

Penny pursed her lips then said, 'It might have been Mrs Desmain.'

When Chris asked for Mrs Desmain's contact details, Penny swung the book around and he copied them.

'Did he kill her, that husband of hers?'

'I don't know,' Chris said. 'What was Margaret Benton like?'

'I never had anything to do with her. Well, apart from once when she came to ask me about the washing machines.'

'I know it was your busiest time.'

'Run off my feet. And thank goodness for it, because look at this.'

'It'll pick up, Penny. Don't worry. Did you see Margaret Benton talking to other campers, other guests?'

'I know you're trying to build up a background, but - '

'But what?'

'Well, they came from Swan Hill. They went back there, didn't they? That's where she was killed.'

Chris did not attempt to respond to this. When he asked Penny if she'd seen the couple leave, Penny shook her head.

'Don't be too hard on Ben,' she said.

'What's Ben done?'

Penny said firmly, 'Nothing wrong, so far as I know.'

Chris gave her a searching look. When it was clear she wasn't prepared to say anything more, he thanked her and wished her good afternoon.

Chris phoned Mrs Desmain from the station, feeling lucky that she seemed willing to talk. She'd only met Margaret Benton at the caravan park, hadn't known her before, and they hadn't spent much time together, just half an hour or so in the laundry one morning.

'She didn't have the right change, and I was able to help her out.'

'What sort of washing did Mrs Benton have?'

'Well, the usual things. There was one thing I noticed. A yellow cardigan. Nice, it was. I said the machine might be a bit hard on it.'

'What happened on the Wednesday night?'

'We were having a barbecue tea. I've got two little kiddies and my youngest - he's only seven, but his father was showing him how to cook the sausages. I guess you've heard about the argument - that's why you're ringing me?'

Chris said that he had.

Mrs Desmain's account tallied with what the McIntyres had said.

'What did Mrs Benton do when the argument broke out?' Chris asked.

'She tried to calm her husband down, but she wasn't having much success. Then Alex came over and had a go at him.'

'Did you see where Mrs Benton went?'

'Not then, I didn't. We finished our tea, and my husband took the boys to the games room while I did a bit of cleaning up. Then, when I was on my way back, Margaret came to the door of her cabin. I could see that she'd been crying. I went inside and we talked for a few minutes. I asked if there was anything I could do, but she said there wasn't. She said they'd have to leave in the morning.'

'Did you see any signs that Jack Benton might be violent towards his wife?'

'Beat her up, you mean?'

'I'm not making suggestions, Mrs. Desmain. I'd just like you to cast your mind back and tell me what you remember.'

'I was upset when I heard she'd gone missing, and then when her body was found - I mean, it wasn't as though we were friends or anything, but I felt upset. I never saw any signs of violence. Maybe she was the sort of person who hates a fuss. That husband of hers was the opposite. The more noise he made the happier he was. I do remember her saying to me that they wouldn't get in anywhere else without a booking. Not over the Christmas break.'

'Did you see Mrs Benton again?'

'No, I didn't. It was a lovely day the next day. The weather hadn't been too good, but that morning was lovely. We got up early and took the boys to the beach. I remember looking over to the Benton's cabin, and that big car of theirs was gone.'

'Did any of the other campers talk about the argument?'

'Not to me. Well, we weren't the Bentons' neighbours. Maybe they talked about it. And they were a lot older than we were. We tended to mix more with other parents of young kids. The Bentons had never had children.'

'Did Mrs Benton tell you that?'

'It was when we were in the laundry. There was a little girl there with her mother. About the same age as my Josh. I could tell by the way Margaret looked at her that she had no kids of her own. And then she said how lucky I was to have Josh and Nathan. I must say, I felt a bit taken aback because I hadn't realised she'd noticed. They weren't in the laundry with me.'

'She knew their names?'

'Oh, no. "Two great kids", she said.'

SIXTEEN

Anthea spent Sunday morning cleaning her already spotless flat.

She looked across at her neighbour's garden. The weatherboard walls, painted white, were thick with vines, as was the fence that separated his cottage from the units. A man was living in the cottage on his own. At least she'd only seen a single man, sturdily built, with a self-sufficient air.

The cottage was tiny. Anthea couldn't imagine that it contained more than three rooms, at the most. The pear and apple trees were in flower, or trees that she guessed were pear and apple. The plain concrete surrounds of the units were easy to keep clean and involved practically no maintenance. Anthea found herself regretting that the fruit blossoms did not blow her way.

With the last of her boxes unpacked, her rooms looked spartan, as though something was missing. Not some*thing*, but some*one*, thought Anthea. Other tenants had pot plants on their balconies. She could buy a pot plant. She could buy twenty pot plants. Tears came to her eyes.

Her neighbours in the units were quiet and hadn't bothered to make her acquaintance. Anthea missed her boxes, missed staring past them to the view outside. As long as they'd remained, they were a testimony to her hope that her stay in Queenscliff would be temporary.

Graeme's absence hit her doubly. It would have been better if he'd never come. He blamed her for ruining the one weekend he'd set aside for her. In any approach she made from now on, she would have to deal with that. Yet whatever else happened, she knew that she was not prepared, ever again, to accept the way that Graeme brushed aside her working life.

Anthea crossed the road and stood looking out over the seagrass meadows. They were golden-green, with the faintest of blue washes over them, the water darker in the channel, where the tide was coming in. Once she'd tried walking along the edge of the seagrass, and had been startled by the way her feet sank into it, how the mud squelched up and covered her shoes.

She spotted the Bar-tailed Godwits. After she'd first noticed the thin, delicately shaped birds, she'd looked them up on a tourist guide listing features of Swan Bay. The name had amused her and she'd thought it might amuse Graeme as well. 'Godwit', and then to cap it off, 'Bar-tailed'. She had thought she might invest in a pair of binoculars. She had gone so far - the foolishness of it gripped her - to imagine Graeme with his eyes fixed to binoculars, remarking, 'Look at that!'

The small migratory waders would not fulfil their function as providers of amusement, and were suddenly dear to her because of this.

Anthea had stocked up so well in anticipation of Graeme's visit that she wouldn't need to do any grocery shopping for the next two weeks. She made herself some lunch, choosing from amongst her delicacies those that would go off soonest. Then she checked the Geelong hospital's visiting hours and decided she would pay Camilla a visit.

Anthea felt no particular emotion on entering a hospital. The smell caused her heart to beat faster, but she supposed that this was true for many people. She'd stopped at a roadside stall and bought some flowers. She buried her face in them for a moment before making her way to an inquiry counter.

Camilla was sitting up in bed, looking uncomfortable, her broken leg covered by a green cotton blanket. She smiled when she recognised Anthea, and pointed to a shelf above the bed, which held an empty vase. Then she touched her mouth lightly with the fingers of her right hand, and shook her head apologetically.

Anthea found a tap and filled the vase with water, no longer nervous that she'd have nothing to say to a woman who could not reply. She wished she'd thought to drive by Camilla's house on the way, so she could assure her that all looked to be in order.

Camilla took up a notepad and pen.

'Have you found Riza?'

'No,' said Anthea, 'unfortunately.'

'How is Julie?' was Camilla's next question.

'Not so good.'

Camilla nodded - a small, economical gesture. She'd had her hair cut. It was neat and fitted her head like a silver-grey cap.

'Can I get you anything?'

Camilla indicated a drinking glass and jug of water on top of a chest of drawers. Anthea half filled the glass and, while Camilla drank, moved the chest so that it was closer to the bed.

'Where were you going when you fell and broke your leg?' she asked.

'To Riza's paddock.'

'What were you going to do there?'

'Watch.'

'In the middle of the night?'

'Riza was stolen in the middle of the night.'

'How do you know?'

Camilla shook her head and looked confused.

'Did you see anyone?' asked Anthea

Camilla shook her head again.

She hated being trapped in hospital, she wrote. She had to get away.

Anthea frowned. Camilla tried to make her expression reasonable and to focus on the young policewoman's questions. Another drawing. That might be better than words.

Camilla drew the lighthouse with fog swirling around it. She drew herself in the bottom corner of the page, remembering a summer morning and a woman's cry. She pencilled in a figure in a black coat, with a blank, white face.

Anthea sat with her hands folded in her lap, knowing that she must be patient, schooling herself to it.

Camilla handed the sketch to Anthea, who studied it, then began asking questions, gently and carefully. It had been between Christmas and New Year, Camilla wrote, one of those summer fogs that descended without warning. She hadn't followed the woman, or seen where she'd gone. She'd stayed by the lighthouse for a while, and then turned for home. She was sorry. She knew she should have gone to the police.

Having done her best to apologise, Camilla leant back and closed her eyes.

Anthea reached out and gave her hand a squeeze. She said she had to go, but she'd be back to visit later.

Anthea stopped by the nurse's station on her way out to mention the chest of drawers and ask that water be left within the patient's reach. The nurse on duty eyed her grumpily and blamed the cleaners.

On her way back to Queenscliff, Anthea hummed a song from *Priscilla, Queen of the Desert* and smiled to herself, reflecting on how little it took to give a person the illusion of travelling towards a brighter future. She'd left Chris a voicemail message, wondering how he was spending his Sunday. Working in the garden would be her guess.

Anthea's phone rang when she was nearly home and she pulled off the road to answer it. Chris was pleased that she'd been to see Camilla, and agreed that it had probably been Margaret Benton on the cliff path. When Anthea offered to bring the drawing over straight away, he said there was no need for that. Tomorrow would be fine.

Anthea had a bad moment, opening the door. Her clean flat, which should have made her feel a certain pride - at least she wasn't living in a slum like Julie Beshervase - was loud in its emptiness. The silence hurt her ears.

Exhausted but unable to sleep, Camilla replayed sequences in her mind.

Her night-time walk to Riza's paddock returned as though every move she had made was magnified.

A rustle in the undergrowth could have been a bandicoot, but was more likely to have been made by a bird. Frogs called from the dam. A yellow glow behind the hill came from the farmhouse. The surf, always louder in the dark, had filled Camilla with a wild gladness, as though Riza had been found and was safe and well.

The walk had made her warm. Though frightened of showing herself at the paddock in the daytime, she understood that night brought its own form of courage - fugitive, stealthy and reliable. As the days had passed since Riza's disappearance, she'd gone about her simple routines, shopping and preparing food, all the time feeling as though she was on a cliff edge that at any moment might give way.

Her thoughts returned to the woman with the white face, who, in her haste, a stranger to the area, could have walked clean off the path. Perhaps she had; but then, of course, her body would have been found on the rocks below.

Camilla had seen the news, and knew Margaret Benton's body had been found. She might not be able to talk, but she still had a working brain. Who had been after her? Who had made her scream?

On the path to Riza's paddock, Camilla had sniffed the air, as though she might smell whoever had taken him away. She'd tripped and fallen over a heaving root, mouth open on a wordless cry.

SEVENTEEN

It was Monday morning, the start of a new week, and the footpath outside Queenscliff police station rang to the heavy tread of a tall, self-confident man - not yet middle-aged, but no longer young. Anthea realised that he was deliberately walking in the middle of the path, had no intention of stepping aside for her, and that her uniform confirmed him in his determination to provoke.

From his appearance, it could be Simon Renfrew. If Camilla's son was on his way towards a confrontation, he'd be disappointed. Chris had just left for Geelong. Simon might be twice Anthea's size, but she'd been trained to deal with big men on the lookout for a fight.

When he was three or four paces away, she asked politely, 'Can I help you?'

'I don't think so, *Miss*.'

The path widened immediately in front of the station's gate, and the man passed without either of them having to move aside, but he did what he could to maintain the insult, refusing eye contact, not slackening his pace.

Anthea decided to keep going, hearing behind her the sounds of impatient knocking. She did not think he would come after her, not in the echo of that *Miss*, delivered with such scorn. No, it would be more his way to pace, provided that he had the time, or to ring and leave a rude message on the answering machine.

She wondered what Simon would make of the lavender and rose beds, and recalled her first impressions of the house as a fairytale confection. Now she'd grown used to it, it did not seem so strange to her that the garden of a police station should be tended well, and by its senior officer.

She was too curious not to risk turning around, and saw that she'd perhaps misjudged the man. He was striding along the footpath in the opposite direction. The glance he threw over his shoulder held the contempt of a few moments before, mixed with a troubling animal appraisal.

Anthea walked over to the park and her favourite bench. The black lighthouse rose above her. Who would have thought to make a lighthouse *black*? They were meant to be beacons, to stand out in the night. And in fact there was one like that, a proper normal white one, just around the headland. Close up, the pillar became dark blocks of bluestone, the same as the oldest houses in the street. Still, its presence was menacing, ornate, matched by a dark grey water tower and the walls of the old fort.

A container ship, directly in front, revealed spaces between the containers that made them look like a giant's chimney stacks. Anthea wondered what it was about Camilla Renfrew's son that reminded her of Graeme.

She remembered holding Margaret Benton's coat up to the light and how, for a few moments, the office, the whole building, had sprung into a different kind of life.

Common sense should have told her that police work would mostly be routine. Common sense told her that the Swan Hill police were investigating Margaret Benton's murder, in the town where she'd lived, where her body had been found. Why should they bother to keep two constables at the opposite end of the state informed?

To hell with common sense, thought Anthea. Time for that when she was forty. Someone from the CIU ought to be in Queenscliff, asking questions, following up leads. In their absence, she and Chris would just have to do the best they could.

Anthea went back inside and made a list of all the people she knew who might have seen Margaret Benton in the township, people who had not come forward, but whose memories might only need a nudge. The first of Camilla's speech therapy sessions, undertaken on that Monday morning, left her throat so sore it felt as though scalding liquid was being continually poured down it. She had decided to be stoic; but the painkillers she was given seemed hardly to make a dent.

Simon had insisted on the treatment. It seemed to Camilla that her son and the speech therapist were conspiring to make her stay in hospital as miserable as possible. She turned her face to the wall and contemplated the notion that her son wished her dead. Could it be that ever since Alan had died, Simon had wished for her to follow her husband, that, in his boy's imagination, with his boy's ideas of shame and honour, he'd conceived of this conclusion as the only right one? Never mind the question of who would bring him up.

Alan had read Simon war stories from an early age. One of their disagreements had been about this; she'd considered that their son had been too young. The stories had given him nightmares, which Alan had said were good for him to face up to and overcome. If Alan had lived, Simon might have learnt to judge him in return for all the judgments Alan handed down. Instead, the father's virtues became fixed in the son's fierce mind. Camilla did not think that anything would happen now to change that. Simon felt no need to change. She was left with the fear that he wanted her to die.

It was after Alan's death, Camilla reflected, that she had gone wrong, living first of all in shock, and then, as the shock lessened, in blessed relief. Simon had misunderstood, but his misunderstanding had not been complete. He'd known that his mother despised his father, and from this to the next step - believing that she'd been responsible for his death - had been a small one for a grieving ten-year-old.

Camilla cupped her cheek in one hand, staring at a brown spot on the wall. Her strength was going; soon she would have none left. It was ridiculous the way this realisation brought relief. She felt that she could face the therapy sessions with something approaching equanimity if she knew that they would soon be coming to an end. Simon wanted what was best for her, he said. She contemplated the enormity of that, and her resolve foundered once again.

Camilla would give limbs in order to get her voice back, so that she could cry out against the cruelty of that 'best'. A non-believer, she nevertheless prayed that desperation would work when all other means had failed. The irony, if it ever happened this way, would escape her son entirely.

In Simon's world, obstacles existed to be overcome. He was fearful of any kind of ambivalence or contradiction. Had she taught him that? But how could she be blamed for a person grasping with a claw-like grip at the letter of a lesson, while totally ignoring its spirit? In Simon's view, since doctors had found no physiological basis for his mother's loss of speech, she could and *should* be made to speak again. Sometimes, Camilla wanted to tell Simon, obstacles existed for a different reason. Wasn't there an alternative viewpoint, equally as valid, that said the origins of her affliction were destined to remain in shadow, and that this lack of explanation ought to be respected?

Camilla shook her head, refusing food, scornfully regarding the painkillers that didn't do their job, passionately wishing that she could give up on her treatment. She hadn't slept, but at least the night had allowed a dulling and a fading of the day's troubles, chief of which was a new theory of the therapist's, which returned in all its ghastly detail now.

The gist of the new theory was that Camilla's loss of speech had been caused by a virus she'd contracted five years earlier. The therapist had made Camilla go right back through her childhood and youth, listing all her illnesses. Camilla recalled the Ah-ha! look on the therapist's face when she'd come to this particular virus.

Camilla had noticed a difficulty in pronouncing certain words a few weeks after she'd recovered from it, a thickened slurring of her tongue, a verbal stumbling which had deteriorated, at first gradually, then more rapidly, into her present state. To Simon, Camilla *in herself*, the person who was his mother, had become a repository for disease. She'd seen this in his face when he'd appeared in the doorway of the ward, taking in at one glance the bed, her trussed-up leg, then moving to her mouth.

Nurse Pemberton pursed her lips, but forbore expressing in words her disapproval of the untouched meal. 'Here's a visitor for you, Mrs Renfrew,' she said.

Camilla turned towards the door. What could have brought

Simon back?

But it was Chris Blackie, pausing in the doorway as though uncertain of his welcome.

Chris said hello and sat down on a chair next to the bed. He asked Camilla if there was anything she needed, then, with a glance at the nurse's departing back, took a folded sheet of paper from his pocket.

Camilla recognised the drawing she'd done for Anthea the day before. Chris spread it flat between them on the bed, while Camilla eyed it warily, as though it might move of it own accord.

As Chris began to point and question, Camilla forced herself to concentrate and to write as clearly as she could. Chris held her notebook for her when he saw how her right hand shook. She had thought about it during the night, in between worrying about Simon and the therapy. It was possible she'd seen the woman in the street, wearing other clothes, but she didn't think she had.

When Chris showed her a photograph of Jack Benton, she shook her head. There was nothing special about that face and no, she didn't recognise it. He could have been up by the lighthouse, but she'd heard no second pair of footsteps, and certainly he hadn't appeared out of the fog. Did she think the woman had been running away from someone? It was a possibility. She couldn't say for sure.

Chris had looked up the meteorological records, but he wanted Camilla's confirmation. December 30 had been foggy. Camilla nodded yes.

'Have you ever ridden a camel, Mrs Renfrew?'

Camilla jerked her head up and made a sign for Chris to repeat what he'd said.

She smiled then, wishing she had coloured pencils, to draw the sunrise in the background. She wished that her soft black pencil might take on colour as a gift. She recalled with absolute clarity that early morning on the beach, the tide running out, the glitter and the feeling that it was here at last, the culmination of all those weeks of waiting for her birthday treat.

Camilla picked up her notebook and drew that long-ago camel

for this patient policeman who'd managed at last to ask the right question. A female, with wide, careful feet - how she'd turned her head and stared, once the small girl was settled on her back, before the driver's command, sharp as a slap, resulted in that first incredible lunge forward.

There had been forbearance in the camel's expression; also the mild surprise of, well, this one's a lightweight. Oblique sunlight had emphasised the planes of her face, thick jowls and lips, eyes half covered by sweeping lashes whose single glance had said so much.

Camilla drew the camel facing forward, towards the rocks at the eastern end of a beach whose every detail she recalled. She drew herself as a stick child, proudly upright. She swayed backwards and forwards in her hospital bed and filled in the remainder of the picture quickly - her father and mother, riding either side of her, the other people who'd booked for the tour.

She handed the sketch to Chris, who studied it, then asked softly, 'Where was this?'

'Broome', Camilla wrote at the bottom, adding the month and year. 'Broome?'

She nodded, turned over the sheet and wrote, 'My father was working there. It was my eighth birthday.'

Chris smiled at the picture of the small girl on the hump, imagining how long before dawn she would have been awake and ready. He wondered what the Indian Ocean looked like, never having been further west than Adelaide.

There was something odd about the child's expression, then Chris realised that she didn't have one. Her eyes looked down, though her straight-backed little body was all anticipation.

Camilla put a hand to her throat, wishing Chris had the power to take her away, out of the clutches of the speech therapist, some place where even her son would not be able to reach her. What would happen if she committed some awful crime and had to be locked up? There would be a ward in the jail for the criminally insane. Her leg could be held in traction until the bones knitted, if they ever did. Nobody would badger her to get her voice box working. The authorities would label and then, if she was lucky, ignore her.

But she would never see the beach once she was officially classified as mad, never watch that film of water shine before it dried, that space between the tides. She saw the camel's large foot, with its pneumatic lift, perfectly designed for sand, two feet down on one side, then two on the other; and herself a small and lofty girl, who'd waited confidently for her treat, who'd had no concept, then, of promises that turned out to be false. How protected she'd been! How could she have failed to divine even a hint of the future that would one day be hers?

'I don't feel well. I'm sorry,' Camilla wrote on a clean page of her notebook.

Chris nodded and said he'd come back later. Camilla made a gesture of regret and apology.

After he'd left, she lay still, staring out the window, and thought how Riza would have loved the beach, loved to feel the sand between his toes. It was his birthright, and he'd been so *close*. She went red, remembering what a hash she'd made of it when she'd tried to indicate this once to Julie Beshervase.

The beach was less than three hundred metres away from his paddock, and Riza was as good as gold. He would have allowed Julie to lead him there and back. And she, Camilla, would have had the joy of watching the lovely creature plant his feet on sand. Recognition would have been there.

Camilla put her hand to her throat again, and gently massaged it. Pain kept her awake and made her aware of exactly where she was. But in her mind's eye, she saw Riza turn his head as though he smelt his own mother, trotting towards her on soundless feet. She patted him, and held her face close to his, smelling his grassy breath. Living in this memory, Camilla felt the tide's pull, and the moon's in the same direction, impossible to resist, and the wet sand splashed by a shore break beginning to gather strength. It was time to walk your camel, before the tide came in.

When the orderly came to wheel her to the speech pathology room, Camilla pretended to be asleep. She heard the orderly whispering to the nurse and clenched her fists, contemplating the logistics of a hunger strike. Surely she was too old to be force fed. But then she recalled her son and the speech therapist, heads side by side above her, the thin, straight indignation of their mouths, the awful tubes that would carry the unwanted food. No, the punishment that reared up in the face of any further protest was worse than what she currently endured. She must just last the weeks until she was allowed to go home.

Chris decided to buy himself a coffee in one of the small streets near the hospital.

He took out Camilla's drawings and looked at them, one by one. He knew that Ben was holding out on him, as was Ian Lawrey. Either of them could have taken the camel; or another boy whom Ben and Ian were protecting.

Chris's coffee was put in front of him and he drank it quickly. He liked his coffee hot and this one was barely warm. It didn't matter. The small café was quiet, somewhere to think without being interrupted.

He had no doubt that the scream Camilla had heard had been made by Margaret Benton. He would write another report. Surely this time it would not be ignored.

Margaret Benton might have dropped her coat in the sandhills, or left it somewhere else, which meant somebody besides herself had taken it there. It had been a good coat, expensive. Chris was inclined to think that, if a stranger had found it, then he or she would have kept, or sold it.

He'd been back to look and there'd been nothing else where he'd found the coat, no signs of a disturbance. He'd dug around to make sure that nothing had been buried there.

Chris spoke to the school principal, and obtained permission to question Ben during school hours. The principal offered the use of his office. When Chris said he wanted to speak to the boy alone, the principal frowned, but did not object. He left the office door open and Chris knew that he wasn't far away.

'When you found out that Margaret Benton had been murdered, you got scared. I don't blame you. Especially when she'd been staying at your van park. But I need to find out where she and her husband went after they left, and I think you know something that can help me.'

Ben's face had gone pale again. The dark hairs on his upper lip stood out strangely, as though he was both too young to have grown them, and too old to have left them unshaven.

'Rasch - ' he began, then bit his bottom lip.

'Yes?'

'Rasch said he'd seen this old witchy sort of woman on the cliff path.'

'When did Raschid see the woman?'

'I don't know.'

A cough from next door reminded Chris that he could be interrupted any moment.

Chris returned to the dare and how it had been carried out, asking questions until he had the sequence of events reasonably clear.

When Zorba's bet to ride Riza had been interrupted, the four boys had left the paddock; but they'd been keyed up, too excited to separate and go home. They'd gone back to Zorba's, whose older brother, Theo, had been down from his farm. Zorba had taken a packet of Theo's cigarettes and they'd smoked them on the beach.

'Who took the camel, Ben?'

'I don't know.'

'Could it have been Zorba?'

'I don't know!'

'It's time to tell the truth.'

'I'd never lie about that, honestly!'

'Ben, listen to me. There's more at stake than loyalty to your mates. What if one of the others stole the camel without telling you?'

'They couldn't! Specially that Zorba! He's so up himself he'd *have* to skite about it.'

The principal knocked on the door and Ben made his escape, head bowed, shoulders hunched protectively.

Chris drove to the station, where he checked for messages. There was one from Simon Renfrew that could keep. Chris looked up Theo Kostandis in the phone book and spent the time before school got out writing his report.

EIGHTEEN

At first, Raschid was inclined to deny everything, but after fifteen minutes of calm, persistent questioning, Chris got him to admit that he *had* seen a woman in a black coat and that she'd been 'acting weird'.

'How do you mean, weird?' Chris asked.

'She was stumbling, kinda. I thought she might be - like, drunk.'

'Where were you when you saw her?'

'On the bike path. I never stopped.' Raschid looked wary and suspicious, trying to guess the next question. Chris thought he would have been terribly ashamed to realise how transparent his expression was.

'When was this?' Chris asked again, to make sure.

'New Years Eve. I'd been at Zorba's helping with the lights and that.'

'You went to Zorba's party?'

'*Did* I? It was awesome.'

'What time of the day did you see the woman on the path?'

'In the morning.'

'Did you ever see her again?'

'I wouldn't know, would I? Maybe she went by in a car, or something. I gotta go now. Mum'll chew me over if I'm late.'

Raschid fidgeted with the handlebars of his bike, jumping the front wheel up and down the curb outside the school.

'It's you kids who've been wasting my time,' Chris said, 'not the other way around. Was the woman on her own?'

'I dunno. I never *saw* anybody with her.'

'And the coat?'

'Well like, it was summer, wasn't it?'

When Chris pulled out his photograph of Margaret Benton, Raschid stared at it for a long time, before he nodded and then shook his head.

Chris sighed. 'Come on, Raschid, you'll have to do better than that.'

'*I don't know,*' the boy almost shouted. 'All I know is, she was acting weird and she was in a hurry.'

Chris climbed the path where Raschid had seen the 'weird' lady. The lighthouse was half a kilometre further on, the spot where he'd found the coat almost a kilometre behind him, in a much less frequented part of the dunes.

He lifted his head and mentally measured the distance, then lowered it again to avoid stumbling over a tea-tree root.

He stopped to examine a small clearing to one side of the path, a hollow in the sand that would make a good resting place on a windy afternoon, sheltered and private. There was nothing to see except bushes overhanging a depression, scattered with leaves and twigs.

There were no human footprints, apart from the ones he'd just made. If there'd been a fight, a struggle, what evidence could be expected to remain after nearly nine months? Some, perhaps, but he lacked the means to find it. The whole area needed to be examined, but Chris knew in advance what response he would get to this request.

What a difficult area to remove an unconscious or dead body from, he thought, how awkward to carry her all the way to the road and whatever vehicle was waiting. If it had happened that way, the attacker had taken a great risk. Chris had to admit that it was much more likely Margaret Benton had been killed close to her home.

He told himself he ought to be feeling hungry and wondered why he wasn't. Instead, he felt light-headed from the effort of interviewing adolescent boys. He phoned Anthea, who was trying another house-to-house, then rang Simon Renfrew and left a message.

It was cold on the path, and Chris pulled his jacket tighter, keeping his back to the sea. Other people had perhaps seen Margaret Benton in her unseasonable black coat, but the locals weren't volunteering anything, and tracking holiday-makers down would be impossible unless they were very lucky.

The ocean heaved below him. Chris told himself he didn't need to walk along the cliff; nothing would be proved by it; but he turned up his coat collar and trudged forward anyway.

On New Year's Eve, Raschid would not have been alone on the path. There would have been other cyclists and plenty of walkers as well. Not too many people would have ventured up there in the fog on December 30, but Camilla Renfrew had.

If his witnesses were right, and he believed they were, Margaret Benton had been seen two days running in the same area. Had she been trying to escape from her husband, and if so, why had she chosen to go there, of all places? Why hadn't she called for help? Had she been contemplating throwing herself over the edge?

Chris stopped walking. Rising before him, without warning, came a nightmare vision of the dead woman being pushed over the cliff, falling to break her neck on the rocks beneath. The insistent, restless water, never still, always worrying at the rocks, lifted her body, billowing the black coat like a pirate's sail.

Chris let himself into the station and turned on every light. He didn't question this. He simply knew he had to make the place as bright as possible. He checked the front door twice to make sure he'd locked it behind him.

He made himself a cup of tea, though he didn't want one, and stared at the hot liquid without drinking it. But the simple actions of boiling water and getting down a mug were calming. He told himself he'd had some kind of waking nightmare, that was all.

The night his father drowned had been pitch black, with a southwesterly gale and the ebb tide running at six knots. The conditions were bad, though not uncommon - the southwesterly holding the waves up against the current, the pilot boat plunging almost vertically between them. After so many years, Chris needed only to walk at night and smell the ocean, particularly if there was a strong southwesterly, to picture it as though he'd been there.

In the maritime museum, there were photographs of pilots climbing rope ladders away from the safety of small orange boats, scaling the huge flank of a container ship or liner, in the dark, above a raging sea. There was a time when he'd forced himself to look at these photographic records, though they made him sick - the man caught in silhouette, black against a ship's white bulk, like some horrible elongated spider. Yet those pilots were the lucky ones; they'd made it and gone on making it, time and time again.

No camera had caught the pilot who'd fallen from the ladder on a vicious night, nor the crewman on the tiny vessel waiting underneath, who'd heard the yell, who'd seen the fall and jumped overboard to save his master.

After sitting for a long time staring at his desk, the mug of cooling liquid still untouched, Chris gave his shoulders a hard shake and got down to work. He made a new list of questions, writing steadily and keeping his mind focussed on the task.

He printed off every single piece of information he and Anthea had unearthed about the Bentons, gathered the pages into a neat pile on his desk, then checked his watch. If he hurried, he'd get to the fish and chip shop just before it closed.

The proprietor, another Greek, not nearly so rich as the Kostandises, looked tired and grey-faced.

He gave Chris a sharp look and Chris wondered about his own appearance, how much of what he'd been remembering showed in his face. Of course, Janaros knew his family history. He wondered who'd told Anthea, if anybody had. He fancied he'd know, by the look on her face, her manner. But maybe he was wrong about this. Maybe she couldn't care less.

'Got a nice piece of whiting left,' Janaros said. 'For you, same price.'

'Okay. Thanks.'

Janaros sank his order into hot oil, then inquired with his back turned, 'Found that camel yet?'

'No,' Chris said, aware that his answer was abrupt.

He sat down on a plastic chair to wait, wondering what Janaros would be doing after he shut the shop. His kids were grown up. His wife had gone back to Greece, ostensibly to help look after her sister; but it was already four months and people were beginning to wonder.

No sound but his own footsteps had followed him along Hesse Street. During the summer holidays, the fish and chip shop was a production line, three men behind the counter, two girls taking orders at the till, phone ringing non-stop from five in the afternoon. Sometimes, when it was very late - Chris rang his order in, twenty minutes before he came to pick it up - the cooks were hunched over with exhaustion, and Janaros was leaning on the counter as though it could barely support his weight. For all that, the fish was always fresh, and freshly cooked.

Chris wondered why Janaros didn't give it away, retire, follow his wife to Greece, or go someplace else.

He pulled out his photograph of Margaret Benton.

Janaros bundled up his order and wiped his hands on his apron before saying flatly, 'It's that woman got herself murdered up along the Murray.'

'Did you ever see her down here?'

Janaros glanced towards the door. 'I couldn't swear to it, but I reckon she came in here one night. It's, well, it's not a face a man would remember.'

Chris nodded and waited. Finally Janaros said, 'She looked like she'd been crying.'

'Do you remember when?'

'No, mate. Not a hope.'

Chris took his dinner back to the station. This time he didn't feel the need to turn on all the lights. He read through his file of papers while he ate, shoving chips and bits of steaming fish into his mouth, washing the lot down with Carlton Light. He wondered if the fishy smell would still be there in the morning, and if Anthea would notice. He opened the window, waved his arm about for a few seconds, shut it again and settled back to his reading.

Jack Benton had first reported his wife missing on January 3. They had returned from their annual holiday, which was supposed to have included a week at Swan Bay caravan park. It seemed that Benton had not been questioned in any detail about this. According to his statement, they had driven back on Friday the 2nd, arriving late in the evening, and the next day Margaret had taken the car to the supermarket, or at least had said that this was her intention. She was not on the supermarket's CCTV film, nor had anyone been found who'd seen her in the car park, or inside at the time she was supposed to have been there. When she failed to return, Jack had gone looking for her, and found the locked car. Her bag, which he knew she'd taken with her, was not inside. He'd gone home puzzled, but not immediately alarmed. Six hours later, when there was still no sign of her, he'd rung the police.

NINETEEN

It seemed everyone had a theory. Penny and Alex McIntyre were rung up ten times a day, mostly by nutters, Penny complained to Chris, who was busy fielding his share of nuisance calls.

One woman, who didn't even live in Queenscliff, thought he should know that she'd heard a car pulling up outside her place in the middle of the night. Another had seen Brian Laidlaw riding past with a suspicious-looking bundle tied to the back of his bike.

Chris listened politely. Where were the townsfolk who really might have seen something relevant, he asked himself as he put the phone down. Why did he have to put up with fools and busybodies instead?

In a single morning, they received three confessions to the murder, two by phone and one by a note pushed under the station's front door. The calls, and the note, which Chris found on arriving at work, had to be followed up. A smudge of blue paint in one corner led him, by a somewhat roundabout route, to a handyman called Joe Fisher, who lived in a cottage by the wharf that was painted half-a-dozen shades of blue.

Fisher readily admitted to having written the confession and looked surprised that it had taken Chris half a morning to find him.

'Why didn't you sign it then, Joe?'

The handyman replied that that would have made his job too easy.

'How did you get the body back to Swan Hill?'

'In me van,' Fisher said with a satisfied smile.

Chris sighed. The van would have to be examined, and the workshop - but what a waste of time. Everyone knew Fisher was several sandwiches short of a picnic. He was harmless; or he had been.

Chris looked around the workshop, which Fisher had added onto his cottage at a time when building regulations were less strict. It was filled with what mostly looked like junk, but obviously had value to the handyman - hundreds of tins of paint, many of which looked empty, wood of all shapes and sizes, hammers, wrenches, chisels, jars of nails. Chris knew that Fisher got by on his age pension, very seldom employed by anybody, even as a favour. He thought of Brian Laidlaw, and other old men who'd lived in Queenscliff all their lives, and wondered if he'd end up like them - or, more precisely, *which* of them he'd end up being like.

He questioned Fisher, going over details of the note, where Fisher had been the night Riza disappeared. It took a while to establish which night they were talking about, since Fisher was vague about dates and times. That night, he claimed with a sly, delighted grin, he'd been 'out on a job'. He wouldn't say what kind.

Chris sighed again, audibly this time, and wondered at the familiarity he'd encouraged with the townsfolk, leading to an insolence he had surely not intended, but was probably his fault. He thought of the debacle over Frank Erwin's horse float, a mistake he was determined not to repeat. Yet Joe Fisher owned a van big enough to transport a young camel. And he was always driving round, 'on the look-out for this and that'. His van was such a common sight nobody would have remarked on it.

'We'll have to take your van, Joe.'

'What? You can't do that!'

'You shouldn't have written that note, then.'

'I need me van for work!'

'You'll have to walk, or ride a bike.' Chris thought once more of Brian Laidlaw, while Fisher looked as though he was suggesting that he sprout wings and fly.

Chris thought of the jokes that would go the rounds. He was already close to a laughing stock. But why? What was inherently absurd about his questions? Was the joke so obvious that everyone but him could see it?

Chris could hear the chortles, yet he still found it difficult to understand except in terms of a false judgement and premature conclusion. *Fancy yourself a detective, Blackie? Better leave that job to real men.* Could a trained detective tell by looking the difference between hairs belonging to a palomino pony and a camel?

'How did you kill her, Joe?'

He was conscious of being deliberately cruel, and felt ashamed.

'I never killed nobody! Can't you take a joke?'

Chris left the van where it was. He wrote another report and filed it. He endeavoured to separate, as much as possible, two crimes that threatened to plait together in his mind. He felt the whole town laughing at him, with Joe Fisher's manic cackle followed by an old sheep's cough. He woke with a headache and dragged himself to work. He heard laughter as he left his cottage in the morning; and the life that he had made for himself, woven out of partly unwanted, partly cherished strands, seemed to dissolve with every step he took.

There were those who could embrace absurdity, even turn it to advantage. Joe Fisher was one of them. Chris wondered if Camilla Renfrew was another. But no, Camilla suffered too much. Her performances - the notes, the drawings - were a product of her disability, a combination of necessity and will-power. A crank call would, of course, have been beyond her; but a mischievous letter or a practical joke Chris felt to be beyond her as well. What was it about murder, he wondered, when its black wings touched down in a place, that made innocent people behave irresponsibly?

TWENTY

Everywhere Julie Beshervase looked she was met by a fluffy whiteness, caught at the corner of her eye, a kind of tunnel vision - though didn't people with this affliction usually see shadows? The outline of a young imprisoned creature was fixed on the inside of her curtains when she went to bed. She took to walking with her head down and her eyes half closed. Sunlight through kitchen windows brought to life a dust pile on the floor. Julie shut her eyes and groaned. She could not walk around in total darkness. Even then, the backs of her eyelids shone.

After catching sight of her reflection in the bathroom mirror, she spent ten minutes fixing a T-shirt over it with bluetack. There was nothing else to hold the edges and she considered the bluetack a logical and sensible idea. She'd been frightened and dismayed by the look of wild exhaustion that had met her in the mirror, hair sticking up at all angles, dirt around her ears. I look madder than Camilla, she told herself, and then, I mustn't lose it altogether. I must keep going for Riza's sake.

Julie had never asked herself why she loved Riza. This was a question it was simply not worth bothering to ask. Having lost the rebellious, self-destructive urge of fifteen, she'd been persuaded that, on balance, it might be better to remain alive. A counsellor had convinced her of that much and it had seemed childish at the time not to agree, provisionally. For years she'd gone on functioning without any sense of purpose. Until she'd found and purchased Riza, she'd felt that her life was on probation, and might fail to make the grade. Extinction, total blackness, might turn out to be preferable after all.

Julie decided that fresh air was what she needed, and that to be shut up inside the house was doing her no good at all.

'Here!' Julie exclaimed, pointing at a muddy patch in front of her.

'Riza's prints,' she said, dropping to her hands and knees.

Chris and Anthea bent, obligingly, to look.

Anthea expected camel prints to be wider and flatter than those made by cattle. None looked particularly wide to her.

When Chris asked Julie when she'd found them, she said, staring at the ground, 'This morning.'

Anthea lifted her head, sniffing the distinctive tea-tree smell. Papery twisted branches caught the light, their shadows resembling tiny dolls. They were in a paddock which sloped uphill towards the Erwins' farmhouse. Half way up was a dam, and it was to this that Julie had led them. It felt like a procession, as though there were more than three of them, as though others waited in the wings. The ground was churned up and fresh droppings covered it. Anthea kept expecting Frank to appear.

Chris studied the prints. He looked funny with his bum stuck out, trying not to get muddy. Anthea drank water from a bottle she had brought in order to hide her smile.

Chris stood up, lifting his cap to scratch his head. They exchanged a glance. Anthea understood that the last thing he wanted was to tackle Frank Erwin again with so slight a piece of evidence. Frank would laugh in mockery and scorn.

Chris photographed the prints, walking carefully around the muddy patch and recording it from different angles. 'Pity we don't have a dromedary here,' he said, 'to make the comparison.'

'It's Riza's print!' Julie's voice was waspish with an undercurrent of hysteria.

'Don't go tackling Frank, now, or anybody else. Leave it up to us.' Chris held Julie's eyes until she nodded.

Green shoots were everywhere. It was the impatience of the spring, brooking no excuse. Anthea thought that, when they found Riza - if they found him alive - he would have grown heaps.

Chris recalled what he'd been like at Anthea's age - keen to succeed, respectful of authority. What had happened to that respect? If he'd been asked two weeks ago, he would have replied that nothing had happened to it, that it was intact. He would have replied without needing to think.

A police force depended on hierarchy. The alternative was chaos. But once Chris began to doubt the wisdom of his youthful conclusion, other doubts sprang up behind it. It was as though the failure of the CIU to respond to his reports had operated like a curtain, pulling back to reveal a gaudy and undisciplined spectacle, a show that drew him towards it, even as it alarmed him and made him afraid that all his beliefs and values, up until then, had been false.

Chris hurried away before he lost his temper with Julie Beshervase, and the whole damned lot of them.

TWENTY-ONE

On her way to the caravan park, Anthea recalled how Julie's older brother had lent her the money to buy Riza. There were questions still needing to be asked about that, but was Julie too distressed to answer them?

The cold wind hit her and she pulled the jacket of her uniform more tightly round her chest. She realised how open and exposed the van park was on a windy day.

Penny had two heaters going in the office and did not look pleased to see her.

Anthea smiled and asked Penny how she was, receiving the briefest nod and 'Fine thanks' in reply.

'I was just wondering, when the Bentons made their booking, whether they said if your park had been recommended to them by a friend or family member.'

Penny shook her head. 'If it was, they didn't tell me.'

'Did they say anything about where they were intending to go after they left here?'

'I think Jack Benton did say something to Alex, after that ruckus over the barbecue. Alex told him he'd have to calm down and accept his ruling as park manager, or leave. And Jack said, where would he go? And Alex said that wasn't his problem. Then Jack said something about the Ocean Road. That's what I think anyway, but it would be better to ask Alex.'

Penny hesitated, then went on determinedly, 'I'd just as soon you and Chris left our Ben alone. He's been that *touchy*. You can't look at him sideways. I'm sure if he knew where that camel was he'd have said so by now.'

Anthea couldn't give any such assurance. Indeed, hearing Ben's reaction made her feel sure that he was still hiding something. She knew Penny saw this suspicion in her face.

Anthea felt like a walk before heading back to the station. She told herself she'd earnt it. The tide was out, the high point it had reached a wavering line marked with brown and green seaweed and bits of broken shells. The soil, pock-marked with white salt circles, felt spongy under her feet. She was careful not to step on the patches of dark, oozing mud. When she looked up, she saw an old man walking slowly along the shoreline. He disappeared around the curve where Swan Bay met the much larger Port Phillip Bay, with its dangerous Rip and shipping lanes carrying container after container to Melbourne.

It was still a novel idea to her, to think of commerce in this way, passing by them constantly. It was a different way to think of Melbourne, a way that Graeme would hardly be aware of. From where she stood, the city was visible as no more than a faint pollution smudge, coloured as usual by his rejection of her. As Anthea put this firmly out of mind, another thought surfaced. If she were going to hide something - even something as big as a camel - she would choose a city to do it in.

The station was empty. Anthea settled herself at her desk, and began looking up caravan parks along the Ocean Road.

She was interrupted by a metallic thump, followed by angry voices and banging car doors.

A car reversing from a parking spot had backed into an oncoming one. Each driver blamed the other. They would have stood in the street shouting till they came to blows.

Anthea got both men inside, thought of phoning Chris, then decided she could handle the incident without him.

She put the drivers on opposite sides of the counter to fill in their reports. When she was confident they'd settled down, she photographed the cars. A small crowd had gathered and were debating the rights and wrongs of the accident. It was obvious that the parked car should have given way; but the townsfolk, Anthea was aware, did not allow the obvious to get in the way of a good argument.

The two men handed over their reports like schoolboys at the end of detention. Anthea told them they could move their cars. When she tried ringing Chris, she found that his phone was switched off. She sent him a text, then returned to the yellow pages.

What if the Bentons had driven back to Swan Hill on New Years Eve? If she could prove that, then there were a couple of days at Swan Hill that did not seem to be accounted for. If the Bentons had managed to find somewhere else to stay, then that time was still a blank.

Half an hour later, she'd made no progress at all. If Jack Benton had tried to book somewhere along the Ocean Road, would any of the park managers remember? At peak holiday time it was most unlikely.

On her own in the quiet building, Anthea was suddenly gripped by a sharp physical memory of the night Graeme had spent in her flat overlooking Swan Bay, how her tiny bedroom had seemed to expand in order to take in the two of them; a wavering, fluid expansion of white sheets and night air and the unbelievable luxury of her lover's skin. She had felt herself blessed in a thousand ways, as though nothing had happened to sour their relationship.

They hadn't talked about themselves, or Melbourne and the distance that separated them. They hadn't talked much at all. They'd drunk the wine she had so carefully selected. They'd joked about a television program, then they'd gone to bed.

Anthea tried to put the memory out of her mind, and couldn't. But then, on her own in the office, staring at lists of caravan parks, she thought - we had that time. I had it. It was mine, no matter what the next day brought.

She sighed, embarrassed by how loud her sigh sounded in the empty room, feeling the beginnings of anxiety about what Chris was up to, and why he hadn't turned his phone back on. She tried his landline home phone, letting it ring out before hanging up.

Anthea kept going with her systematic search of van parks, wishing again for a decisive boss, a big metropolitan station, a clear chain of command. She would be at the bottom, the youngest and least experienced member of a team; but she would be given straightforward tasks and orders; she wouldn't feel as though she was trying to achieve something in a vacuum.

At Apollo Bay, she had a bit of luck. Jack Benton had rung the park and the manager had told him sorry, they were fully booked. Jack, who'd introduced himself at the start of the conversation, had argued, then become abusive. The park manager had jotted down his name in case he ever rang again.

'Trouble I don't need,' he told Anthea, who thanked him and then made a note.

She felt pleased and decided to go for another walk. She locked the front door and headed down to the pier, breathing in the kelp that the last tide had deposited. There were piles big enough to live in, if you could stand the smell, make castles of, and forts, and rank, slippery hideaways.

She thought of Margaret Benton's body emerging from its grave. Jack's story about his wife leaving the house to do the shopping and never returning could have been invented after she was already deep in the fertile river soil. But if she'd been killed in Queenscliff and his Landcruiser used to transport her body to Swan Hill, some evidence of this had surely remained.

Anthea's courses at the Academy had dinned into her just how hard it was to erase all evidence of a body from a car. Of course it was a long jump from arguing over a barbecue to murdering your wife. But Anthea was satisfied in her own mind that Margaret Benton had been trying to escape, and that her husband had prevented her.

The white ferry was half way across the Rip, returning from Sorrento. The orange pilot boat, tiny by comparison, was on its way back too. Terns had located a shoal of fish and were diving; vertical, exact. Anthea imagined the view from under the water, from the fishes' point of view - a calm surface, nothing out of the ordinary, then all hell breaking loose.

She fetched her car and drove to Julie's house, relieved to see Julie's bike in its usual position. She realised that concern for Julie was a constant nagging presence at the back of her mind. More than once she'd imagined Julie deciding that, without Riza, there was no point in hanging on. When she knocked on the front door and there was no answer, she decided to go around the back.

Julie was in the yard, breaking up stale bread and scattering it on the grass. She turned to look at Anthea with a small, self-conscious frown. Exhaustion had thinned her face; her body had lost its long-legged grace.

'I suppose you want to come in?' she asked abruptly.

'We could talk out here.'

'There's nowhere to sit down.'

Anthea conceded the point with a nod. Inside the house, the smell didn't seem so bad. The kitchen window was open, and the garbage bin, overflowing on Anthea's last visit, had its lid firmly on.

When Anthea asked Julie if her brother had set a time for paying back the loan, Julie said, her frown deepening, 'Is that what they teach you in police school? To grow a hide as thick as a rhinoceros?'

'Have you told the previous owner about Riza's disappearance?'

'I rang him. He was sympathetic, but what could he do?'

'Can you think of any reason why he might want your camel back?'

'I sent some photos a few weeks ago. He was happy that Riza was doing well.'

'Are you sure you never saw Margaret Benton anywhere around here?'

'Yes.'

'Nowhere round the paddock?'

'I just told you!'

Riza's saddle was arranged across two chairs, directly in the light. Each mirror shone. The leather had been polished so that it looked wet.

Anthea stared at the saddle, conscious of Julie to one side, a sullen rag doll after her outburst. She walked across and saw herself reflected from this angle then that, long blue legs and face foreshortened to a dot of white. She moved her arm and there it was, a line transfixed and multiplied. It seemed each mirror had a small mind of its own.

Julie said, 'Did you know that a camel can't see behind itself, like a horse? I mean, a horse can't either. In that way, a camel is just like a horse.'

There was something menacing in Julie's tone. Anthea felt the hairs rise on her forearms

'So if someone came up behind Riza, he could have been surprised. Though camels have excellent vision otherwise, and an excellent sense of smell.'

'We'll get him back,' Anthea said, trying to put into her voice the conviction that she did not feel.

Anthea sat in her car and felt how reality could split, how Julie straddled a split that was growing wider. She wondered what she ought to be doing if she really believed that Julie was contemplating suicide - arrange someone to stay with her, which Julie would almost certainly refuse - invite her to stay at the flat, which she would hate?

She could contact the relevant social services. Julie might be offered counselling. Anthea knew in advance that Julie would consider this kind of interference as a form of betrayal. Was it better for Julie to be angry with a police officer who couldn't solve a simple crime, or be left alone to follow her own worst inclinations?

Anthea went on sitting, trying to collect her thoughts. Her unease seemed in some odd way the fault of all those mirrors on the saddle, reflecting her back in pale ovals and blue lines without being able to convey anything of what was in between.

On her way home, she called in to the library and took out a book on bird migration, surprising herself by feeling her spirits lift as she filled out a membership form and provided proof that she was a local resident. She sat on her balcony with the book open in front of her, reading about the orange-bellied parrots, rare and endangered, who wintered on Swan Island.

There was quite a large section on the Bar-tailed Godwit. Their wing bones, thin as skewers, served the waders on a ten thousand kilometre journey to their nesting grounds in Siberia. Anthea learnt that the Godwits used the same migration route as half the world's shorebirds, the Asia-Pacific Flyway, which led them over the steppes of Mongolia and Northern China to the mudflats of northeast Asia, where they rested, stocking up on worms and shellfish, before crossing the Pacific.

It grew cold and windy, but Anthea scarcely noticed. She'd never taken an interest in birds before, and knew nothing of their feats of navigation and endurance. The golden seagrass was almost covered by the rising tide, yet the Godwits, along with stilts and dotterels that she could now identify, continued foraging along the shoreline. What an encumbrance, to be named for the creator, she thought, narrowing her eyes to watch them - a top-heavy name for such a slight, self-effacing creature. And whose 'wit' had it been? She'd found no reference to the origin of the name.

The black swans stretched their long necks underwater. Anthea loved the way the tide came in here without a wave, on most days scarcely a ripple. The swans called to each other, a soft, conversant honking. She lifted her head and smelt the rich stink of dead plants composting. She wondered what building had been there, where she was now, before the block of units; whether there'd been a couple of old weatherboard cottages similar to the one next door, and whether their owners had died in order to make way for concrete, aluminium and glass.

Anthea made herself a herb omelette and ate it on her balcony with chunks of bread, having put on a thick jumper to keep out the wind, thinking about journeys. There was the Bentons' Christmas holiday, a modest trip from Swan Hill to Queenscliff, and her own small, unremarkable relocation, to set against the massive journey the shore waders faced each year.

The last few paragraphs of the chapter in the library book described how the parent birds left Siberia weeks before their young, who followed the navigation routes and arrived at Swan Bay by instinct. Each year, there would be some, many perhaps, accidents along the way; birds drowning, or dying of exhaustion or starvation. It was the Godwits' ordinariness that moved her, how nondescript they looked, with their brown and buff-coloured feathers, methodically picking their way along the tide line. What did they think of their birthplace in Siberia? Did they hold pictures of it in their minds?

To the Godwits, the bumpy seagrass, the black mud, crusted and drying at the edges, only to be soaked again by the incoming tide, had the proportions of great mounds and bog-lands full of food. Their light feet did not sink. What was their impression as they looked up and saw humans stumbling through their territory, shaking their great feet like princes and princesses whose carriages had been unaccountably delayed? What did they think of the swans, twenty times their size and weight, who lived off the seagrass meadows all year round, who never had to travel further than their backyard to find food, or lay their eggs? Great humping creatures the swans were, effortlessly graceful.

After her customary walk along the cliff, Anthea lay in bed thinking about Julie. She'd suffered bouts of insomnia from time to time, and knew how desperate it could make you feel. She recalled Julie crouched by the station's back fence like some half-hidden feral animal, one that knew it had to hide, but wasn't clever enough to do so properly. If she'd had a gun that day - if Julie had been a rabbit, she a hunter - then Julie would be dead.

TWENTY-TWO

When Chris didn't show up for work next morning and still wasn't answering his phone, Anthea called around to his place.

It was a dinky house, she thought, pulling up outside it, a toy house held up off the ground by foundation blocks that looked as though the next gale would split and sunder them, bringing down the child-sized wooden structure in a heap. Yet the building had survived for a hundred and fifty years. One wall was dominated by a crumbling brick chimney, and Anthea was reminded of her neighbour's cottage with fruit trees cleverly arranged around it. If a developer bought three of these and wanted to replace them with units, advertising first-rate water views, would anyone complain?

Chris's car was parked outside. The blinds at the front were drawn. The chimney looked stuck on, an afterthought, and yet would have been a central feature of the original construction. The family would have gathered round the stove to cook and keep warm, and would have slept near it as well.

When Anthea had learnt that Chris had shared the house with his mother until her death from cancer, she'd thought that this partly explained his character. Three years was a long time to nurse somebody. She did not think that she would have the patience, and had no idea, really, how she would feel about her parents had they lived. She was still young enough to want life to grab her under the armpits, take her by the hair. She pictured the strong wind that would lift her up, scouring the small, dark cottage that had been built by a fishing family, the house where her boss had been born. She imagined the wind blowing grief away.

Anthea knocked and, behind the sound of her fist on wood, thought she heard a cough. When no one answered, she found a narrow path that led around the side. A vegetable garden at the back, clearly long established, took up all the available space. She noted a large and flourishing variety of herbs and heard the cough again, louder this time.

'Why didn't you phone the doctor?'

Chris shook his head, incapable of words.

His bedroom was barely wide enough for a single bed, and the cottage, Anthea had noticed as she stepped inside, had only four rooms, or five counting a bathroom which had obviously been added later.

Anthea phoned the medical centre and made an appointment. She found a carton of juice in the fridge and made Chris drink some. He shook his head to indicate that he couldn't eat.

The kitchen caught the rising sun, and Anthea caught it too, feeling it red and golden on her arms. Chris lay with his eyes closed while she bustled about. She knew her presence in his bedroom would have embarrassed him dreadfully if he hadn't been too sick for embarrassment.

She checked his landline phone, then his mobile for texts and voicemail. There was one from Frank Erwin saying he'd remembered something. Frank's voice trailed off in the way of people who dislike leaving messages.

Anthea wondered if she should drive Chris to Geelong hospital, and not waste time with the medical centre, but the hospital was half an hour away. What if he collapsed in the car? She checked her watch. They'd go to the centre early.

It was an effort for Chris to keep his eyes open, and he stumbled as Anthea helped him to her car.

A doctor saw him almost straight away. Anthea wondered how she'd manage if Chris had to go to hospital; but she couldn't nurse him and work at the same time. She felt an irrational anger with her boss for being so alone. How dare he have no friends! Surely there had to be someone, a neighbour or an old acquaintance.

The doctor came out and told Anthea that Chris had glandular fever. He wrote a prescription for antibiotics and strong painkillers.

When she asked about the hospital, he grimaced and said, 'We'll see.'

They spoke about practical details. Anthea was to ring if there was any change for the worse. She wondered if there was something she'd done to make the doctor short-tempered with her, then noticed the dark shadows under his eyes, the blank-faced patients lining the walls. His attitude implied that she should be grateful for his curtly offered information, and do or say nothing that would waste his time.

Chris had fallen asleep and didn't wake even when he was moved on a stretcher from the medical centre's minibus to his bedroom. The stretcher had to be tilted because the cottage's hallway was so narrow. Chris lay in the middle of it, wrapped in a green cotton blanket, his face swollen, child-like, vulnerable.

When the paramedics left, Anthea did what she'd been wanting to do. She opened all the doors and windows and let the wind blow through the cottage. The wind felt clean, hard and indifferent, and the sun was strong and hard as well. She breathed in southerly air unused to being interrupted by a landmass. In the power it gave her, the animal exhilaration, she ceased worrying about how she was going to cope.

When her phone rang, she pulled it out of her pocket and answered without thinking. It was Julie. Frank Erwin had complained about her hanging round his dam. What had Anthea done about those camel prints? And the next lot of rent was due. She didn't know whether to pay it or not. She wanted to pay, because that meant she believed Riza would come back. But she didn't know!

Anthea responded as calmly as she could. She didn't mention Chris's illness, guessing that Julie, rather than backing off in reaction to the news, would be inclined to add it to her list of burdens. Nor did she apologise for the lack of a result concerning the hoof prints.

'Did Frank want anything else?'

'Beyond harassing me, you mean? I haven't been hanging round his stupid dam. I just went to see if there were any fresh prints. When

I told him that, he laughed at me! Well, he'll be laughing out the other side of his face if I discover that he's been hiding Riza all this time!'

'Are you okay, Julie?'

'Of course I'm fucking not fucking okay!'

Anthea sighed, staring at her phone. Probably all Frank wanted was to complain about Julie trespassing, but she'd have to call him back.

Frank Erwin did want to complain. Anthea listened in silence and let him get it off his chest. Julie Beshervase was a bludger, a no-hoper. He should have seen that from the start and not let himself get tangled up with her and her camel. He'd thought he was doing her a favour. The rent he charged was laughable. Anthea could have interrupted to ask who else would have paid him for the use of his paddock, but she didn't.

As for hiding Riza, then letting the animal out to drink at the dam, well, Frank said, that was past a joke. Assuming he had, for whatever mad reason, stolen the beast, why would he risk it being seen like that?

Anthea murmured that yes, it was a bit far-fetched.

The farmer carried on in the same vein for a few more minutes, ending with a warning that he wasn't going to tolerate Julie or anybody else trespassing on his land.

When Anthea asked who else had been trespassing, there was silence on Frank's end.

'Well?'

Frank cleared his throat, then said, 'I did see someone by the dam one night.'

'Why didn't you say so before?'

'That boss of yours annoyed me. Too big for his boots. People sometimes use the paddock as a short cut. They wander along the beach too far, then think they'll cut back to the road through my place. Usually day-trippers in the summer. It's irritating, but I never make a fuss.'

Frank paused, so Anthea could thank him for this consideration, which she did.

'That's probably who it was. And that's the only time I saw him, coming round by the dam.'

'A man?'

'I think so.'

'Did you say anything? Call out?'

'I was right up near the top of the hill. I did call out hello, but he didn't answer. He probably didn't hear me. I watched till he got to the fence on the other side, and climbed through to the road.'

'When was this?'

'Now you're testing me.'

'It might be important.'

A noise in the background that sounded like a heavy object being dropped was followed by a bellow, whether of pain or fury it was hard to tell.

'I have to go,' Frank said.

'Please answer my question first. Could it have been the - '

'It was round Christmas,' Frank said, and hung up.

Chris slept on. Anthea wondered if she'd have to stay the night, and who to ask for help. She decided on a neighbour, and told her story to an elderly woman who answered promptly when she knocked next door. The woman looked rather grim, but didn't waste time making Anthea repeat things, or asking silly questions. When Anthea said she needed to call by the station, the neighbour offered to look in on Chris in half an hour.

Anthea didn't know what to expect, entering the station as temporary officer in charge. She checked the phone for messages. There was only one, a complaint about a speeding fine. She'd met the complainant, a multiple offender whose idea of fun was to hoon up and down the main street from midnight until two in the morning.

She realised that she was hungry. There was some ageing avocado dip in the fridge and some biscuits in a tin. She ate them washed down with water from the tap, reading from the file on Chris's desk, pausing every now and then to brush crumbs from the paper.

Anthea stared at a photo of Jack Benton. Chris had shown it to Camilla and Julie, as well as the four boys. Apart from Ben McIntyre, none of them had recognised him. She had no reason to suspect that Benton was the man Frank Erwin had seen, and schooled herself against jumping to conclusions. She searched for a report detailing forensic tests on Benton's Landcruiser. It wasn't in the dossier Chris had put together.

Almost without thinking, Anthea sent off a query, then blushed at her audacity. She pictured Chris asleep in his room, telling herself that she had to be strong and competent in his absence, giving way to a righteous, noble feeling, a feeling of unexpected confidence that she could make decisions and act on them.

There was a lot to be done in an hour. She planned to call in on Frank, talk to him in person. He could show her where he'd seen the man. Re-visiting the spot might jog his memory.

'Where's Blackie?' was Frank's first question. There was a trick to his voice, as though the village grapevine had already reached him, but he wanted to hear what Anthea would say.

Anthea kept her account of Chris's illness to a minimum, stating simply that he had a fever.

'I heard it was glandular fever.' Frank watched for Anthea's nod, then continued, 'Highly contagious, that. They call it the kissing disease. You need to wash everything he touches.'

Anthea thanked Frank for his advice. They were walking quite quickly and had almost reached the brow of the hill on the farmhouse side. She wondered at the ease with which the farmer assumed she'd be doing Chris's washing and who, exactly, he'd been talking to. She guessed that, if she fished for this information, he'd withhold it, and that withholding it would give him pleasure.

Perhaps Frank disliked young women out to make careers for themselves. On the other hand, it might be more the case that his back was still up about the horse trailer.

'Was there a full moon the night you saw the man?' she asked.

'Funny you should say that. As a matter of fact, there was.'

They crested the hill and began their descent. Anthea lifted her eyes to the dunes covered with Moonah and tea-tree, cutting Frank's property off from a view of the sea.

'It was about here I saw him. There.' Frank pointed to where a path followed the contour of the hill, then wound along the right side of the dam.

'Did it look to you like he knew where he was going?'

'Hard to say. He was going the right way to link up with the road.'

'On his own?'

'Well, I didn't see anybody else.'

'Perhaps someone was waiting in a car.'

'I didn't see a car, or hear one.' Frank shrugged, the expression on his face difficult to read.

'When you called out, what did he do then?'

'Kept going.'

Mentally, Anthea measured the line the trespasser would have taken if, as Frank said, he'd decided to take a shortcut from the beach to the main road.

They turned around and began retracing their steps. Frank broke the silence to say, 'You know what happened to his father, don't you?'

Anthea said nothing, but looked at Frank inquiringly.

'Eric Blackie drowned trying to save a pilot who fell off a ladder.'

'Drowned?' Anthea heard the echo of her voice bouncing off the hill.

Satisfied by the reaction he'd produced, Frank told the story of the storm, the hazards of climbing rope ladders even in calm weather. With carefully timed pauses, he worked up to the fall, Eric the crewman watching from below as his master fell, then jumping in after him.

'They both drowned. The pilot's body washed up at Point Nepean. Chris's Dad was never found.'

'Do they still do that?'

'Do what? Oh, you mean the ladder. Tried all sorts of things, including helicopters. Come back to the ladders. Ten to one, you're looking out across the channel, there's a pilot boat - '

'I know.'

'And just out past the heads there's some poor bugger swarming up a ladder like a monkey. Every twenty minutes on a busy day.'

'But why?'

'Why do they need pilots? Know how narrow that channel is? Know how big those container ships are? They need 'em all right.'

'Why do they do it?'

'Honour. Prestige. They're all master mariners. Skippered their own ships for years. Navigational certificates as long as your arm. And I'm sure the money's nice as well.'

But not for the crew, thought Anthea. No honour and prestige for them.

'I suppose pilots work with the same crew for years,' she said.

'Some do. The ship, it was a Swedish one, let down lifeboats straight away, of course. And the pilot's driver - he stayed out there searching on his own all night. At first light they brought helicopters and the Coastguard. I felt sorry for the driver. The boats only carry one crewman and a driver. Three on board, that's all. The driver quit his job.'

'And Chris's father?'

'"The sea took him", his widow used to say. You'd bump into her in the street and she'd come out with it. Couldn't get her to say anything else. Went funny in the head.'

'Where was Chris?'

'When his father drowned? In Melbourne. He came back here to be with his Mum. I don't think he meant to stay. But then his Mum got sick.'

They were almost at the farmhouse. Frank asked Anthea, in a voice that was unexpectedly gentle, if she'd be all right.

She was about to react with a brisk, 'I'll be fine', except that Frank's voice might have come from a different person, not one who always seemed to be enjoying a private joke at her expense.

'Why don't you come in for a cuppa?'

'Okay then.' Anthea smiled. 'A quick one. Thanks.'

A kettle was on the stove, steam coming out the top. Knowing nothing about farmhouses except for the little she had read in children's books, Anthea supposed that a kettle might always be ready on the stove in a farmhouse kitchen.

Frank asked how she took her tea, and she told him, 'White. No sugar,' thanking him again and sighing, wanting suddenly, with a kind of desperation, to go home to her flat and shut the door. What if Chris would resent her staying in his house? He hadn't asked her to. He might bitterly resent it.

'Might as well make yourself comfortable if you've got to stay there overnight,' Frank said with neutral practicality. 'We've got a mattress you can have. Easy enough to pop it in the ute and drive it over. How about we do that once you've had your cuppa?'

Anthea's flat looked strange to her, like a place she'd never lived in. She found herself moving from room to room with her eyes down, almost as though she was an intruder, as though she might surprise the real tenant, who might reply with a cry of 'Halt!'

She shook her head and told herself not to be stupid. While Frank waited in the ute, she hurriedly packed an overnight bag with pyjamas and a change of underwear, a clean shirt to put on under her uniform. She threw in a towel, toothbrush and paste, her phone charger. Chris had good coffee and plenty of breakfast food, but he was nearly out of milk. She took hers out of the fridge and put it in a plastic bag, after a moment's hesitation adding a tub of yoghurt as well.

Chris's neighbour had left a note on the kitchen bench saying that he hadn't woken. Frank helped Anthea carry the mattress into what she assumed had been Chris's mother's room, now empty of furniture. After Frank left, Anthea stood at the window, feeling the cool air on her face. The room had recently been vacuumed and dusted. In the linoleum were marks where a bed and chest of drawers had been.

Anthea walked quietly down the corridor to where Chris was sleeping. She bent over and touched his hand, which was hot and dry. She managed to take his temperature without waking him, or perhaps he was so sunk in unconsciousness that it would take a great deal more than a small plastic tube under his tongue to make him wake up. His temperature was 39. She thought of getting Frank back, or asking for the neighbour's help to drive Chris to the hospital. If she mistrusted the doctor's judgement, that's what she ought to do.

But what if they spent hours waiting in casualty, and the only result was that Chris was sent home again? A few weeks ago a woman had miscarried in the emergency room toilets. She'd been waiting for three hours to see a doctor. It had made the headlines, of course; but Anthea doubted that the publicity had resulted in more beds, or staff. Chris was probably better off staying where he was. Though a world of doubt might hang on that 'probably', it was where she decided to leave him.

The kitchen was clean and well stocked, the stove and fridge relatively new. Anthea took a tin of tomatoes from a cupboard, found spaghetti in a jar, olives and chilli sauce and parmesan cheese in the fridge. She made what had been one of her and Graeme's favourite scratch meals, thrown together in ten minutes. It gave her a small start to realise that these meals had always been cooked at her flat, that she'd been the one with ingredients on hand. When they'd met at Graeme's place after work, they'd gone out to eat. But those times at her flat had been good times. They'd laughed over their bubbling sauce, and salted water bubbling, ready for the pasta.

To say that Graeme had broken up with her - not that she'd actually said the words to a living soul - would give their separation a formality she shrank from accepting. On the one hand, Graeme might prefer to disappear without any more words being exchanged between them; but, on the other, he might be deliberately leaving his options open, leaving open a crack which he could push wider if and when he chose, confident that she would be waiting.

When had Graeme started to withdraw? Had it been when she moved to Queenscliff, or weeks earlier, when she received her appointment? Anthea remembered one evening, a dinner - there'd been others present, eight or six - she couldn't remember the number now, or any of their faces. Dinner at a restaurant, with Graeme playing host. It hadn't been the time for any kind of personal discussion, but it had suddenly dawned on Graeme, the result of a chance remark made by one of the others, that Anthea was about to graduate, and that meant she would be working out of a police station. She couldn't imagine what he had been thinking - that her training had been undertaken somehow for its own sake, a hobby, or a way of passing time?

On another evening - it couldn't have been too long after the restaurant dinner - she had challenged him. Could he conceive of studying architecture for five years, and then not *working* as an architect?

Graeme's response to this had been swift. There was no comparison.

There was a time, about eighteen months ago, when she'd believed Graeme was going to ask her to marry him. She would have said yes like a shot. She would have given up her training once she was Graeme's wife, though she was not at all sure what would have taken its place. Something bland - a secretarial course of some kind.

Anthea wondered what would have happened if her weekend with Graeme had not been spoilt. The glow would have carried her, buoyed her up for weeks, but then anxiety would have crept up once again. For she knew, deep down, that Graeme would not soon have repeated his visit. She would have been left to wait, and eventually to worry that the glow had been all of her own making. She told herself that it might not have happened this way, that Graeme might have invited her to Melbourne; but deep down she knew.

What joy there was in the lift of a dark eyebrow, what delight the shine of pale olive skin and a brightening smile. They had delighted in each other once. She had not imagined that.

Lost in her memories, Anthea almost didn't hear a knock on the front door.

It was Chris's neighbour, who, this time, introduced herself as

Doreen. Doreen Ramsey was a slight woman, though the muscles in her arms looked tough. The two women glanced at one another, conscious of an unspoken reluctance when it came to certain of the sick man's needs.

When Doreen said, 'Mike, that's my husband, he'll drop by in an hour or so', Anthea thanked her warmly.

The sauce was burning on the bottom of the saucepan, but Anthea didn't care. She put the saucepan in the sink to soak, and ate at the small kitchen table, scalding her tongue and adding grated parmesan by the handful. She recalled how Chris had gobbled, that night she'd invited him to eat her lover's share of the meal she'd pictured in advance. But of course Chris hadn't known this. She thought of the phrase 'fell on his food', how it summed up a certain kind of man. But not her boss, who evidently looked after himself in the food department, or had the makings and equipment to do so. His utensils were good quality, his pans heavy-based and strong, his olive oil thick and greenish-gold.

Anthea looked in on Chris again after she'd washed her few dishes and tidied up the kitchen. It was said that murder destroyed privacy - murder investigation, not only the act of it. People caught up in a homicide case were asked to reveal all sorts of secrets about themselves and their lives. But illness destroyed privacy as well, she thought, looking down at Chris's sleeping face. Unless the sick person had a special nurse to guard this privacy, or family members prepared to work around the clock. Those less fortunate dealt with the emergency as best they could. Complaints could be kept for afterwards, when the mind was active, the body well again.

Anthea was thinking about Camilla Renfrew when Mike knocked at the promised time. Gently and without fuss, he woke the patient and helped him use the lavatory.

TWENTY-THREE

Anthea woke with the sun on her face. Thin curtains were covered with a floral pattern faded almost past recognition. Whoever had made them - Anthea assumed it had been Chris's mother - had skimped on material. The curtains were unlined, did not meet in the middle, and were useless as any kind of insulation.

She found that she was smiling at the sun's warmth, the feeling of being well rested. She hadn't woken at all during the night. So much for being on call. Frank's mattress had been surprisingly comfortable and she'd been exhausted by the time she finally undressed and lay down.

Deliberately making a noise as she entered Chris's room, Anthea was pleased to see him lift his head and smile.

She smiled back and said good morning, poured water and helped Chris to drink. Looking embarrassed, he gestured towards the doorway. She helped him to stand up, but then he indicated that he could manage by himself. Anthea waited outside the bathroom door, feeling both foolish and relieved.

Ten minutes later, she was arranging breakfast in bed, balancing the tray, saying, 'Well sir, I hope you've got an appetite.'

Chris made a face in which the necessity of acknowledging weakness, gratitude and annoyance with himself all fought for expression. He avoided his assistant's eye, concentrating on nibbling a piece of toast.

But then he looked up, and surprised Anthea by speaking in a strong, decided voice. 'I don't know what kind of fool I've made of myself. I don't suppose I need to, not right now. I can remember waking up yesterday - was it yesterday? - and feeling absolutely lousy.'

'Do you remember being taken to the doctor's?'

'Was I? Well, of course I was, if you say so.'

Anthea became aware that she was wearing only a cotton dressing down over her pyjamas. 'You've got glandular fever,' she said.

'Good Lord. I suppose I'm contagious.'

'Very.'

'What are you doing here, then?'

'Someone - ' Anthea began defensively, then saw that he was teasing her. She laughed.

What had Frank Erwin called it? The kissing disease. She'd been careful not to use any of Chris's kitchen utensils without first washing them thoroughly, and he was most unlikely to kiss her.

Chris ate slowly, as though eating was a duty he was required to perform, watching Anthea with a guarded, half-admiring expression. Perhaps the best thing would be to dress quickly, then leave, she thought. She excused herself and went to have a shower. When she came back, Chris's face was flushed and he was panting slightly. An unnatural brightness in his eyes warned her that he wouldn't welcome any more questions about his state of health.

He coughed, then asked, 'What's Frank been up to?'

'He saw a man crossing his paddock. The one with the dam. From the beach side to the road.'

Chris listened while Anthea went over her conversation with the farmer, surprised at how easily the words came back to her. She'd admired Chris for his ability to recall interviews word for word, and did not think she'd shared it.

'Frank called out, but the man just kept going.'

Anthea recalled the story of the drowning then, and bit her lip.

She went on with her account, how she'd tried to trace the Bentons' movements after they'd left Queenscliff, and had found a van park in Apollo Bay where the manager said Jack had rung him wanting to make a booking.

She looked from Chris's tense hands to his over-bright eyes. 'They could have stayed in Geelong or Melbourne.'

Chris agreed that it was a possibility.

'But if they didn't, if they went straight back, and Jack's story about Margaret going to the supermarket is a lie because she was already dead, then why the extra days? Why not say they drove back on New Year's Day?'

'He had to get rid of the body. Perhaps he drove to Swan Hill late at night. That way, although the Landcruiser might be seen, it would be impossible to know how many people were inside it.'

'But there's nothing in the Landcruiser that - '

Chris nodded and then coughed again.

Anthea poured more water. Chris's hand shook so much that she had to help him drink it. His condition seemed to have deteriorated in the last few minutes, and again she was in a quandary as to what was the best thing to do.

She suspected that it was more than glandular fever. There'd been an instability in her boss long before. Underneath his calm demeanour - keeper of the peace, everybody's friend - there was a more turbulent person, one whose demons might rise up to get the better of him when they sensed a crack.

Anthea wished she'd found out about Chris's father earlier. Did he believe she'd known all this time, and had deliberately said nothing? He hadn't asked about her family. Was this because he'd looked up her file? She couldn't guess what it might mean to him if he did know. She wondered if it would shock him to learn that she hardly ever thought about her parents. She'd been too young. All she could remember was walking down a path between tall trees, hand in hand with two people who must have been her mother and father. She could not recall their faces, just that they were large and she was tiny, and that the three of them were walking in step, so they must have slowed their pace to hers.

The path had been dense with shade. Before her grandmother died, Anthea had asked her about this memory, and her grandmother had confirmed that yes, there had been such a path beside the house. Anthea felt sure that it had been warm, the trees in summer foliage, which might make it just a few weeks before the accident.

She'd grown up with the certainty that, if her grandmother hadn't been looking after her while her parents had a night out, she would have been killed as well. She'd often felt that she was alive owing to a lucky chance, that her continuing to live was some sort of mistake or oversight. She wondered if Julie felt like that as well. But she did not share Julie's guilt. Her grandparents had been kind and loving. They'd never made her feel unwanted, or a burden. As a child, she'd often wished for a sister or a brother, but this desire had faded.

'I need to go to Swan Hill,' Chris said, his jaw clenched and shoulders braced as though to combat a physical attack.

Anthea stood up and took the breakfast tray, in order to have something to do with her hands. Chris clearly wasn't asking her opinion. But how did he think he could just take off? He could barely walk. She could put his 'need' down to the fever, or that other, deeper malaise of which she'd just caught a glimpse. She decided that she would go ahead and pursue the course of action she considered best. She hoped that Chris would spend the morning resting, but knew that nothing she said or did could persuade him to do this if he decided otherwise.

She was saved from having to speak by a knock on the front door.

It was Doreen Ramsey. Anthea welcomed her in.

They chatted for a few moments, then Anthea excused herself to tidy the room she'd slept in and collect her overnight bag. She left the mattress on the floor, not knowing what else to do with it. She supposed that Frank would be happy enough to pick it up eventually. As for tonight, she'd cross that bridge when she came to it.

Chris's neighbour offered to do a bit of shopping, dealing with the invalid by jollying him along and mothering him discreetly. Chris agreed to stay in bed, but asked Anthea to fetch his file on the Bentons. Anthea had been planning to go through the file again herself, but of course she didn't say this. She picked up the file from the station and left it with him. She didn't think it would matter if she went home for a short while.

TWENTY-FOUR

Anthea's neighbour appeared in his driveway as she was unpacking her car. With smooth practised movements, he hoisted his kayak onto roof racks and tied it in place. He didn't look her way. His skin was brown and smooth, his body compact, the sort that never gave trouble, always did what was expected of it.

Anthea considered her own body, her city-pale skin, the pull on her arm of her overnight bag, that slight weight yet how it pulled. A moment returned to her, Chris stumbling on the path to the surgery, how she'd steadied him. He weighed a lot more than she did, but she'd acted without thinking and prevented him from falling.

Anthea smiled to herself and swung her bag, whose weight now seemed negligible. When she raised her head, the man had finished tightening the ropes. He straightened at the same moment and met her eyes.

Anthea took another shower, as a kind of homecoming present to herself, made toast and smothered it with butter and raspberry jam. She'd dressed in her uniform again, but left her feet bare. She sat on the balcony with her feet up while she ate, rubbing her soles and the ends of her toes against the chair's heavy cotton cover.

She lifted her face to a sun that turned the bay into a huge, reflecting plate. The kayak man was out there, brown line of his craft no more than that, tentative and slight against the gold-green profusion of the seagrass. He paddled steadily across the dazzle of the morning, his figure coming and going through reflections that were suddenly too bright. For a whole minute, sun-blinded, Anthea was unable to see him at all. She thought of fetching her new binoculars, but was afraid of the conspicuous glancing of sunlight off glass, of the man looking up and noticing.

She knew that she should get a move on, but lingered, eating more than she really wanted, washing it down with coffee so strong she felt instantly dehydrated.

Wildflowers were out along the top of the low, raggedy cliff. On impulse, Anthea crossed the road and picked a small bunch, returning to her flat to put them in a kitchen glass. Later, she would rearrange them properly, or maybe she would not. She might leave them as they were, more connected somehow to the cliff top in their hasty, unselfconscious combination, in their makeshift vase. She told herself that it was the flowers she'd come for, not a final glimpse of her waterborne neighbour.

She remembered Graeme's ironic half smile, a way he had of making her feel inadequate simply by the way he stood, the way he looked around a room. She thought of how she'd bought her furniture, her few ornaments, even her food with this in mind. It suddenly seemed fortunate - not that she'd wanted such fortune, but the way things had worked out in *spite* of what she'd wanted - that there was nobody to disparage her flowers. The critic in her head, who wore Graeme's smile, who'd taken up residence inside her when they met, vanished in the morning glare, in the reflections off the bay.

As Anthea washed up her few dishes, her thoughts returned to Chris and the way he'd spoken, through gritted teeth, about needing to go to Swan Hill. She guessed that he'd been thinking about it for a while. She pictured him collapsing on the highway and guessed also that he'd played out the scenario this way too, and that it only added to his frustration.

On her way to the station, she thought about being a reluctant witness. She'd scarcely put her bag down when the phone rang. There'd been an accident in Hesse Street. The caller was the chemist and he asked for Chris. When she said that Chris was sick, but that she'd come straight away, there was a short but eloquent silence on the other end.

The accident proved to be a complicated one, involving three cars and a bicycle, and it was over an hour before Anthea had sorted it out. She put up witches hats and diverted traffic. She photographed the cars and bike, establishing positions, taking close-ups of the damage.

She had to take statements from five people - two of the cars had only had their drivers in them, but the third had had a couple. The cyclist had been taken to the medical centre by the time she arrived on the scene. The chemist had taken charge, and Anthea was grateful for this. He'd made sure the bike had stayed where its rider had been knocked from it, and had photographed the scene himself.

Anthea listened to the motorists' voluble complaints about each other, but mostly about the hapless bike-rider. They all agreed that he'd dashed out from the lane that ran beside the post office, straight into the traffic. Loudest was the female passenger, who was certain she had whiplash, though Anthea very much doubted that she'd be waving her head and arms around in such a manner if she really were in pain.

Anthea recorded the statements, not trusting her memory with four people gabbling at her. Once they'd left, she rang the medical centre, where she learnt that the young cyclist's name was Raschid, that he'd suffered bruises, scratches and a bump on the head, and that his mother had taken him home.

Not only the chemist, but each of the three drivers, and the passenger as well, had asked how Chris was doing. They'd let their disappointment show that the policeman they knew and felt comfortable with hadn't been there to take their statements, and listen to their advice about what to do with boys on bikes who didn't wear helmets, who thumbed their noses at the road rules.

But they hadn't made her feel that she was stuffing up completely, and Anthea supposed that she should feel grateful for this. It wasn't her job to explain Chris to his flock.

The Abouzeids lived in a newish brick veneer house on the Geelong Road. It was a fair ride each day to the high school, but a fourteen-year-old boy would probably think nothing of it.

Raschid's mother was waiting for Anthea, and was prepared, not to defend her son - she'd got enough out of him to be satisfied that he probably had caused the accident - but to stand between him and the unforgiving hand of the law.

The boy was sitting up in bed with a bandage on his head. He might have looked pathetic if he hadn't also looked too pleased with himself for someone who'd caused a three-car pile-up.

When Anthea asked why he'd been in such a hurry, Raschid patted his bandage. She could see that he had no answer to this question. If she'd phrased it differently and asked *if* he'd been in a hurry, his answer would have been no. Raschid had been riding the way he always rode, at the pace he always rode when there was no immediate obstacle in his path, that is to say recklessly and without consideration for anybody's safety.

Anthea sighed. She had no wish to make trouble for this boy or his mother, who was hovering in the doorway. Selafa Abouzeid touched two fingers to her right cheek. Her glance towards her son was both a warning and a supplication.

Raschid did not ask where Chris was, and Anthea guessed that it was not his way to ask direct questions of adults, particularly adults who had some hold over him. His way was rather to work out what kind of hold it was, how much of a danger, and how he might wriggle out from under it. Freedom, to a boy like Raschid, was to be grasped in the moment, for the moment, because the future most likely held punishment of one sort or another. His internal, private balance of innocence and guilt had nothing to do with the fact that he was used to punishment, used to finding it waiting for him.

Anthea was suddenly reminded of Julie Beshervase. But she saw also, from the way their eyes caught and held, that this boy loved his mother and did not want to cause her trouble.

'You've made four people angry and upset,' Anthea said.

Instead of replying, Raschid touched his head again, more lightly this time, as though afraid that the gesture, if repeated, might fail to impress; but unable to resist it even so. His thought processes were transparent. He would have been terribly ashamed to learn how easily readable they were.

'You'll have to apologise.'

Anthea didn't ask if Raschid thought an apology would be in

order, guessing that he'd accept punishment and put it behind him, but that the hypocrisy of those in power pretending to take his views into consideration was deeply galling to him.

'And we'll work out a few hours of community service.'

Raschid nodded, eyes bright, rest of his expression sober.

Anthea changed the subject. 'That day you claimed to see a woman in a black coat walking on the cliff path - '

'I did see her! I told Mr Blackie. I never made it up!'

'Constable Blackie asked if that was the only time you'd seen the woman, and you said you thought it was. But you added, and quite rightly, that you might have seen her without knowing it was the same person, going by in a car, for example, or walking down the street. Anything you can tell us, anything you might have seen, even if you're not sure about it, might help.'

'Well, like, I dunno.' Raschid chanced another swift pat at his bandage.

Anthea forbore asking if his head hurt. He'd be quick to take advantage of whatever opportunity her sympathy provided.

'Like, I did see *some*body,' he offered with an air of divulging an important secret, 'who *might* have been that lady. I dunno.'

'When? What was she doing?'

'In Hesse Street. Well, when I like first seen her that's where she was. Then this guy pulled up. He opened the door. She didn't get in, but. She kept walking.'

'What makes you think it was the same person?'

'I didn't say it was, I said it *could* be.'

Raschid frowned. He was trying to be helpful and he didn't see why he should be rewarded with more questions. He glanced at Anthea from under long black eyelashes, with an expression that always worked on his mother.

Anthea returned the boy's gaze steadily. She took him through the scene forwards, back and sideways. The woman hadn't been wearing a coat. The vehicle might have been a Landcruiser. He hadn't noticed the number plate or who was driving.

But Raschid was certain of the date. It was January 1, New Year's Day. His holiday job had been delivering groceries, or helping with their delivery, since he was too young to drive. He'd just carried a box out to the van. They'd been short-staffed, since the boss was too mean to pay penalty rates on public holidays. And the Kostandises had had their big party the night before. He hadn't wanted to get up and go to work, but his Mum had made him.

'Did you see what happened then?'

Raschid hadn't. He'd had to go back into the shop to fetch another box. When he returned to the street, the four-wheel drive had gone and the woman too.

Anthea thanked him for his help, gave him a card with her mobile number on it and asked him to contact her if he thought of anything more.

Raschid took the card and slipped it under his pillow. He looked tired suddenly, and very young.

Anthea said goodbye. 'And Raschid? Wear your helmet from now on. I'll be watching out for that.'

She felt excited on the way back to the station, but once inside the silence and emptiness unnerved her. She would even have been pleased to see Julie Beshervase's head poking up by the back fence. She sat down and wrote up what Raschid had told her while it was fresh in her mind.

Anthea looked up, surprising herself by picturing Chris's cottage, where she'd slept so deeply. Ugly and squat it might be, yet the funny, fragile box returned to her as an attractive memory. Comparisons with the cottage next door to her unit sprang to mind. Her neighbour was no more than average height, but muscular and fit, his skin brown as a seal's.

When Anthea called in on Chris, she found him sound asleep. Doreen came out as she was leaving, and said that she'd taken in some soup, which Chris had eaten for his midday meal.

Anthea thanked her. She did not feel hungry, and made do with orange juice and fruit. She found herself wondering, irrelevantly, if there were, or ever had been, swans living on Swan Hill.

TWENTY-FIVE

Anthea's questions in Hesse Street brought forth only disappointing responses. New Year's Day was one of the shopkeepers' busiest. The street was parked out from early in the morning until late at night. Why should one car be noticed, let alone who was inside?

She hoped she might do better with the supermarket staff. Jack Benton's Landcruiser - if it had been Jack Benton - had pulled in next to their loading bay. It was late afternoon before she managed to track down the driver Raschid had been assisting with deliveries, but when she did he was no help either.

He frowned and repeated what everybody else had said. He'd been far too busy to notice which tourist parked where, or what they said to one another.

Anthea was about to give up when she received help unexpectedly from Raschid.

She answered her phone to a boy's voice saying, 'Hello, Miss?'

Raschid's voice sounded childish, higher-pitched than when she'd spoken to him face to face. He told her that a mate of his who worked in the ice-cream shop over the summer had seen 'that lady you were askin' me about.'

'Yes,' said Anthea. 'Go on.'

'He doesn't know if it was the exact same day, but he saw a lady rushing past and he reckons she was crying. It sounds like the same one, you know. I reckon if you show him that photo he'll be able to tell you.'

Anthea took down the boy's name and address and thanked Raschid warmly.

Peter Drayson lived in a renovated weatherboard house not far from the harbour. His mother answered the door, frowning when Anthea introduced herself. She was dressed in a silk blouse and fine wool skirt, tinted grey tights and shoes with higher heels than Anthea had ever worn. Even before she spoke, she made Anthea feel provincial and dowdy.

Anthea explained what she wanted, and was greeted with the information that Peter was doing his homework. Couldn't Anthea's questions wait until tomorrow?

No, said Anthea. They couldn't.

Peter regarded her curiously, not at all put out that his homework was being interrupted. He seemed tall for his age, not that Anthea had much of a standard of comparison, but he was certainly taller than Raschid. His straight black hair covered a pale forehead, and his eyes looked directly into hers.

'Sit down, Peter,' she said gently, guessing that this was a boy who would see through a pose of authority.

Mrs Drayson stood with one hand on the door. Anthea said that she would prefer to talk to Peter by himself, but that, if she wished to be present, that was, of course, her right. Peter wasn't in any trouble. Anthea hoped he might be able to help in identifying a person of interest to the police.

Two small children appeared behind Mrs Drayson. Her skirts weren't the sort that you could hide behind, but they did their best, peering out at Anthea with dark brown eyes. Anthea smiled. One smiled back, showing two enormous front teeth.

The children were well dressed. Peter's jeans and T-shirt weren't bargain basement either. Their mother shooed them away, then took two steps forward and sat on the very edge of a chair, in front of thick curtains. Anthea took out her notebook and began by repeating what Raschid had told her, first of all about the scene he'd witnessed, then his conversation with Peter about the woman who'd run past the ice-cream shop. She watched Peter carefully for his reaction as she took out a photograph and asked, 'Was this the woman, Peter? Do you recognise her?'

'It could have been. I guess.'

His mother held out her hand for the photo. 'Who is this?' Her voice was impatient and dismissive.

Anthea repeated mildly that she was a person of interest to the police, reflecting that Mrs Drayson might be the only person in Queenscliff who didn't know about Margaret Benton.

A quick glance at Peter confirmed what Anthea thought must be the case. Raschid had told Peter that Margaret Benton was dead. It was interesting that Peter apparently wanted to keep this information from his mother, who apparently didn't watch or read the news.

'I saw her through the window,' Peter said.

'Which way did she go?'

'I was serving behind the counter. I just looked up and saw this lady running by.'

'Which way?' Anthea repeated.

'To the church.'

'The Anglican church on the corner of Crystal Street?'

Peter nodded.

It was one possibility, thought Anthea. If the church was open, Margaret might have gone inside.

'Was someone following her?'

'I don't know.'

'What about in a Toyota Landcruiser?'

Peter thought for a moment, then shook his head.

Anthea opened her mouth to ask another question, but Mrs Drayson interrupted. 'You heard what my son said. He had a job to do. He couldn't pay attention to what was going on in the street.'

Anthea nodded, realising that she wouldn't get any more out of Peter while his mother was there. Perhaps there was no more to get. Still, she knew what Peter looked like now. If need be, she could wait for him after school.

The church was locked and the vicarage, or what she assumed was the vicarage next door, was locked as well.

Anthea called in on Chris, who was sitting up in bed. His eyes were clear and there was a more normal colour to his skin, but Anthea felt again the turbulence, some kind of unspoken fury, just underneath the surface, and how he struggled to control it.

He listened while she told him her news, leaning forward and nodding as though she'd confirmed something for him, more than the stated facts. Anthea held out her hand in a gesture of solidarity and he grasped it briefly.

Chris knew the Anglican vicar. Anthea could see that he was annoyed with himself for not having pursued the possibility that Margaret Benton might have sought refuge in a church.

In a confusion of images, she saw again the kayak man as though painted on the seagrass, the mass of golden green supporting him, a frightened woman knocking on a locked church door.

Chris was sweating at the hairline, and along his upper lip. Anthea wondered what she would do if she caught glandular fever: pull up the doona and stay in bed? Open the curtains when she was feeling a bit better, and sit on her balcony?

She liked to think so. She liked to think she would be sensible enough to let the illness run its course. She wanted to tell Chris that it would be professional suicide to tear off up to Swan Hill, barge in on someone else's patch, when only the day before he'd been too sick to know what he was doing. Yet she couldn't help admiring him for wanting to.

Chris smiled, and Anthea took this as a good sign. A memory of the wildflowers returned, in their modest yet substantial beauty. She should have brought a bunch with her. She would have, if she'd been surer of her patient.

Chris leant back against the pillows and said, 'Raschid's not a bad kid.'

'But thoughtless. He could have got himself killed.'

'Oh, you'll never convince him of that. All fourteen-year-old boys believe they're immortal.'

There was a silence, then Chris cleared his throat. 'No need for you to come back here tonight. I'm fine.'

'Are you sure?'

'Mike's coming over later.'

'That's good then.'

Anthea knew she should feel pleased that she didn't have to spend another night away from home. A part of her *was* glad, and thought with pleasure of her own bed. Another part felt sidelined, even when it came to the amateurish nursing care she'd tried to offer.

They said goodbye, Chris adding that if he felt better in the morning he'd come in to the station for a while, and Anthea assuring him that she was managing and he shouldn't rush.

She felt tired and told herself she must be starting to operate on local time. How to organise the next few days was the question. She would have to deal with whatever came up. Beyond that, she might be free to ask her own questions, as she had been that day. She wondered how the village would react. What if there was an outbreak of theft, and the local motorists decided to break the speed limit all at once? This thought made Anthea smile again.

She cooked herself a simple meal. The setting sun on her balcony was warmer than it had been since she arrived. Maybe spring was really here at last. She would have to get some sort of awning for the summer, or else the sun would turn her flat into an oven. Anthea kicked off her shoes and sat with her feet rubbing the seat cover.

The kayak man was there again, paddling slowly in the dusk. His movements looked drawn out, elongated, as though time, out there on the seagrass, obeyed different rules. As before, his image seemed to come and go through the reflections off the water and the rich, luminous plant life. Anthea would be sure that he had disappeared. Then she would blink and he would be back.

He obviously did not work nine to five. Perhaps he worked from home; or had inherited money, or won it. Almost without thinking, Anthea fetched her binoculars, hooking them around her wrist by their fine leather strap, and returned to her position on the balcony.

It startled her to see the kayak and its occupant close up, paddle registering as an enlarged brown smudge, but the man himself in sharp and human outline. His squarish hands looked like an extension of the paddle, but were at the same time clearly flesh, absorbing and transmitting their own share of the fading light. His body was perfectly balanced and upright, and he moved forward without haste or nervous impulse, his expression focussed. Anthea understood how foolish she had been to think he might be affected by the reflection off her glasses, and the knowledge that she was behind them as they swept the bay.

The water became more mirage-like than ever, with no line at all between it and the air, but all a pearly blue-grey that seemed to move with one accord towards nightfall. Anthea wished that she could hold the moment, or else share it with someone. She poured wine, wondering at the kayak man's ability to find his way to shore after the last light was gone. She raised her glass - she hardly knew to what - pride that she was managing perhaps, or solitary, unexpected pleasures.

TWENTY-SIX

An object, blown by wind, sand-coloured, was not sand, but something more substantial.

Julie Beshervase shaded her eyes and squinted, then began to walk towards it. Day after day, she'd scoured the sandhills, though what was left of her common sense told her that if there ever had been footprints, if Riza *had* been taken that way, then they were long obscured.

The hoofprints around the Erwin's dam had proved to be those of cattle. Julie knew her credibility was fast approaching zero, but she didn't care. She was used to people backing off in disbelief, in wariness or puzzled amusement, from the things she said and did. The one exception was her brother. Julie knew she tried his patience sorely, and his generosity; knew that his guilt for having survived was only slightly less than hers, though he bore it so much better.

She spotted the object, covered in blown sand, and made her way towards it, head down and shoulders hunched. It was a woman's yellow cardigan.

Julie shook the sand out, or attempted to. She asked herself if it was possible that whoever had stolen Riza had been wearing such a garment. She tried to remember if she'd ever seen Camilla Renfrew dressed in yellow, but Camilla's clothes were dun-coloured, as though she'd long ago chosen camouflage.

Chris bagged and labelled the cardigan. Anthea drove to the dunes so Julie could show them where she'd found it.

Julie had marked the place with a stick shoved deep in the sand; but even so, by the time they got there, the rising wind had almost pulled it out.

It was hard for them to hear each other speak. Anthea fixed a more solid marker, then stood for a few moments, teeth into the wind, hair pulled straight back from her scalp.

Shoulder to shoulder, they made their way back down. Chris stumbled once, and Anthea was surprised by how swiftly Julie moved to steady him.

Back at the station, Julie told them what she could, which wasn't much. She had seen something rolled along by the wind, and, thinking of Riza, had gone after it. She did not say she'd been in the sandhills looking for hoofprints. There was no need for that.

She told the two constables that she would walk home, that she would be all right. It was too windy for a bike, and she'd run all the way to the station with the cardigan inside her parka.

Once Julie was gone, Chris said he was sending the cardigan to the forensics lab in Melbourne.

A coldness came off Chris's skin and hair. An hour like that, in the freezing wind, was enough to send him back to bed.

Anthea phoned for a courier. Something about her boss's determination reminded her of bushes that the wind bent, but did not break.

'Margaret Benton dropped her coat, then this. Whoever killed her didn't have time to go back for them. And he mustn't have known about her name being on the coat. He needed to get her body away as quickly as possible.'

'Jack Benton? In the Landcruiser?'

'Maybe,' Chris said. 'Yes to the first one, anyway.'

Anthea was thinking that the cardigan had been found a long way from the coat. She reflected that, from the little they knew of her, Margaret Benton had been a woman who liked expensive clothes.

Who could link the cardigan to her? Mrs Desmain from the caravan park? They could hope for traces of skin on the collar or cuffs. There were no hairs, or other identifying marks visible to the naked eye.

Two days passed and they heard nothing from the lab. On the afternoon of the third day, Chris announced that he was going to Swan Hill.

Anthea said goodbye, wondering if she should have offered to drive him. He wasn't well enough to make the trip alone. But she knew that, if she offered, Chris would refuse point blank. And someone had to remain on duty at the station.

Returning to the empty rooms, Anthea realised something else: she didn't want to follow Chris into the downward career spiral his impulse was about to lead to. She had come to respect, even to admire her boss, but she had an instinct for self preservation too.

She kept expecting Chris to call; or worse, to be told there'd been an accident. She remembered the way his hands had grasped the wheel, the tension in his arms and shoulders as he'd said goodbye. A contrary impulse surfaced then, making her itch for the chance to question Jack Benton herself, to ask without preamble where he'd gone that first morning of the new year, after Margaret had been seen running towards the church.

TWENTY-SEVEN

Chris woke the next morning with an extraordinary feeling of wellbeing. He had slept deeply, and his hands were no longer shaking. He showered in the motel's tiny shower cubicle and went in search of breakfast. It was too early for any of the cafés in McCallum Street to be open, but, after walking for ten minutes, he found an all-night service station and ordered sausages and eggs. As he ate, he felt the town coming to life around him, and fancied he could smell the water, though, by his calculation, the river must be over a kilometre away.

On impulse, after he had paid, he walked towards the Murray, thinking of the belief that the sea was supposed to stretch a person's horizons and induce far-sightedness. He felt an enormous relief to be away from it. All his senses were alert. A dullness that had been at the back of his eyes, he realised, since long before he'd fallen ill, was replaced by a child's unspoilt curiosity.

Chris almost ran the last few hundred metres, drawn by what it was not sufficient to imagine, and towards an idea that was new to him as well - a boundary of which both sides were visible and touchable, one river bank opposite another.

Across the border was a different state, with a different administration. Margaret Benton's body had been found on the very last unstable, crumbling edge of Victoria, and for the first time Chris asked himself if this might be significant.

The trees parted and he was there, standing right above the river which flowed swiftly, green and purposeful. He looked across at New South Wales. The bank was damp and covered in leaf mould. He picked up some soil and smelt it. The smell was heavy, thick and saltless. He wondered how long it had been since he'd breathed in air that did not contain at least a hint of salt. He breathed again, taking the river air deep into his lungs.

That morning he'd be shown where Margaret's body had been found - it was a request that had already been agreed to - but for now he was content to picture a spot very like this one. The grave would have taken only a short time to dig. Lambent light might have been enough. Of course, the body did not have to have been buried at night. But why take the risk in daylight, especially if you knew the area well and were confident of finding your way about?

Chris could not, even then, standing on the river bank, have said why it mattered so much that his and Anthea's findings should be acknowledged in some way. He knew that only a tiny percentage of cases ended neatly like the ones on TV. Decisions had to be made and blame apportioned; but that didn't mean the victim's family thanked you for it. Much more frequently, friends and relatives griped behind your back, sometimes forming astonishing alliances. The griping could go on for years. It helped to know your townspeople, to be able to predict what they were, and were not, likely to get up to; but Chris admitted to himself, taking another deep breath, that over the years people he'd thought he'd known well had been capable of extraordinary surprises.

If Swan Hill had been his patch, he would have known the Benton family. If they'd lived in the district for a long time, he would have been familiar with quarrels and alliances going back several generations. He felt again the humiliation of unanswered phone messages, of the reports he'd sent off seemingly into thin air.

After this morning, he would be richer information-wise, but still, of course, without the authority to act.

Two sides to the river: a far bank that could be seen and touched. The river - river bank rather - had given up the body. Well, it was a combined effort, of rain, strong currents, and that absence of other factors which militated against a body breaking loose. At sea, these factors were many, and he knew them by heart. Not for the first time, Chris reflected on the fact that Margaret Benton had no children to mourn for her. As for her husband, well, he hoped that he would get to meet Jack Benton. He felt that he would be able to tell at a glance whether or not the man had loved his wife; he would be able to see through Benton's lies.

Pondering all of this, Chris began walking back the way he'd come. At a T intersection, he checked his watch and took the left-hand way, instead of the right, which led to the centre of town. It was barely eight. His appointment at the station wasn't until ten. Presumably now there would be cafés open, but he wasn't hungry or thirsty. He preferred to walk, rather than sit around and wait.

This time he looked at the buildings he was passing, not in a fever to get to the river, but with a solid sense of the river at his back, the smell of freshwater soil still on his hands. He read billboards with the vague prurience of a tourist.

One caught his eye. He hadn't forgotten that the stud where Riza had lived for a short time was close by. Indeed, visiting the manager was on his list of things to do. But he hadn't paid attention to exactly how far out of town the stud was, and in what direction. Eleven kilometres along the road that he was facing, the billboard said. If he got the car now, he could easily drive there for a look and be at the station in good time.

Chris started to run. A proper jogger, in shorts, T-shirt and headphones, passed him, heading towards the river. Chris hadn't noticed a jogging track along it, but there probably was one, a cycling and jogging track combined. It was what country towns went in for these days.

Within twenty minutes, he was pulling up outside the stud. On impulse he'd booked to stay at the motel for another night. He had no intention of questioning the manager just then, assuming the manager was there and willing to be questioned. There'd be nothing worse than starting an interview and having to break off.

That Wallington was a large stud, and camels no more than a sideline, had been apparent from their website. The land was rich and green and gently sloping, not right on the river, but close to it, with at least one good-sized creek visible from the main road. Instead of driving in through the gates, Chris parked at the side. One sign advertised equestrian show-jumping, lessons for beginners, and everything in between. A smaller one was decorated with a camel and her calf.

The main buildings, stables and farmhouse, were a long way from the road, well screened by trees. Chris could make out red roofs and at one end a smoking chimney. He decided to keep walking along the road, since it was public land and he could do so without drawing attention to himself. He was aware, however, that a solitary man on foot was an oddity, and if anyone drove past him they'd probably take note and remember.

Two young camels came over to the fence to check him out, regarding him from under eyelashes so long and thick they looked as though they must be false. Chris stopped, picked some grass from his side of the fence, and held it out on the palm of his hand. He had no idea whether the principle of grass being greener on the other side applied to camels. On the whole, he thought not. They were probably smart enough to see that it was exactly the same, and not waste energy hankering after what they couldn't reach.

These two sniffed his hand curiously, bumping each other with their hips and shoulders. Chris transferred half the grass to his left hand, and held his hands apart. The animals went on sniffing, then one nuzzled at his offering, lifting back her top lip gently to reveal a row of large, gleaming teeth.

They were relaxed and confident in the presence of a human stranger. Perhaps they'd been handled regularly from birth. Chris wished he'd taken the time to ask Julie about her training, or to watch a session when he'd had the chance. So often in his life, it seemed, he found out about something good, or potentially good and valuable, only after it had been lost or spoilt. Then people came to him to complain, to demand or plead, all with the expectation that he could put right, retrieve or mend what he had never himself experienced.

He'd never expressed this difficulty to anyone, never even thought it out properly before. Of course, his life would have been very different if he'd been part of what he thought of as a normal family; if his father hadn't died, if his mother had not become dependent on him. He'd loved his mother. That he'd never doubted. But one love had had to cover, compensate for, other kinds he'd missed.

Though he feared otherwise, Chris hoped that Riza was alive and safe with a more personal hope than he'd acknowledged until then. He swung round at the sound of a heavy vehicle approaching, and then as quickly swung back so that he was facing the fence again. It was a Toyota Landcruiser. Chris's eyes took in the registration number with a shock of recognition. The Landcruiser pulled in through the gates, at its wheel a dark-haired, thickset man.

The camels were regarding him as seriously as though he might be part of their curriculum in the study of human behaviour. Chris felt ridiculous, with his hands stretched out and bits of grass clinging to them.

'Don't laugh,' he said under his breath.

But he was glad that he'd had something to occupy himself with when the Toyota had passed him, glad that he was out of uniform and could pretend to be a tourist. There was no reason why Jack Benton should recognise him, though he was glad he'd parked on the other side of the gates and Benton had not passed his car on the way in.

Chris dropped the grass on the camels' side of the fence and wiped his hands on his handkerchief, then drove to the police station.

His briefing was as comprehensive as he could have wished. Sergeant Fowler seemed determined to smother him with facts, and assured him repeatedly that all the points he'd raised about the Queenscliff connection had been properly considered.

It seemed irrelevant now for Chris to ask why no one had phoned him in order to tell him this, and he reminded himself that he did not want to get off on the wrong foot.

Fowler was sandy-haired, built like a rugby player. Unless invited to do so, Chris thought, you'd hesitate to call him Chook. His wide-spaced blue eyes sought Chris's and held them, with no hint of resentment or embarrassment; but with the awareness that, in this encounter, he held all the cards.

They spoke about the black coat. Jack Benton had no recollection of his wife having left it behind in Queenscliff. The most likely explanation, Fowler said, was that she'd left it at the caravan park, and that 'one of the boys' had taken it to the sandhills.

Chris thought this unlikely. He said he'd seen Benton driving into the stud whose owner had sold Riza to Julie Beshervase. He would not necessarily have raised the camel theft just then; but the connection couldn't be ignored.

Wallington was one of the best known and most prosperous studs in the Riverina, Sergeant Fowler told him, in the manner of a teacher delivering a primary school lesson. Practically everyone in Swan Hill had an association with it of one kind or another, whether it was riding lessons for their kids, or the camel rides they organised at the local show - all proceeds to charity - or even picking up a load of horse manure for the garden.

Chris repeated what Julie had said about seeing Margaret Benton at the gates, glancing at the file on Fowler's desk as he registered the sergeant's patience and tried to guess in advance what its limits might be. Presumably his reports were in there somewhere, in that pile of paper. He described what Julie had referred to as Margaret's desperation as she climbed into the Landcruiser.

'If the Beshervase girl thought she was in that bad a state, why didn't she ring up and report it?'

Chris knew it was a reasonable question. He also knew, as Sergeant Fowler didn't, that Julie was mentally unstable. But he did not believe that she'd been lying about the encounter at the gates. He said that the police only had Jack's word that Margaret had gone to the supermarket on January 3. There was most of Thursday and all of Friday to account for. The drive home would have taken five hours maximum.

Fowler scratched his chin and frowned, but he didn't contradict or interrupt, and Chris, taking heart from this, pressed on.

'Jack and Margaret had been fighting. I think the fight started at the caravan park. He spoilt her holiday by getting into an argument and being told they had to leave.'

Two witnesses had seen her on the cliff path. Her coat had been found in the dunes. Another witness had seen her running down the main street.

Chris wanted to mention the cardigan as well, but he had not yet received the forensic report, and he knew he'd been out of line in sending it to the lab himself. Perhaps Fowler knew about this, and perhaps he didn't.

Fowler said, 'That Landcruiser shows plenty of signs that Mrs Benton drove around in it, but what would you expect? Look, Blackie, no one's blaming you. No one's saying you've done less than you could.'

A drum began to beat behind Chris's eyeballs. He suppressed a cough.

'Jack's got a temper. He admits that. But he swears that they returned to Swan Hill together, that Margaret left to go to the supermarket, and never came back. She ran away. She took her chance and scarpered.'

'Who killed her then?'

'I never said it wasn't Jack, but we haven't got enough to charge him. We've turned his house upside down. As soon as we found the body and it was identified, we were up there.'

Chris forbore from pointing out that Benton had had plenty of time to get rid of any incriminating evidence.

'What was he doing while his wife was supposedly at the supermarket?'

'Working in the garden. He's got a large vegetable garden with an adjoining orchard. There was a lot of work to do after even a few days away.'

Chris bit his tongue to stop himself from arguing. He forced himself to listen to what Fowler was saying, to look at him without unreasonable prejudices rising up to spoil a meeting the sergeant could end at any moment.

'Who found the body?'

Chris knew the answer to this, but he wanted to hear Fowler's description.

'It was kids. Kids and a dog.' The sergeant's voice expressed both lack of surprise and sorrow that it had been, as it so often was, children who found what they weren't supposed to. 'There'd been that week of heavy rain. We were all so glad of it up here.' He managed to convey that he expected Chris to be ignorant of the drought. 'The dog found the body. The kids had to stop him making a picnic of it.'

A crease appeared between Fowler's eyebrows that in a couple of years would be permanent. It had fallen to him to reassure the children and their parents. He made no mention of how hard this had been. He didn't have to. Chris could imagine the parents' outrage; the sequence of chance events that had led to children making the discovery, and their children in particular. He could imagine, too, the suspicion with which they'd treated the police once their initial shock was over, as though the police somehow shared the responsibility for murder - keepers of the peace who had not kept it, who had allowed, instead, this horror to emerge.

Chris had felt this public hostility himself, on numerous occasions. From one second to the next, he stopped judging the young colleague sitting opposite him. Instead, he felt Fowler's need to make an arrest as soon as possible, and his frustration that he lacked hard evidence. An arrest was necessary for the sake of those kids and their parents, for the sake of the town and in some way to make up for having left a body rotting in the river bank until a rush of water led to its exposure. The sergeant hadn't been responsible, but he'd been made to feel as though he was.

He was willing to give Chris any written information he wanted, but his answer to Chris's question about whether he could interview Jack Benton was a polite but emphatic no.

Chris knew that he had no grounds whatever for insisting; but he was disappointed, and he was sure his disappointment showed. They talked around the periphery of the case for another ten minutes, both withdrawing by degrees. Chris was given copies of more statements to take away. Sergeant Fowler looked relieved.

Chris's visit to the spot where Margaret Benton's body had been found was both a pleasure and a disappointment. A pleasure in that he smelt again and tasted on his tongue the rich, black soil. Gulping in one breath after another, he turned to Sergeant Fowler and felt his face grow hot, but Fowler didn't seem to notice. The police tape had been removed; only the churned up earth and foot and tyre prints remained to mark the interest that had once been concentrated on a few square metres of river bank. There was nothing new to be learnt from it, and Chris had known there wouldn't be.

Margaret Benton's grave had been a destination, a goal that had, for reasons of his own, been necessary. Standing over it, Chris understood that this had as much to do with his father's lack of any kind of grave as with finding the woman's killer.

He felt faint, and rested his forehead on his left hand, which was cold and damp.

When he raised his head, Fowler was looking at him with concern. He swallowed hard and felt his stomach drop, a sensation he'd never experienced with such absolute physicality before.

Stumbling over the words, he thanked the sergeant for his time. They returned to their cars. Chris sat in his and watched Fowler drive away.

It seemed to him a foolish notion then, that humans should consider they had earnt some right to shelter from the elements, when the elements were so clearly and effortlessly superior. When he'd walked along the Murray, the fact that he could see both sides had seemed to give him ballast. The ocean was too large, too filled with danger. Chris felt an immense weariness, and that his own small victories and successes were behind a veil of water, laughing at him.

The Murray had acted according to its elemental character in freeing Margaret Benton's body. There was a kind of symmetry to it, and yes, if he was honest, a mockery as well. Policemen came along with their equipment, made pronouncements and pontificated; but the release, the revelation and the mystery that remained unsolved had been the river's doing.

This time, Chris drove in through the gates of Wallington stud and pulled up on a paved area in front of a building labelled both office and reception. To the right was a painted sign offering 'Horse Poo $2 a bag', above a tin with a slit in the top. If all you wanted was manure, there was no need to trouble the staff. You could drop your coins in the tin and be on your way.

Chris hesitated over leaving the folder he'd been given in the car, but he didn't want to take it inside. He put it on the floor and covered it with a rug that he kept on the back seat.

The office was smaller than he'd expected, judging by the building's exterior, and dominated by a large sign advising visitors: 'Go Broke, Buy A Horse'.

Chris asked to see whoever was in charge.

His first and strong impression was that the stud manager had nothing to hide. Very tall, a good seven centimetres taller than Chris, with long loose limbs and light-brown hair tied back in a pony tail, he asked Chris to take a seat with the easy confidence of a man whom it was almost impossible to catch off guard. It crossed Chris's mind that he might have been forewarned.

They introduced themselves and Chris asked about the camels.

They were a fairly recent addition, the manager said. When Chris raised the subject of Riza's disappearance, he looked mildly surprised that the theft of a camel should have brought a policeman all the way from the Bellarine Peninsula. He confirmed that Julie had phoned him. There'd been nothing he could tell her, and he was afraid he had nothing to add now. Riza had left the property in good health and condition. He had no idea why anyone would want to steal him.

'How well do you know Jack Benton?'

If the manager was surprised by the change of subject, then he didn't show it. 'Jack buys manure from us, for his orchard.'

Chris blinked, moistening his lips, and said he'd noted their honour system.

'We practically give it away. And our receptionist can see the money tin from her desk in the office.'

'I also noticed the security camera.'

The camera was clearly visible, if you knew where to look and what to look for, but the sign warning visitors that they were being filmed was tiny.

'Last year someone broke into the stables,' the manager said, with a suspicious upward glance. 'Stable doors were left open, valuable equipment was stolen. None of our horses escaped from the property, thank goodness, but it gave us a fright.'

'No one sleeps here, then?'

'The house is half a kilometre away. It's the original farmhouse, over a hundred years old. I live there with my wife and daughter.'

'What about the owner?'

'Mr Ling visits four or five times a year.'

'And the rest of your staff?'

'They live in town.'

'Is there one person in charge of the camels?'

'Not exclusively. It's interesting you should ask, because it came up just the other day. Mr Ling wants us to expand our breeding program.'

'The camels are a particular interest of Mr Ling's?'

'Becoming so. Not that he's losing interest in horses. That will never happen.'

'What's he like to work for?'

'Mr Ling is an excellent judge of horseflesh.'

'From Hong Kong is he, originally?'

The manager nodded as though this was none of Chris's business. 'Will that be all? You'll appreciate that I've got a few jobs waiting for me.'

'Did Margaret Benton ever come here?'

'I couldn't answer that.'

'If Margaret had come inside and spoken to you, or the receptionist, you'd remember?'

'What are you getting at, constable?'

'Did you ever see Margaret Benton waiting at the gates?'

'You mean our gates? No.'

'Did any of your staff?'

'I don't know.'

Chris decided to let it drop. Even if Margaret had been running away, or trying to, the day Julie had seen her, what did it prove? He had much stronger evidence that she *had* been running away from her husband in Queenscliff, but apparently it wasn't enough.

'How's Jack Benton taking his wife's death?'

Anger made the manager's face white, his lips hard and flat. 'Jack's personal feelings are none of my business, but I will say this. The discovery of Margaret's body has shocked and distressed the whole community.'

Well, I know which side you're on, Chris told himself as he drove away. Another headache was beginning. He longed for the clarity and wellbeing of the early morning.

The folder of statements waited for him in his motel room, while his feet took him back to the Murray. He remembered a story a cousin of his had once told him, about the Mekong River at night, how alive it was with people and activity. This cousin had been what was called a seasoned traveller, as though moving about the world had something to do with adding flavour to a cooking pot. Chris recalled both the stories and his attitude to them, which had been one of detached interest. He realised that he could no longer claim detachment from people who moved about from country to country, as if by right, and spent the intervening dull times entertaining stay-at-homes with their adventures.

His recollections and his former, outdated responses came back to him as though carried gently and without fuss by the river current. He felt a vague kind of nostalgia, which was overtaken by an immense and deep frustration.

The cousin had begun his travels early. His father, Chris's paternal uncle, had sent him to an expensive boarding school when he was eleven. Chris wondered what effect this had had on his adult life. He never came to Queenscliff. He'd sent Chris a card when his mother died.

It was funny how moving just a few hundred kilometres could bring back a cousin he hadn't thought about for years. It really did have something to do with the forward-moving water, and his slow and steady progress along the embankment.

When he'd sorted out the business with the camel - if Riza was alive, he was going to find him, and, if dead, find proof of that - he thought he might take extended leave, perhaps even resign from the police. The prospect of resigning caused him a moment's shudder, as though he'd slipped and plunged his leg into cold water. Then it seemed a possibility that had been inside him so long he was amazed he hadn't paid attention to it before.

But within half a minute, he was cudgelling his wits for a way to catch Jack Benton out. He was tired now, and his brain felt sodden. He was glad that Sergeant Fowler hadn't said anything about his illness. Condescending sympathy would have been more than he could bear. He shivered at the vision of a kelp forest underneath the sea, its branches thick as pythons, reaching out to trap a man and hold him down. Fish would eat his flesh. His bones would glitter in the dimness of the forest.

He realised that he felt bound to Benton, this widower whom he had never met. He understood that he might have left the real man behind, replacing Benton with a creature born of his imagination, a creature in whom ordinary compassion and constraint had been replaced by vindictiveness and hate. As an antidote to this, Chris clung to the facts as he knew them, the aggression and the arguments, the discarded clothes.

He woke feeling feverish, and decided to take it easy on the drive back to Queenscliff. He stopped at the gold-mining town of Bendigo, which he'd visited as a child, but never returned to as an adult.

Anthea rang while Chris was eating lunch. She said that everything was fine, and reminded him of the address of Zorba's brother's farm. He'd practically be driving past it.

TWENTY-EIGHT

The farmhouse Theo Kostandis' parents had bought for him was built of pale gold brick, no later than the 1960s, Chris thought, and lasting well. Trees hid it from the highway, where there was a sign offering horse agistment and horse trailers for rent.

Chris parked and walked towards the front door. An unseen dog began to bark. He quickly looked around, wondering where the stables were. An open shed, containing a tractor and an assortment of machinery, faced the house. The barking came from what Chris assumed were kennels behind it. He thought the shed housing the rental trailers might be there as well. There was only one road in from the highway.

The man who answered his knock was an older Zorba, with black hair and self-confident black eyes.

Chris introduced himself. Theo shook his hand with a superior smile which, Chris guessed, seldom left his face.

He was shown into a small office adjacent to the living-room, and was pleased to see that, although the room had only one small window, it looked out over the driveway.

Without explanation or preamble, he pulled out his photograph of Jack Benton and asked Theo if he'd ever seen him.

Theo studied the photo for a long moment, then raised his eyes and asked why Chris wanted to know.

'In connection with a homicide inquiry. The man I'm interested in would probably have been driving a Toyota Landcruiser, registration YLB 371.'

'I - ' Theo began, then shut his mouth again.

'Did this man rent a horse trailer from you?'

Theo rubbed his chin vigorously with his right forefinger. 'I take rego details,' he said. 'Just give me a moment to check.'

Chris thought he heard Theo speaking on a phone.

He came back looking more relaxed. 'Here you are. On the first of January.'

Chris swallowed his excitement. 'I'd like a copy of that, please. When Mr Benton arrived to rent the trailer, was he on his own?'

'When I saw him, he was. We weren't really open for business, it being New Years Day.'

Chris asked the time and Theo said, 'I don't recall exactly. In the afternoon, I think.'

'When did Benton return the trailer?'

'The next day.'

'Why did he need it? Did you ask him?'

'Presumably to transport a horse.' Theo allowed himself another small, ironic smile. 'Isn't that the usual reason?'

'Did you ask him?' Chris repeated.

'No.'

The noise of wheels on gravel made Chris swing round to face the window. A ute was heading towards the highway, with a small horse float attached.

'Stop the driver,' Chris said.

'What?'

'Stop the driver now.' Chris was half way out the door. He ran to his own car, accelerated quickly and caught up with the ute.

The boy looked barely old enough to have a licence and was clearly scared. He made no protest when Chris pulled him over.

Chris opened the trailer doors, and there, at last, was Riza.

An hour later, he had the story pretty well sorted out. Theo was apologetic. Neither he nor his kid brother had meant to cause trouble. Zorba had been going to take Riza back after a couple of days. He'd just wanted to prove to his mates that he could get away with it.

'You mean they knew?' Chris asked.

'Guessed, more like it. I've taken good care of the animal. You can see how well he's looking.'

'Tell me what happened. From the beginning, please.'

Zorba had rung his brother to see if he could borrow a trailer. 'I asked him what he wanted it for. He's too young to drive, of course. When he told me, I tried to talk him out of it.'

I bet you did, thought Chris.

'When I could see he was determined, I thought I'd better make sure the camel came to no harm.'

'So you took a trailer down to Queenscliff. How did you catch Riza?'

'Zorba did. It wasn't any problem.'

'And after you brought him back here?'

'He's been in a paddock with the horses. Perfectly happy. He's enjoyed the company.'

'What about your parents?'

'They know nothing.' Theo looked surprised that Chris would ask.

'How will your parents react to you and your brother being charged with theft?'

'Isn't that a bit harsh? We were going to take him back. As a matter of fact, your arrival's a coincidence. He was on his way back today.'

'Oh, you'll be charged all right,' Chris said. 'I can understand stupidity in a lad of fourteen, but I expect more from a man of your age, who's had your start in life.'

While Riza's transport home was being arranged - Chris didn't have a tow bar on his car, and was reluctant to entrust the camel to Theo or any of his employees - Chris rang Julie, who sounded drunk or drugged, then, when she realised what was being said, cried with relief. Next he spoke to Anthea, whose praise went down a treat, and whose questions about Jack Benton reminded him that he still had a lot to do.

Anthea agreed to pick up Zorba and take him to the station. His parents would no doubt insist on being present too. The main interviews could wait until Chris got back, but he didn't want Zorba getting any brilliant ideas about hopping on a ferry, or performing some other kind of disappearing act. He knew that, as soon as he was gone, Theo would phone his brother.

Theo's amusement vanished, and was replaced by barely contained anger. He tried bribery, and, when this failed, became sullen and uncooperative, answering in monosyllables, and only when forced to.

Chris asked to be shown the trailer Jack Benton had rented. Theo first of all claimed he couldn't remember, but with a little persuasion, and a few examples of extra charges that could be added to theft, his memory improved.

Backing onto the shed with the tractor was another one. Theo pointed out a horse float at the far end.

'Has it been rented since?'

'I'd have to check.'

'Do that please. I'm making arrangements for it to be fetched.'

Theo went pale then, as if the full import of what Chris was saying had only just found its way underneath his skin.

Chris was glad he wasn't towing Riza. His hands shook on the wheel. He recalled the way the young camel had turned to look at him when he'd thrown open the trailer doors. Riza had been securely tied so he wouldn't fall and hurt himself if the driver had to brake suddenly. He'd looked back over his shoulder at the sudden burst of light and noise, not fearfully or apprehensively, but rather with the curiosity of a creature whose fears have been short-lived. It was a look such as a human child might have given him, a child whose courage has already been put to the test.

Chris pulled over and shut his eyes for fifteen minutes, then phoned Anthea again. She'd done everything he'd asked. He left a message for Camilla at the hospital. He wasn't sure when he'd find the time to get in to see her; but he knew that, of all the people concerned, after Julie she was the one who would most welcome the news.

There was quite a gathering waiting for Chris at the station - Anthea, with Mr and Mrs Kostandis either side of Zorba, who tried to look cool and succeeded only in looking scared - Ian Lawrey standing with his head down while Mrs Kostandis threw him furious glances. If she was going to blame Ian for any of her son's fooleries, Chris thought, he'd have something to say about that.

Julie Beshervase was there, and Frank Erwin. Chris guessed that Anthea had had a hard time keeping the opposing sides from attacking each other.

He told Julie and Frank to go to the farmhouse and wait there. They left to pick up his neighbours the Ramseys, who, it seemed, Frank had invited to have a look around the farm.

Though exhaustion was beginning to drag at all his cells, Chris was determined to get through this first and most difficult of interviews with the Kostandises. He knew that, in spite of their older son's confession, they'd continue making trouble, loudly throwing blame around and hoping that it stuck to someone else's children. Maybe that had been part of Zorba's problem: that, and having far more money than his mates. He flashed Ian Lawrey a swift, sympathetic look, and saw, by an easing in the boy's clenched forehead, that it had been noted.

Ushering them in and finding places for everyone to sit, Chris wondered why the bet had been so important to Zorba in the first place, and why Ian hadn't picked Zorba as a boy who would go to great lengths in order not to lose.

Zorba sat on the edge of his chair, staring at Chris out of black eyes half defiant, half afraid. Chris told Ian to go home and that he'd call for him when he was ready.

When Ian looked particularly glum at this, Chris amended it to, 'Come back here in an hour.'

He wondered why the Kostandises hadn't brought a solicitor. They'd had time to arrange it. Perhaps they wanted to keep their sons' little felony personal, involve no one outside the family.

Zorba's mother began speaking, offering a version of events so absurd, flying in the face of everything Theo had told him, and that he'd worked out for himself, that for a moment Chris felt like laughing. Theo hadn't known who the camel belonged to, much less that he was stolen. Her older son had been looking after a stray camel, feeding him, and this was the thanks he got. How did the police know it was the same camel the girl claimed was missing, and where was the animal anyway? Until it was positively identified, no one could be sure. And she didn't look the type of girl to be able to afford to keep a pet like that. How did they know she was telling the truth? And why blame Zorba? He'd never been near that paddock. He didn't even know of its existence.

Chris glanced across at Zorba, who was looking smug. He was glad he'd taken an extra twenty minutes to type out a statement and that Theo, worried about having rented a horse float to a suspect in a murder inquiry, had signed it.

Chris handed the statement across. Husband and wife read it together. Mrs Kostandis' voice rose again, in high, resistant argument; but this time her husband put his hand over hers, gently at first, then pressing down more firmly. She frowned, staring at the hands and drawing in her breath, then, without missing more than half a beat, turned her invective on her younger son.

Chris said he would get statements typed for all three of them to sign. Zorba kept fingering the phone in his pocket, and Chris knew that he was itching to get away and call his brother, perhaps seeing Theo as a last ally against his mother's wrath. The boy looked unhappy now, annoyed, but still not sorry. Maybe when he was facing a magistrate he might, but somehow Chris doubted it.

It was well over an hour before Chris was able to turn his attention to Ian. He was glad to see that Anthea had produced sandwiches, and the boy had eaten. He munched cheese and tomato on brown bread while Anthea told him that Riza was safely back in his paddock with Julie fussing over him, and that the horse float that had been used to bring him was waiting at the Erwins.

'I'd like a word with the driver. Let him know that, will you?'

Chris wiped his mouth and looked at Ian. He knew the boy would cop at least one hiding from his father. He could talk to Phil Lawrey himself, but would have to be careful, in case this made it worse.

'So,' he said, 'when did Zorba tell you that he had the camel?'

'He never - ' Ian began, but Chris cut him off.

'I've got a full confession from his brother. So no more denials.'

Ian licked a stray breadcrumb from the corner of his mouth. 'Zorba reckoned he had the camel, but he wouldn't tell me where. He reckoned I had to give him a hundred bucks because he'd won the bet.'

'A hundred?'

'He said that snitching the camel was worth more than riding him. At least twice as much he said.'

'What did you say to that?'

'I said I'd already given him twenty and how did I know he was telling me the truth.'

'And?'

'He said just give him the hundred and he'd bring Riza back and that would be the proof.'

'Did you guess where Riza was?'

'I thought of Theo's farm. But I didn't want to ring and ask him in case I was wrong and in case - '

When Ian's voice trailed away, Chris finished his sentence for him. 'You didn't want your parents finding out about the bets. Did Zorba threaten to tell them?'

Ian was silent in response to this. Chris said, 'Where did you think you'd get a hundred dollars?'

'Nowhere,' Ian said.

The rest of the story came out, at first haltingly, then in a rush, how Ian had borrowed a metal detector from his boss and scoured the beach for coins, all the time hoping for the bonanza of a wedding ring. His boss had lent him the metal detector before, and didn't ask questions. He knew that practically all of Ian's pay was given to his mother. But by the end of a whole weekend's searching, he'd barely ten dollars worth of coins.

'When I told - told Zorb I couldn't raise the money, he said make it fifty and he'd call it quits.'

'Or he'd tell your father?'

'He said I'd get into even more trouble if the camel never came back.'

Chris looked grim. He thought it likely that Theo would have kept Riza. There was a risk he'd be caught returning him, and he doubted whether Zorba would have confessed to his brother how much Ian knew. Once Riza was on his property, Theo would most probably have reasoned that it was better to sit tight and hold onto what might be a valuable animal once he was fully grown.

TWENTY-NINE

Ian rode home. Chris had offered to speak to his father, but the boy said no. After her initial shock, Zorba's mother would return to being protective of her sons, keen to shift as much of the blame as she could onto the others, to make Riza's theft part of a game that had got out of hand.

When Chris arrived at the Erwins, he discovered that, not only had the driver of the horse float been fed and looked after, but there was practically a party going on. The driver proved to have a tricksy, wicked tongue; waves of laughter met Chris at the door. Julie was there, a different Julie, glowing and carefree. She rushed up to Chris and hugged him.

'You haven't left your baby all alone?'

'He's fine. He's fine. He's gone to sleep.' This was Julie and Frank both speaking at once.

'I'm going back there soon!'

Julie ducked her head and made a face, then hugged Frank too. Chris recalled how he'd suspected the farmer, who'd paid him back by causing that 'accident' on the Ocean Road.

'Look at him. That's the second time I've asked you, Blackie. Do you want some dinner?'

Chris accepted with thanks. He was glad that no one asked him about the Kostandis family. He did not want to talk about them, and even less about Ian. He'd have to see Ben and Raschid in the morning, and the three sets of parents.

Chris would have been happy to put his head down on the table and close his eyes, or better still, go home and collapse into bed; but there was too much nagging at him, too much unresolved. He satisfied himself that the driver would return the trailer the next day

- Frank had offered the man a bed for the night - and took his leave.

He hoped a walk would clear his head. He felt a sudden need to feel the cool night air on his face, but he didn't want to go anywhere near the sand dunes or the beach. That side of town felt infected somehow, as though not only had Margaret Benton's body been buried there, however briefly, but that he had seen it, touched it, smelt it. Death had its fingers in him and would not let him rest.

Chris drove the long way home, and then, finding himself within a stone's throw of Anthea's flat, decided on impulse to call in.

Anthea answered the door as though she'd been expecting someone else, but recovered immediately and smiled.

'Have you eaten?' she asked, leading the way to the kitchen.

'At the Erwins. I was thinking - I could do with a walk - '

Chris let his suggestion hang in the air, aware of how odd it must sound.

Anthea half turned and looked at him over her shoulder. 'Such a long day,' she said. 'And you're still not recovered. Congratulations, by the way.'

'To you too.'

'To us. A celebratory glass of wine? Or would you rather coffee?'

'How about a walk first?'

'Okay.' Anthea made an admonitory face. 'A short one.'

She slipped on a jacket and put a small silver torch in the pocket. Chris noted with approval, as he had before, how everything about his assistant was neat, each of her movements fitted to the task at hand. He was aware also that this care, this composure, made it hard to know what she was thinking, but, with a spurt of optimism, decided that this didn't matter. They had time to learn each other's ways, make allowances for each other's shortcomings.

Chris recalled, with something of a shock, his resolution while walking along the Murray - could it have been as recently as yesterday? He could resign, or take extended leave. He could tell Anthea right now that this was his intention. But he had to nail Jack Benton first.

Chris smiled to himself in the dark, realising that Anthea had not spoken for some time. He heard a panting sound and understood that it came from him.

Anthea took his arm. By unspoken consent, they started to go back. Chris wanted to talk, but felt exhausted. If he confessed to Anthea how little he'd done with his life, would she mock him gently, or offer him a sympathetic hearing which was worse than mockery? He was glad of the dark.

'I only hope there's something in that horse trailer,' he said. 'A bit of blood, or - '

Torchlight played over the uneven ground, accentuating dips and rises scarcely visible in daylight. Chris was once more overcome by the sensation, more powerful this time, of being close to a dead body. He shuddered and gagged, imagining *he* was the murderer, returning for his dead wife, his mind busy with how to carry her down the path to the road. He occupied himself with this, noting the wider places where he might stop to rest for a second or two, how to avoid making it obvious that some sort of load had been hauled down the dune; not that he expected anybody to connect that with his wife's disappearance, having already decided that the river bank would be her permanent burial place.

He came to with a jolt, realising that Anthea was holding him upright.

The celebratory glass of wine wasn't mentioned. He said he'd get himself home, that he'd be all right.

Chris lay in bed, but, as he'd feared, was unable to sleep. A great deal remained to be done, not the least of which was tracing Margaret Benton's movements from the moment when Peter Drayson had seen her running along Hesse Street. If only he could find a witness who'd seen Margaret and Jack together after that; better still, seen them quarrelling. Of course, what would really sew the case up would be finding traces of Margaret's blood or clothing fibres in the trailer. But for these results he'd have to wait. And they might not be there.

He had no reason to suspect that Theo Kostandis would tamper with what evidence there might be, or shield Benton, who was, after all, nothing more to him than a man who'd rented one of his horse floats. But still, Chris had left nothing to chance. He'd stayed at the farm until a police vehicle arrived to tow the trailer to the lab and he'd kept it in his sights till then. Theo had looked on with a worried frown. Benton might have swept the trailer, even hosed it down, but he needed to bury the body quickly and get the trailer out of Swan Hill before dawn.

What had Benton done during the daylight hours, given that he would have waited until dark before fetching the body? Sunset at that time of year was around 8.45 and it stayed light for at least a good half hour after that. He may have pulled in with the horse float somewhere off the highway and slept for a few hours. Chris tried to imagine, and couldn't, how sleep might come to a man who'd bashed his wife to death. And how had he cleaned the blood off his clothes and hands, before turning up to hire the trailer? A swim in the sea would have done the job. Chris was willing to bet that, while Margaret lay in a temporary, shallow grave, Jack had plunged into the surf.

THIRTY

Anthea woke to cold, wind-driven rain and a freezing southerly. She opened her bedroom curtains, checked the time, then fetched her spare doona from the cupboard, snuggled underneath the extra warmth and tried to go back to sleep.

By ten o'clock, Chris, looking tired but determined, was leading the way along the path into the dunes. He was wearing a heavy fisherman's raincoat and sou'wester. He'd lent Anthea a spare one, dismissing the coat she'd brought as a 'bit of fluff' and laughing when she'd produced her umbrella.

When Anthea suggested that maybe they should wait until the wind had died down, he dismissed this idea as well. They reached the spot where Julie had found the cardigan, and Chris began to pace in widening circles.

Anthea felt superfluous and cross. She watched her boss's face, what she could see of it under the sou'wester. He looked both ill and oblivious of her. He ought to be at home in bed.

She reminded herself that Chris had grown up with one foot in Bass Strait. These sudden, vicious throwbacks to winter, that in Melbourne were cushioned by buildings, and by the habits and layers of a city, were normal to him. Perhaps he even enjoyed them.

They couldn't search the whole of the sandhills, particularly not in this weather. She thought that maybe Chris was going mad, and wondered, now that Julie was better, if there wasn't a kind of madness that floated about under the surface of country towns, and every now and again fixed itself on someone. When would it be her turn?

Chris glanced at Anthea, whose face was set in an expression of endurance. He knew she wouldn't complain aloud, and that she would follow whatever instructions he gave her. This certainty surprised him. It hadn't been there when she was new to the district and the job.

He could not have said exactly what had made the change, whether her training had been solid enough, sound enough, to emerge intact after those first weeks of turning up her nose at everything - emerged like good, solid scaffolding under a flaky exterior.

He remembered that Saturday he'd called her out, instructed her to meet Julie Beshervase, how she hadn't complained, even though she'd obviously been anxious and upset. Now she would trudge along in the rain until he said, 'Enough'. You could call it training if you wished, or loyalty, or a sense of duty. The quality pleased him, whatever name he gave it.

Chris heard a noise behind him. He turned and saw Anthea pointing to the right. The rain had caused a small area of subsidence where the path made a sharp turn. Tea-tree branches had been broken, though not recently, and the ground under them had sunk in a rough rectangle. They made their way over to it. Chris didn't think Benton would have wasted time digging down to any great depth. His mind would already have been working on how to get the body away after dark.

Chris bent down and studied the hollow on his hands and knees, then took a trowel out of his coat pocket and began lifting samples, some from the centre, some from around the edges. Rain dashed his eyes, but still he searched, as carefully as he could, for some sign that a body had been buried there. Rain got in between his hat and the collar of his coat. He felt it trickle down his back. His trouser legs below the coat were streaked with grimy sand. He glanced at Anthea again, working on the opposite side of the 'grave'. Her hat hid her face, but her hands looked bloodless, freezing. He'd offered her gloves when they started out, but his were far too big. He felt a spurt of irritation that she'd come so poorly prepared, but almost immediately this was replaced by the acknowledgement that it wasn't her fault.

Chris wiped a hand across his eyes and decided that they'd taken enough samples. Reluctantly, he accepted that there was nothing in the sandy soil but twigs and leaves, nothing, at least, that he could see with his naked eye.

He led the way back, Anthea falling in behind him. All the way down, he thought about death, as though each step was taking him closer to his own, which was true, theoretically, but what he felt had nothing to do with theory. It was a trick of the harsh conditions perhaps, but he couldn't get the sight of Anthea's white hands out of his mind. The world had gone topsy-turvy and would never be the right way up again. He felt as if Anthea's hands belonged to the corpse whose traces they were seeking, and told himself the waking nightmare was his illness catching up with him. He'd pushed himself too hard for a man with glandular fever, and this was the result.

Benton would be wet after he'd buried Margaret, having just come from washing himself in the ocean. He'd be wearing swimming trunks, his blood-stained clothes and shoes wrapped in a towel. He would fold the lot into a plastic bag to be dumped in a public garbage bin once he was well away from Queenscliff. He would examine his hands and feet and the backs of his legs carefully, before he climbed into the Landcruiser, then, not taking any chances, place another towel, to be discarded in its turn, on the driver's seat.

He would be shivering slightly, from excitement, not from cold. By now he would have a plan clear in his mind, and the events of the next few days would turn out pretty much as he had scripted them. No witnesses would come forward to say they'd seen his four-wheel drive pulling a horse float. His arrival home without his wife would not be noted. The police would listen to his story that Margaret had set off to do some shopping and had not returned. He would allow the inference that she'd left him to emerge and be built on. He would act the part of a deserted husband well. The police, not necessarily believing him, would be unable to prove his story false.

Chris compared himself with officers of his rank who worked in large city stations, where the detectives were housed in the same building as the uniformed men and women. From time to time he would have been roped in to assist with homicides. Procedures would have become familiar. His supervisor had tried to talk him into coming back. Chris had used his mother as an excuse, though he hadn't seen it that way at the time. His supervisor had argued with him, pointing out that there were other considerations, that he needed to challenge and to stretch himself. But Chris had had enough of such talk.

He wondered what had happened to that supervisor. He'd heard, a few years back, that she'd retired. Of all the senior officers he'd come across, she was the one he'd have liked to talk to about his predicament, the one who struck him as most likely to listen and to understand. Had she been thinking of herself as well, when she'd advised him to take risks? Perhaps the jumping and the risk-taking - or the failure to - had been in her past. She was divorced and had no children. Back then, she'd seemed to him quite old, but she'd probably been no older than her middle forties.

Chris had almost forgotten that Anthea, his flesh and blood assistant, was trudging along behind him. He thought of the Murray at night, the way light was reflected in the river, its two banks side by side. For now he need do nothing more than contemplate the change that this body of water had brought about inside him. He would visit Camilla again. He wasn't sure why, but he felt that Camilla had more to tell him - not tell, of course - something important to convey.

THIRTY-ONE

Anthea offered to drive the samples to the lab herself. Chris, after looking blank for a moment, murmured an agreement, then settled down to type his report.

With the address noted down, the samples next to her on the passenger seat, Anthea turned onto the highway, wind at her back, windscreen wipers batting at the rain. She decided to think of herself as a courier, nothing more. It was unorthodox, but in view of all that happened over recent weeks, hardly remarkable.

Her cargo was precious, but if a semi-trailer hit her and it got spread all over the highway, along with her body parts, more samples could be dug up and sent. Instead of upsetting her, Anthea found a kind of backhanded comfort in this ghoulish picture, in the reminder of her own mortality.

Her neighbour's car had been in the driveway when she'd called by her flat to change into a clean uniform. Anthea had delayed for a few moments, watching him carrying his kayak as though it weighed no more than a thimble. He'd tied it onto the roof racks without haste. She pictured him paddling in the rain. He was certainly determined, if not a little mad? Par for the course, she thought. Maybe everyone in Queenscliff was a nutter.

For a few moments, Anthea nourished an irrational desire to sit in the kayak and be transported over water. She would forget her place of origin and her destination. Her mind would be cleansed; she would focus only on the present. She would become one with the kayak, as her neighbour appeared to be, without apparent strain.

Anthea shook her mind clear of this vision and concentrated on the traffic, on finding the lab in an unfamiliar suburb when visibility was poor.

Once her errand was completed, the samples handed over and

signed for, she stood under the awning at the front of the building. She needed hot food and coffee, but wasn't sure whether to leave the car where it was and walk until she found somewhere that looked decent, or drive to a suburb she knew. Chris had given her no instructions for the rest of the day. Timing the trip, allowing a bit extra for bad weather and a meal break, Anthea supposed that he would expect her back by mid afternoon.

She fetched her umbrella from the car. Around the corner, as though fate had decided to give her a treat, she found just the café she was looking for - warm and well lit without being noisy - tasty lunch dishes on the menu. She ordered soup and a focaccia. Both were delicious. If she got sick of police work, Anthea thought, she could open a café like this one in Hesse Street. Then she remembered that she'd have to make a year's income over the summer months. On a day like this, she'd be lucky if she had two customers.

Anthea checked her watch, feeling that she'd earnt a little time off, an hour when she wasn't following anyone's instructions. It would take no more than twenty minutes to drive to Graeme's office. She recalled the kayak man again, wondering at his stoicism. Later, she was to see the two as connected - the brief returning picture of the kayaker crossing the seagrass in the rain, and her decision to drop in on Graeme.

Of course, it was likely that he wouldn't be in; or that he'd be with a client. Presented with either of these alternatives, she would turn around and go. But she wouldn't ring ahead and be fobbed off over the phone.

While Anthea negotiated the route and found a parking spot, it began to seem that she'd planned to confront Graeme in precisely this way - not a confrontation unless he chose to make it one - using a small gap of time so that she might, with luck, present herself unheralded and find a welcome.

Yet not only did her heart lurch, but all her body's vital parts, when Graeme appeared at the foot of the stairs.

His hair flopped forward and half hid his frown.

'You,' he said.

'Come and have a coffee.' Anthea was amazed to hear her voice sounding normal.

'I have to be in Camberwell in' - Graeme checked his watch - 'fifteen minutes. It'll take me that long to drive there.'

'I'll come with you, then.'

Graeme glared at the receptionist, as though blaming her for allowing Anthea inside the building. He opened his mouth to argue, then apparently thought better of it. Anthea followed him to the company car park. She felt that, having set this collision in motion, she had nothing further to do but remain upright. It would have been different if Graeme had been pleased to see her, or even pretended to be. She could turn around now, knowing it was over, knowing he'd never contact her again. But the die was cast, this car ride to wherever. Funny word that, *die* - surely it should be the singular *dice,* in her case - one throw to determine the future.

'What are you doing here?' Graeme asked as she buckled her seat belt.

Anthea chose to interpret this as, what are you doing in Melbourne? She told him she'd had to deliver some samples to the lab. He looked thoughtful, as though this might be a regular occurrence. Perhaps she was in Melbourne more often than he'd thought. She saw him wanting to ask why she'd sought him out this time, but was glad he didn't. She would have found a truthful answer impossible.

When asked about his work, Graeme replied in monosyllables. He turned to her at a red light. 'It's very awkward, you know, this.'

'I agree it would have been more comfortable to talk over a cup of coffee.'

'What is it you want to say?'

'To know why you left in such a hurry.'

'What did you expect me to do, hang around that boring flat? Why couldn't you have told Mr Plod that Monday would be soon enough?'

'I couldn't do that,' Anthea said quietly. She waited for a moment, then asked, 'Is there someone else?'

'If there was, could you blame me? Long distance relationships never work. You knew that when you took the job.'

'It's only a couple of hours.'

'It might as well be three times that. There can't be any spontaneity.'

'Could you please answer my question?'

'I should have known you'd give me the third degree.'

Anthea reflected that, if she was a temporary prisoner in the car, then so was he. Graeme drove as though the traffic snarls around the junction were put there solely to annoy him. She wondered why she'd ever considered his expression of petulant bad temper handsome.

'No one to write home about,' he said, accelerating when the lights turned green. 'And you?'

'I would have come back to Melbourne every weekend if you'd asked me.'

'Oh yes, and what would you have done when Plod rang up and demanded your presence on a Saturday? It wouldn't have worked and you know it.'

'I know it now,' she said.

It took Anthea an hour to get from where Graeme dropped her at the Camberwell shopping centre back to where her car was parked. She walked to the nearest train station, where she spent her time staring at the opposite platform, then out the carriage window at fences and backyards. The rain had slowed to a drizzle and there were patches of blue sky. She wondered what the bay looked like at that moment, where the swans would be. Her phone didn't ring and she was glad of this, glad she owed no one an explanation of how she was spending her free time.

Rain had scoured the headland before it blew off to the east. The light was dull over the bay, clouds heavy with more rain. Anthea hoped that her familiar cliff top walk would allow the events of the day to settle, bring her to a calmer acceptance than she felt at present.

Her feet slipped in the mud. She thought of the umbrella lying forgotten on the floor of her car. She would bring it inside and dry it. Wasn't it supposed to be unlucky to open an umbrella inside? She thought that, in her case, bad luck ought to apply retrospectively, and be cancelled out by Graeme dumping her; unless she slipped again and broke her leg like poor Camilla Renfrew.

It was odd to think of the formal end of a relationship, as compared with *the end that had already been there* all these weeks. Graeme had implied that she had ended it when she'd taken the job in Queenscliff, but it had not been up to her to say 'send me somewhere else'. She'd tried to explain this, and to suggest they make the best of it. She wondered why Graeme hadn't said the right words, the clean-cutting words, back then. She had taken it upon herself to force the last - I declare this over - conversation. She had to face the folly of a bed far too big for the room it occupied. She had to face the voice in her head which insisted *I told you so.*

Returning home, Anthea looked for lights next door, and was pleased to see one in the front room of the cottage.

THIRTY-TWO

Chris was shocked by how weak and ill Camilla Renfrew looked. It occurred to him that she might never recover, that the broken bone might not heal properly, that she might leave hospital only for a nursing home. Where was Simon, that he was letting his mother suffer and deteriorate like this?

Camilla's eyes were closed and she did not open them when Chris said her name. He did not believe she was asleep. She did not want to be bothered by him, or any other visitor. She had given up.

Chris found a nurse, who reacted to his concern with thinly veiled impatience. Camilla refused to eat, that was her problem. Lack of food made her weak, and she would only get weaker until she changed her mind, or was fed intravenously.

'But why?'

'Heaven knows. She complains that her voice exercises hurt her, that's when she bothers to communicate at all.'

'The message I sent, did Mrs Renfrew get it?'

'What message was that?'

'About a stolen camel. Mrs Renfrew was upset about it. I told the sister in charge to make sure she got the message that he'd been found safe and well.'

'Then she will have, Constable Blackie. But you can see for yourself that Mrs Renfrew is a bit beyond taking an interest in camels.'

'What will happen to her?'

The nurse gave Chris a look which said, spare me idiotic questions. 'After doctor sees her this morning, I believe he'll give instructions for her to be put on a drip. You're welcome to sit with her, but I have other patients to attend to. So, if you'll excuse me - '

Camilla was lying face to the wall with her eyes shut. She had shrunk so much that her broken leg looked grotesquely large and ill-proportioned. Chris wondered if the note about Riza might be in one of the drawers beside her bed. It wasn't. He decided he would write another one and place it so that it would be the first thing she saw when she woke up.

He drew Riza smiling - he thought that might amuse Camilla - and underneath the words, 'I'm back!' He'd recorded Simon's number in his phone, and walked out to the corridor to ring him.

Simon didn't recognise Chris's name and had to be reminded. When it dawned on him that Chris wasn't calling on a police matter, but out of personal concern for his mother, he became defensive and annoyed. The hospital staff were doing their best. His mother was being extremely uncooperative. When Chris asked what Simon planned to do about this, he received the curt answer that it wasn't any of his business.

Chris asked when he planned to visit Camilla again, and was told, after a moment's hesitation, that he hoped to get down on Friday after work.

When Chris returned to Camilla's bed, she opened her eyes and smiled at him, a pale but welcoming smile.

Chris leant across and took her hand.

A nurse from another ward, hurrying past the door, saw a man with his back curved, bent in an attitude of gentle helpfulness, and smiled to herself, thinking that he must be the old woman's son.

Camilla grabbed her notebook and began writing quickly. She held it up for Chris to see.

'Congratulations! You deserve a medal!'

Chris laughed and asked how she was feeling.

'Better for your news,' Camilla wrote.

Many of the tasks Chris had performed, during those years of caring for his mother, had been performed without conscious thought. In recent years he'd been inclined to focus on their more awkward times, times when his personality had chafed and grated against hers, when, for instance, it had needed all his patience not to cry out against her habit of sitting in the car outside the Kostandis place.

He was, and had been for as long as he could remember, the kind of man who was inclined to focus more on his faults and failures than successes, and to feel impatient that he could not go back and change them.

He talked a little about Zorba and Theo, skating over details, then asked after Simon.

Camilla's face dropped from expectancy to resignation, then distress. Her whole body seemed to collapse inwards, as though the name on its own, just those two syllables, carried extraordinary power. She shook her head and closed her eyes.

Before leaving the hospital, Chris asked to be shown to the speech pathology room. A group was in session and he couldn't interrupt. He checked the therapist's schedule at the desk and noted a time when she appeared to be free. He left the hospital wondering how best to occupy himself for the next hour or so. He wished that Zorba and Theo were appearing in court right now, today, and felt frustrated at how long it would be before the brothers, represented no doubt by the best and most expensive lawyers, were forced to account for what they'd done.

Chris had never taken much notice of Corio Bay or Eastern Beach, having plenty of bays and beaches right at his back door. City beaches were tamed and sullied by the proximity of so much human traffic, and less objects of fear as a result. He decided to walk, hoping to ease some of his anxiety about Camilla.

The day was damp and gloomy. The tankers at the oil refinery sat as though stuck on the water, rather than immersed in it. It seemed foolish to expect that Camilla's voice would ever return, now she was so weak. After spending only a few moments in her company, Chris understood that the speech therapist wanted to use him as a sounding board for her puzzlement about her patient. The woman certainly had no problems with *her* voice box, Chris reflected, framing questions in his mind and waiting for a chance to squeeze them in. Camilla suffered from none of the known diseases which caused loss of speech, such as throat cancer, or Parkinson's. The therapist had initiated a program of exercises to strengthen her muscles and a step-by-step vocalisation of basic sounds. Most patients responded well to this regime.

'But Mrs Renfrew was in hospital for a broken leg,' Chris pointed out. 'She was in considerable discomfort.'

'Many of our patients are in pain. That doesn't alter their desire to speak.'

'Who suggested the treatment?' Chris asked, though he knew the answer.

His expression must have given him away when the therapist said Simon's name. 'I'm sure your work would be made easier,' she said, 'if Mrs Renfrew could answer questions like a normal person.'

'That's not - '

'We do our best. We can't cure everyone.'

'What will happen to Mrs Renfrew now?'

'That's not up to me. As far as her voice treatment goes, we've had to discontinue, but I expect you know that.'

Chris tried to talk about causes. The therapist kept repeating that none of the tests they'd done showed any abnormality.

'Are you saying Mrs Renfrew doesn't speak because she doesn't want to?'

'I'm not a psychologist. That's not for me to say.'

'But surely it affects your diagnosis and treatment if the problem is wholly, or partly, psychological?'

The therapist shrugged. 'It may be less relevant than you think. As I've said, the patients referred to me are actively seeking treatment, and even those who might be ambivalent - well, once they feel that their voice production is improving, that gives them the motivation to try harder. The exercises can cause discomfort, especially at first,' she admitted.

'But you persevered, even when it was clear that Mrs Renfrew was becoming weaker.'

'We persevered with the patient's best interests in mind, Constable Blackie.'

Chris wished that people wouldn't use his rank like that, when they meant to put him down.

Camilla's doctor was a young South Asian, who looked worried about what a police officer would want with him. Yes, he said, it was unfortunate that Mrs Renfrew's recovery was slow. Yes, she would need professional nursing care for the foreseeable future. When Chris asked how long it would take for her leg to heal, the doctor refused to commit to a time frame.

'Do you need Mrs Renfrew's help with your inquiries?'

Chris almost smiled at that. He said that Mrs Renfrew had already helped a lot.

He steeled himself for paying Camilla another visit, without having anything to offer her - no escape plan, no words of hope.

While Chris pulled the chair closer to the bed, Camilla reached for her notebook and wrote, 'I want to go home.'

'What about your leg?'

'I have money. I can hire a nurse.'

'Who is your solicitor?'

Camilla balanced her notebook in shaking hands and managed one more word. 'Sinclair.'

Bob Sinclair lived in a part of Queenscliff that Chris seldom visited. His house was on a hill opposite the Catholic church, occupying the highest point of land. The town's richest residents lived up there, people who, if they broke the law, managed to do so without attracting the attention of the local uniforms. Chris's heart had lifted at the sight of the name, because Sinclair had been his mother's solicitor. He was surprised that the old man hadn't retired.

Bob Sinclair's head was bald and age-spotted, covered with incipient skin cancers. In answer to Chris's first question, he replied that he'd retired for all but for a few of his oldest clients and that these included Camilla whom he'd known since she was a child.

Chris described Camilla's state of mind and health. He said he'd just come from visiting the hospital and that, in his opinion, Camilla would be much happier and recover more quickly at home.

The solicitor took Chris's meaning, and Chris was glad of it, glad he did not have to refer to Simon directly, or to his intentions. There was one of those small silences that occur between relative strangers when meaning has been implied and understood. The two men looked at one another, then Bob Sinclair turned and stared out the window. Chris had never been inside his house, had guessed, but never confirmed, how much of the ocean was visible from those wide, clean windows.

'You know the day Harold Holt drowned,' Sinclair said, startling him. 'I was standing right here when I saw the helicopters circling. Someone's drowned, I thought. The search went on for hours, and then of course we heard it on the news.'

Chris went white and could not prevent himself from clutching an edge of curtain for support. Had the solicitor forgotten his father, or was he being deliberately cruel? If so, what on earth was Chris doing there, enlisting, or trying to enlist his help?

The old man stared out across the channel with a faint smile on his lips. Chris cleared his throat. Quickly, he searched his mind for alternatives. There weren't any. What mattered was that he should act on Camilla's behalf.

When Chris was a boy, his mother had told and re-told the story of Prime Minister Holt's disappearance. She'd stood on the headland watching the helicopters and the rescue boats, along with three-quarters of the town's population. The first time Chris went to Portsea, he'd trudged over to the back beach with a school group, and been shown the spot. One of the more imaginative theories was that Holt had been picked up by a Russian submarine. It was the days of Khrushchev, after all. Theories multiplied when no body was washed ashore; not even pieces of the politician's wetsuit.

The story had come back to haunt both Chris and his mother. He hadn't been able to bear her making the comparison. 'Hush!' he'd cried, and, 'Please!'

Here was the horizon he'd escaped from in Swan Hill, the expanse that mocked him by its reach, the blend of sea and sky which had swallowed a country's leader and made him disappear without a trace. The mockery of it filled Chris's mouth with bile.

Clean windows made it worse, the view paid for by a lifetime's professional success. Chris was appalled by the barren expanse ahead of him, the more so since, were he to attempt to express his feelings, the solicitor would stare at him in disbelief. He knew depression had been growing in him; yet at the same time it seemed sudden, unforeseen. And why hadn't it lifted now he'd found Riza, now Julie's camel was back where he belonged?

The shipping channel was full of buoys and markers, defining precisely this human activity, or that. And on land, there were the lighthouses. He only had to step onto the footpath outside his own station door to be aware of the black one's jutting, solid shadow on the headland, its white twin a little further round, and further still the great stick marking the Point Lonsdale reef.

Full of definition, yet none of it availed him. He hated the very idea of commercial shipping, would have swept it out of existence like an angry three-year-old. He had no doubt a psychologist could explain his black mood, in language that was smooth, remote and logical. And he knew in advance that the definitions psychiatry offered would seem as false and alien to him as the ones his eyes sought out only to disclaim.

Yet what truth of his own did he have to set against them? How had he come to this point, that all his inner markers had deserted him? Was he making too much of ordinary grief?

His assistant was a case in point. When they'd rung to tell him they'd appointed her, he'd asked to have a look at her file, and had noted that both her parents had been killed when she was only three. How had this loss marred and shaped her? Of course it was impossible to tell. Even her close friends might not know. All Chris could think was that he'd never meant for it to be like this. He'd never meant to wake up in his forties with so little to show for his time on earth.

Chris forced his thoughts back to Camilla, who was alive and in danger. Bob Sinclair was speaking and Chris had missed half of what he'd said. He apologised and asked him to repeat it.

'There are several ways in which the law might be of use.'

Chris listened carefully while the old man explained that Simon Renfrew would apply for power of attorney if he had not already done so. 'He might persuade the doctors in Geelong to sign the forms.'

'Why not come and see Mrs Renfrew yourself?' Chris suggested. 'On the way, we can discuss the options.'

Camilla was delighted to see her solicitor. The two of them clasped and held each other's hands for a long time.

Camilla wrote in her notebook 'No speech therapy!' and underlined it three times. She drank some water that Chris poured from a jug on the bedside table.

A plan began taking shape. Sinclair would apply to be legally responsible for Camilla after she was discharged. He would arrange for nursing care and deal with the financial side of things.

THIRTY-THREE

Chris dropped Bob Sinclair home, pleased that he could set the problem of Camilla to one side for the moment. He was confident the solicitor would act responsibly and straight away. He hoped the test results on Theo's horse trailer and the soil samples would have come in, and was disappointed to discover that he still had to wait. Perhaps Jack Benton had carried the murder weapon into the surf with him, thrown it out as far out as he could. If that part of the beach had been empty, he might have taken the chance. Chris thought it likely that Benton had used something from the Landcruiser, but, if that were so, whatever it was had not been missed and noted.

He wondered how he might discover who'd been on the beach that day. Holiday-makers, tourists, they could have come from anywhere, be anywhere by now. Benton might have risked throwing a metal bar, knowing it would sink and eventually be buried in the sand.

Chris saw the murder as an act of rage that had been building up over weeks, even months, but impulsive nonetheless. He pictured Margaret jumping out of a moving vehicle, stumbling, righting herself, running off into the dunes. She probably had no idea how isolated it was there, beyond the swimming beach. Yes, a tool from the Landcruiser was the most likely weapon. It fitted with the skull fracture in a general way.

The phone rang. A woman Chris knew by sight wanted him to go to the lookout. Some kids were trespassing on Port Authority land. Chris never went near the lookout, certainly not for any recreational purpose, but the woman couldn't be expected to know that. On a clear day, Point Nepean looked close enough to touch, a paltry three kilometres away. People swam the Rip, foolhardy, stupid people, who risked causing grief to their families.

The lookout mocked him by being the closest point of land to the other side. For all it had done his father any good, Point Nepean might as well be three thousand kilometres away. The pilot and his father had both been wearing life jackets. Why hadn't they been rescued? The pilot boat with its driver had been right there, underneath the rope ladder. If the pilot had fallen straight down he would have landed on it. Why had his father jumped?

Chris had been over these questions countless times, and each time brought him no closer to understanding or acceptance. Yet he'd gone for years with the lid firmly down on all of it. Why had the questions come back now with such a vengeance? He knew why. It was the murder, the body, the woman who'd escaped her hidden grave.

The pilot's driver had testified that Eric Blackie had said nothing to him, had not spoken a word. He'd been at the wheel, Chris's father in the stern when the pilot had fallen. The driver had described the black spider shape against the tanker's white flank, how it had detached itself and dropped, how he'd swung around to see Chris's father jumping overboard.

Nobody had been able to answer any of the questions that began with why. Why had the pilot fallen? Why had his father jumped? Why hadn't they been rescued? The driver had resigned, not that he'd been blamed by anyone. He'd moved his family inland, to the other side of Colac. His mother had kept in touch with them until her last couple of years, and the driver had come to her funeral.

From Chris's reading of the inquiry transcripts, and his at first frantic, then bitterly resigned inquiries, he'd been unable to come close to solving the mystery. The pilot had fallen from the ladder. His father had jumped in, presumably to try and save him. Both men had disappeared. Though the driver had searched until exhaustion forced him to stop, he'd seen no sign of them. By the time Chris spoke to him, the man had moved beyond guilt, or perhaps had never felt it. He was only certain that he would no longer make his living by ferrying pilots out to waiting ships.

When Chris's mother had been offered a memorial, she'd refused.

He'd thought her refusal perverse and ungracious at the time. Now he felt that she'd been right to say no. He never went near the pilot's memorial.

There was no sign of the children who were supposedly playing on prohibited land. The woman who'd reported them had perhaps scared them off, or their game had simply taken them in another direction.

Aware of a feeling of reprieve, Chris stopped for a moment, well back from the edge of the cliff.

A tanker was making its way ponderously through the heads. A swift, slim, orange pencil of a boat darted out to meet it. It was the last hour of the ebb. Almost immediately, the small boat began to buck. At times, cross-waves hid it from view. Conditions weren't bad. Nobody who knew anything would say today's conditions were bad. Chris went on watching in spite of his increasing heart rate, his desire to run away, knowing he was about to witness the most ordinary of events, if daily, nightly repetition could render any event ordinary, which he supposed it might.

The orange sliver hooped and splashed its way towards the tanker, then on past it, whipped and swung around and drew close alongside. Now, even if Chris strained his eyes, he could not see the next stage, though he knew it by heart. The tanker did not slow down. The pilot's driver, cutting his engine to move at the same speed, manoeuvred to within touching distance of its massive side. The pilot began his climb down. Slow. So slow. A less than human pace. Foot beneath foot and hand beneath hand, the great vessel and the tiny one coupled by this strange, unremarkable activity, repeated perhaps forty times a day. The slowly descending man was the weak link between the vessels, for an instant resembling nothing so much as a huge mother and her suckling offspring.

This pilot had brought the tanker safely out from the Melbourne docks. Now he was going home; but not for long. Next time, he'd be climbing up, to steer another tanker, or container ship or liner, safely into port.

The orange arrow, safely received of its human cargo, sped away. Chris looked down at the shoreline.

Scavenging along it was a figure in a long black coat. Recognition came slowly, Chris's heart still racing. The figure was old and masculine. Above the coat, a long grey beard and untidy hair announced it as belonging to Brian Laidlaw.

Chris smiled his relief. He looked down and told his hands that they could now stop shaking.

Brian Laidlaw was known for riding his bicycle as slowly as it was possible to do so without falling off. When he was a boy, Chris and his school mates used to bet on when Laidlaw would take a tumble. He never did, though his stately progress along the main street had been the cause of many complaints, and at least one potentially serious accident.

Chris smiled again at the retreating figure, who had not looked up. Laidlaw wouldn't, not while there was a chance that he could find something of value on the tide line. He seldom spoke, and his answer to a greeting was rarely more than an indifferent nod. But his eyes were sharp, and, Chris believed, his hearing good as well.

Making his way down the nearest path, Chris wondered where the old man had got the coat - St Vinnies in Hesse Street most probably. He waited until he was a couple of metres away before calling out hello.

Laidlaw frowned at him through wiry hair. Chris saw that he was getting ready to refute whatever complaint was about to be levelled at him.

'Relax Brian,' he said comfortably. 'I was just wondering where you got your coat.'

'I never pinched it.'

'Was it St Vincents?'

Laidlaw stared down at the high water mark and kicked at a bit of broken cuttlefish with his salt-stained boot.

'I'll tell you why I'm interested. There was a lady staying here - '

Laidlaw curled his lip, it may have been at the word lady, or at a memory of the town filled to the brim with tourists.

'She had one just like it. I'm wondering if you saw her anywhere about.'

Chris described Margaret Benton as well as he could. For once he'd left his photographs behind. He would have liked to ask Laidlaw to come back to the station, but knew that if he were to get anything out of the old man, he'd do better here, on the beach, where Laidlaw felt at home.

'She was down here with her husband,' Chris finished, aware that it was lamely, and that Laidlaw would only have noticed the Bentons if he'd bumped into them on his bike, or if they'd got in his way in some other fashion.

Laidlaw turned away, gruffly and rudely incommunicative, daring Chris to reprimand him.

The ex-sailor's moods were few, and he expressed them parsimoniously. A person needed to be experienced at reading his expressions in order to tease out any but the most negative and misanthropic. Chris stepped back and let him continue his beachcombing, watching his stooped, deliberate and sharp-eyed progress. He wondered about the thoughts, the mental landscape of a man who'd lived alone well into his eighties; and solitary, by what Chris knew of him, in his younger years as well. He'd bet a year's salary on Laidlaw never listening to gossip, or watching the news.

Laidlaw's lack of interest in his fellow human beings was enough to make Chris pause on his way back to the station. For all the old seaman's cantankerousness, he lived modestly on his pension, didn't drink excessively, and would probably die painlessly in his bed one night. Still, it seemed a sour achievement just then, to end one's days beholden to no one, owing nothing to any living creature, entirely without duty or commitment.

Chris's phone rang. It was Simon Renfrew.

'How dare you force my mother to keep a house she can't look after and to pay for individual nursing care when there are plenty of good nursing homes!'

Chris took a deep breath and said, 'It's your mother's wish to remain in her own home.'

'Nonsense! My mother's not capable of making that decision! She's a sick old woman and her mind is wandering!'

'On the contrary, there is nothing wrong with your mother's mental faculties. Both her doctor and her solicitor have signed statements to that effect, and she has given Mr Sinclair enduring power of attorney, so I'm afraid that any legal questions from now on will have to be taken up with him.'

There was a moment's silence before Simon exploded again.

'Who'll pay the bills when she can't? That's where I come in, isn't it, to finance an absurdity! And why? Because of some bloody-minded idea of yours! You're an interfering, jumped-up little dictator. Have you any idea how much home nursing costs?'

'Mr Sinclair and your mother went over her finances together. She can afford a nurse for six weeks and that's all that should be necessary. Your mother is a strong woman, Mr Renfrew. There's no reason to predict anything but a complete recovery.'

'And you'll make her talk again, will you? I suppose that comes under your godlike powers as well.'

'No one will *make* your mother talk again,' Chris said sharply before hanging up.

Chris and Bob Sinclair helped Camilla move back home. Ian had picked flowers from his garden, and arranged for the house to be cleaned, and groceries delivered. Chris left before the nurse arrived, satisfied that Camilla was in good hands.

When Sinclair rang a couple of hours later, Chris expected trouble, but the solicitor said that Camilla had a visitor with some information for him.

Camilla's bedroom seemed quite crowded, with Sinclair on one side of the bed and Brian Laidlaw on the other. In the middle, her broken leg covered by a brightly coloured blanket, Camilla exerted a surprising authority over both men.

Chris's eyes were drawn to the blanket's colours and patterns, which reminded him of something that he could not quite place.

Brian Laidlaw wasn't a man to come forward with information, having all his life behaved as though even pronouns had a price attached. Yet this antisocial man, who appeared not to know what a conscience was, had suddenly produced one.

Chris drew Laidlaw's story out of him slowly, letting him begin it where he would. He'd heard about Camilla's fall and her spell in hospital. These facts were offered with half a dozen nods, by which Chris understood that the old seaman liked Camilla, for all he appeared to have had no more to do with her than with any of his neighbours.

He liked Camilla and considered what he was doing now in the light of a favour to her; and by extension to Chris as well, because Chris had helped to bring Camilla home. Chris knew that Laidlaw would much rather have died than be stuck in hospital himself.

He'd been trawling along the surf beach on a summer evening, paying close attention to what the sea brought in, as well as what had been left behind by trippers. He'd hired a metal detector for a few days, so he'd been ranging further than he usually did, up into the soft sand of the dunes.

The man had startled him; Laidlaw hadn't expected to meet anyone coming up from the water just there. From the look on his face, the man hadn't been planning on meeting up with anybody either. The two had almost bumped into one another, Laidlaw stooped over his metal detector, the stranger dripping wet.

Once Chris eased him into it, Laidlaw described the encounter with a certain understated flair. The fellow had made an impression on him, no doubt about that. He'd been wearing swimming trunks, seawater pouring off his hair and body. Laidlaw had noticed that his hands were clenched.

He'd stared at Laidlaw as though about to challenge him, but neither man had spoken. The encounter had lasted only seconds before the stranger continued on up through the dunes. He was powerfully built, a little past his prime. Laidlaw was confident he would know the man again. Chris questioned him closely about the date and time, which direction he'd been coming from, and exactly where he'd gone.

A more openly accepting, optimistic character might not have noted Jack Benton's demeanour when he came dripping from the ocean - for who else could it have been but Benton, fresh from washing away the blood of his murdered wife?

Chris stood up. 'I'll take you there now Brian, and you can show me.'

It wasn't a request, but Laidlaw looked mutinous, as though he'd finished co-operating and was going to refuse.

Camilla cleared her throat. The sound was so unexpected that they all looked startled, Camilla in particular. She held out her hand towards Laidlaw. Chris noticed that she'd drawn the folds of bright material closer to her, and kept her other hand on them.

He said goodbye, taking a hastily scribbled note from Camilla, and drove to the surf beach. The spot Laidlaw picked out led directly to the path where he'd found Margaret's 'grave'.

Chris thanked the seaman, recalling the lovely swathe of material that had caught the light back there, in a room where a woman was beginning to get well. Camilla had written him a thank you note. Chris knew suddenly what her blanket reminded him of - it was Riza's saddle.

THIRTY-FOUR

Chris sent off a copy of the statement he'd typed up for Brian Laidlaw to sign, then decided to cook himself a slap-up meal, glad he wasn't one of those Billy Bunter types who only had to look at a three-course meal in order to pile on the kilos. When he was growing up, his mother had encouraged him to eat heartily; it had been the done thing. She had been slim - too slim really - it was advice she might have applied in her own case. Chris's memories were more of his mother watching him eat than of tucking in herself. It wasn't until she died that he understood to what extent meals were a social activity, even if the 'social' only consisted of two people, one of whom had the appetite of a small bird.

He thought of asking Anthea what she was doing for dinner, then rejected the idea. He wanted to think about his plan for leaving Queenscliff. He'd liked Swan Hill, but he wouldn't want to work for the Swan Hill police. Somewhere inland anyway, with a decent river.

Chris concentrated on cooking and let the vexed question of his future dissolve in the smell of roasting meat.

Never having been much of a one for music, he decided that music would be appropriate tonight. He wondered later whether, if it hadn't been for that, he would have heard footsteps, or a rasping at the window and been warned.

Chris was standing with his back to the kitchen door when he heard his name spoken in a low voice, and turned to face Jack Benton, who was standing less than two metres away, holding a hunting rifle.

'Well, Mr Smart Policeman,' Benton said.

'Don't make things worse for yourself by shooting me.'

Chris sounded unconvincing even to himself, and thought, why argue? Let him do what he's come to do, only make it quick.

'Who said anything about shooting? We're going to take a little drive.'

Chris had been threatened often enough in the past by men bigger and stronger than he was, angry men past caring who they hurt, though this was the first time he'd had a rifle pointed at him. He was surprised by his acceptance of it, by how little he cared. He asked if he could brush his teeth.

Benton smiled. He seemed amused by the domestic scene, adopting a relaxed stance in the bathroom doorway, holding the rifle as though it weighed no more than a wooden spoon.

Chris took a last look at his face in the mirror. It did not seem real, or even made of material substances - tissues, cells - ingredients that were, or had been living. He thought fleetingly of the bullock who'd died to provide him with the principal ingredient of the last supper he wouldn't now be eating; but was as detached from this thought as from his own reflection. A mind soon to shut down forever should be concentrating on what was important. But how? And where to begin?

Benton made him turn off the stove, take the meat out of the oven and put it in the fridge, wash the dishes he'd used, then fetch shorts and a towel - Chris told him he had no swim suit - all the time smiling as though he was preparing a treat.

Benton pulled on close-fitting gloves before he got into the front passenger seat of Chris's car, and sat with the gun across his knees, pointed at Chris's stomach. Apart from the gun, he behaved as though they were about to embark on an ordinary, pleasant outing. From the driveway, Chris glanced at the front windows of the house next door. Lights were on behind drawn curtains. He heard the faint sounds of television.

They drove in silence. Benton signalled for Chris to stop at the main path to the surf beach. It was dark enough to need a torch, the moon hidden behind banks of cloud, but if Benton had brought a torch with him, he didn't switch it on. They began walking, Chris in front.

He found some energy, and was suddenly curious enough to hazard a few questions.

'Why was Margaret running away?'

'We had an argument.'

Chris felt the rifle prodding at his back. 'What about?' he asked.

'What difference does it make? She was a bitch, but I never meant to kill her.'

'That horse trailer was a good idea.'

'I thought so too. You're not known as a champion swimmer around these parts, are you?'

'Not at all,' Chris said. His mind filled with irrelevancies, such as a passage from the first chapter of *Moby Dick*, about how Ishmael's cure for depression was to sign up on a whaling voyage. Not his solution, but potentially attractive to a lot of men. Chris understood that his embryonic solution - that luminous, two-sided river - would be still-born, a dead hope known to no one, expressed to no one but himself.

'Why did you leave the clothes behind?' he asked.

'That prick of a sergeant kept on at me about that. The truth is, I forgot about them.'

Chris couldn't see, but he guessed that Benton was still smiling.

'Stop here,' he ordered. 'Take off your clothes and fold them, with your shoes on top.'

'Why should I go swimming at night?'

'Just do it.'

The clouds parted, and there was enough moonlight to see his way into the shallows. All aspects of the sea repulsed him, and now the fear of death seemed strangely to be the least of these. Benton pushed him over, casually, as though expecting no resistance, and Chris offered none. He rolled from side to side as the shore break caught him. He felt glad that his mother had gone first.

Benton steadied his rolling body with one foot, then, suddenly and fiercely, trod on the middle of his back.

Chris had no time to take a desperate gulp of air. He tried to keep his eyes open, but the swirling sand hurt them too much. He raised his head, struggling at last, only to feel a boot kick him in the face. His nose and ears were full of water. His head jerked up once more. This time, no heavy foot thrust it back down.

Aware of a momentary reprieve, Chris thrashed and tossed his head and managed to roll over. He could breathe. He spat and coughed, then sat up. The water was shallow, scarcely thirty centimetres, though deeper when a wave came. Chris half rolled, half crawled a little further from where he imagined Benton was still standing. He heard a woman's voice.

'Who's that? Who's there? Are you all right?'

Hands were pulling him by the shoulders. The woman spoke again, calling loudly, 'No!'

Chris blacked out. When he came to, there were more voices, more shadows. He felt himself being lifted. He tried to speak, but couldn't.

THIRTY-FIVE

Chris woke in the middle of the night, startled awake by somebody taking hold of his wrist. A nurse was writing on her clipboard, pausing to regard him sternly. He whispered questions, remembering the thick, obliterating water, and before that the gun in Jack Benton's hands. He understood that he'd been rescued, but not how, or by whom. He'd been carried somewhere, bumpily. Around him had been voices that he'd recognised, but could not put names to now.

The nurse told him to go back to sleep. His throat and head hurt. There was water beside his bed and he managed to drink some.

He woke again at dawn when the ward became active. Curtains were pulled back and a different nurse came to take his temperature and pulse. Chris asked who had brought him to the hospital, but she didn't know. He asked when he might go home, and she replied, 'Wait till doctor's seen you.' He found that his voice was hoarse, but serviceable. After he'd had breakfast and used the bathroom, he confirmed, by looking out the window, that it was the Geelong hospital he'd been brought to. He got back into bed and closed his eyes.

Memories returned. He felt the gun again, in the middle of his back. Benton had waded in after him, still carrying the gun, and had stamped on him to force his head under the water. Chris asked himself why he hadn't tried to break free, why he hadn't dived through the shore break. Perhaps he would have been shot and bled to death, but how could that have been worse than drowning? At least then his murder would have been known for what it was. Instead he hadn't fought back, or tried to escape. The realisation made him feel cold; but then he recalled the woman's voice, and this time he recognised it.

The doctor was happy to discharge a patient whose bed was needed by somebody else. Anthea appeared, smiling atop a bunch of wild flowers. Chris thought he had seldom been so glad to see a human face. When the doctor told her that he had a temperature, that there was a possibility his glandular fever would recur, Anthea replied that Chris would be well looked after.

Two hours later, Chris was settled in his own bed, though he kept protesting that he wasn't sick. Voices rose and fell in the kitchen, through an open door. There was water by his bed and he hoisted himself on one elbow to drink it. His throat still felt sore and the cool liquid tasted good. He looked up to see two heads peering at him, two young faces which belonged to Anthea, his assistant constable, and Julie, who had saved his life.

Of the many strange connections and streaks of luck that found their way into the light over the rest of that day, the budding friendship between Julie and Anthea was perhaps the least strange, the most easily accounted for.

Chris smiled to himself, after they had fed him, demanding that he shouldn't talk too much, after the first explanations had been given and received.

Julie had taken Riza for a walk along the beach. It had suddenly come into her head that she wanted to, and that Riza wanted it as well. Perhaps it had been the droop in the young animal's shoulder as she'd said goodnight, even though she'd stayed with him until after dark. She'd wondered if he missed the horses who'd kept him company in Theo's paddock, and had decided to give him a treat. She'd unlocked the gate. By now, she knew the path through the tea-tree so well that she had no fear of stumbling in the dark. Riza's pleasure and excitement had made it more than worthwhile.

Julie had been about to begin the plunge down to the beach when a car pulled up. It had passed under a streetlight and she'd thought she recognised it. Two men had got out, little more than shadows, soon absorbed in the shadow of the dunes.

Julie and Riza had run down onto the wet sand. The tide was going out, the sand glittering each time the sea pulled back from it. Julie turned in the direction away from the car; not that she felt afraid, but there was no need for her to bump into the two men, whatever their business on the beach. She ran with Riza on a short rope, loping easily beside her.

They did not go far. It was soon after they'd turned and were heading back that Julie saw movement in the water, close to shore. She was puffed by that time, but she ran faster, calling out. A man ran ahead of her, up into the dunes.

In Julie's retelling of events, it was almost as though finding Chris on the beach had been Riza's doing, that it had been Riza's nose and intention she'd been following.

When Anthea asked if she'd been scared, Julie replied, 'I didn't have time to be.'

Jack Benton must have seen two shadow shapes as well, one human, the other large, confusing, inexplicable. For it struck Anthea, and sharply, that Benton knew nothing about Riza and his misadventures. It must have been a wild sight that he'd glimpsed in the lambent light. He'd probably been too startled to wait and shine his torch in order to be certain who, or what, was descending on him. If he'd done so, if he'd seen it was a young woman with a camel on a rope, there might have been two successful drownings, not one aborted one.

Anthea smiled at Julie, recalling the day they'd sat facing filthy windows. She was proud that Julie had phoned her first. She found herself hoping that Julie would stay after the owners of the house came back. It would be a shame to have to move Riza again. Perhaps she could help Julie look for a small apartment and a job.

The two women returned to their account of the night before. They'd needed extra people and a makeshift stretcher to carry Chris over the dunes. Frank Erwin was the obvious choice. He hadn't wasted time, but thrown a folding camp bed into the back of his ute.

It hadn't been that difficult. Anthea had rung police headquarters, reciting the rego number of Jack Benton's Landcruiser, and approximately where it might be if he'd decided to drive back to Swan Hill. She'd fetched gloves and a bag from the station, pausing for a second in the doorway and allowing herself to consider the fact that Chris had almost died. She'd thought of absence, loss, how suddenly it could occur, a floor falling away - that was how people sometimes put it. In her case, she thought, the floor would have stayed, the office would have stayed, and she would have gone on working in it.

The loss would have been inside her. She rejoiced that it was not so.

Anthea's phone rang. Jack Benton had been arrested. The rifle had been found in the Landcruiser, and a pair of sandy boots, damp with seawater.

They wondered aloud why Benton had made no attempt to hide the gun, to clean up. Perhaps he was arrogant enough to believe he could talk his way out of it. Perhaps he no longer cared.

When Julie excused herself to go and visit Riza, Anthea said, 'I'm sorry about your father.'

She bit the inside of her cheek, wondering why she'd come out with it like that.

After a tense moment, Chris shook his head again, then he smiled and thanked her.

There were people who tended their own pasts and the dead who inhabited them like a garden so precious it left no room for intimacy with living human beings. Watching Chris, Anthea felt sure he had been one of them, and might now be able to change.

The Ramsays came to visit. By now the news of the attempted murder and the rescue was all around the town. Bob Sinclair phoned; half an hour later, he dropped by with a note from Camilla. Frank Erwin brought a casserole, and the McIntyres a cake.

Anthea decided to treat herself to her favourite walk. The tea-tree and wild flowers gave off a faint air of thanksgiving. Jack Benton had overplayed his hand, which could have ended in disaster, but had not.

Stepping carefully around tree roots, Anthea decided that she rather liked mysteries when they turned out well. She thought of Margaret Benton then, and felt ashamed, but only for a moment. Margaret was dead, and Anthea had never known her, but they'd done their best to find out what happened and bring her killer to justice.

The kayak man was out there, paddling slowly across the seagrass, as though no destination could mean more than the one he'd chosen. But what kind of destination was it, to paddle round and round and then return, repeating the same movements both before and after? Anthea bridled, feeling a spurt of irritation of the kind she used to feel for Chris.

She let it go. Her neighbour was who he was, and most probably oblivious of her.

Swans were feeding. Clumps of Moonah framed the bay. Anthea stood still and listened to the swans calling, then reached out to pick different kinds of wattle. She'd become so used to the varied and surprising offerings that she could hardly conceive now of walking into a florist's and paying for a bunch of flowers.

She must have taken longer to get back than she'd thought. When she crossed the road, the kayaker was pulling up in his driveway. Anthea watched as, with smooth, unhurried movements, he began unhooking ropes. He turned and met her eyes and smiled.

THIRTY-SIX

They had a party in the paddock, so that Riza could join in. Jack Benton had pleaded guilty to the murder of his wife, and there was much, besides, to celebrate.

Julie did herself up like an Afghan princess. Camilla wore the multi-coloured blanket as a cloak. Wielding her crutches with quiet determination, she hobbled from Bob Sinclair's car to the chair he placed for her underneath the Moonah. Her nurse was there as well, having bought Camilla, following instructions, a new hat in green and gold. Julie had decorated the hat with seabirds' feathers picked up by Brian Laidlaw.

They were a pair of butterflies, Frank said. Laidlaw fetched Camilla a plate of cakes and a cup of tea from the trestle table covered with a white cloth that Frank and Cynthia had set up in a sheltered corner of the paddock. All agreed that for Brian Laidlaw to attend a social gathering was nothing short of a miracle. From Laidlaw's expression, it seemed he thought so too.

Julie whipped Anthea's police cap off her head. Laughing, Anthea chased her round the paddock and stole it back again. Julie had curled ribbons into Riza's hair, but not too many - he was a camel, after all.

Frank was in his element. He might have been born to play host to just such a gathering. He and Chris talked briefly about the man who'd crossed his paddock; it seemed he'd been an ordinary tripper after all.

Cynthia had been cooking all morning. Chris had provided salads, relishes and chutneys. Anthea had made filo pastry rolls. They drank cordial, beer and wine, and toasted one another, laughing and yet solemn when one or another of them glanced up at the sandhills.

A carload of city people, passing on the dirt road, lost and wanting directions, stopped to stare. The driver, a man, looked embarrassed, barely polite as Chris pointed the way to the main road. The woman passenger was more friendly, smiling at the fancy dress and touching her companion lightly on the arm. In a story with more than a gesture towards the surreal, these strangers would have been invited to join in. As it was, Chris watched them go, dust rising and settling in their wake.

If eyes lingered on the dunes, no one spoke of the body that had, for a short time, been buried there. And if Chris Blackie glanced up more often than any of the others, and his glances lasted longer, this was scarcely to be wondered at.

Laughter drew Chris back to the present. Riza was dribbling a red ball, using all four feet like a soccer champion. Frank Erwin was looking proud and laughing heartily, the ball having been his idea.

Chris looked from one pair, one trio to another, as they grouped and reformed. He thought it wrong that anyone should be sad on such an occasion, and he wasn't sad. He accepted the congratulations of those gathered around him with good grace, while Julie wore praise like a bright and shimmering mantle. Julie's eyes had lost their bitter, hunted look. She laughed immoderately when Frank made a wild swipe at the red ball and missed.

It was an afternoon when you could feel the ground warming underneath your feet. The saddle was back where Camilla had first seen it, gracing the fence on the side furthest from the road. Each mirror caught the light and shared it.

Riza ignored the saddle, having no idea that it was for him, while Anthea walked over to admire it.

She fingered the leather, which felt strong and supple, catching her reflection more times than made her feel quite comfortable - blue uniform, dark hair, pale face, blue uniform. This time, there seemed quite a lot between the lines.

Chris had advised his assistant to go back to Melbourne for detective training. He'd said she would be good at it, that she was a natural. What did that mean - a natural? - and how much detecting had she really done?

Chris was loyal and encouraging. But Anthea had to work out what *she* wanted. If she left Queenscliff, she would never come back again, except as a visitor. A part of her still missed the city, missed the unpredictability of it, how an evening begun one way could end up spent in quite another, with surprising and interesting results. And there was the question, also, of what Chris would do, in the long term - in the short term, she knew. He'd told her that he wanted to take extended leave, to travel overseas.

Anthea could not imagine the station without him. Who would do the garden, for example? This suddenly seemed to be a question worth asking, whose answer might influence her own decision.

Anthea turned away from her multiple reflections. Someone would have to fill the gap, unless they closed the station. This was another possibility, of course. If that happened, would Chris care? Would she?

In the pocket of her jacket was the drawing Camilla had done for Chris in the hospital. Anthea had discovered it when she'd put the jacket on, and could not recall exactly how it had got there. She unfolded it, glancing towards Camilla, who was leaning forward, smiling and watching Frank playing with Riza. Next to her, Brian Laidlaw, in deeper shadow, was watching her, watching over her, ready to move if she needed anything.

The drawing was both more and less accomplished than Anthea remembered. The seashore was a single line with waves above it, the sun a pimpled circle sprouting a few more lines, the remaining background tentative rather than assured.

But with the camel and the girl-child, something more had taken place. True, they were simple lines as well, stick figures that might as easily have been produced by, as about, a child. But there was something charming in the way the camel's long, straight legs were reflected in the girl's straight back. A pride was there, and the joy of anticipation. She could not think the camel very old, though full grown certainly, easily able to take the weight of a birthday child. The child's head and the camel's - was Anthea mistaken in finding a resemblance here as well? A chin raised towards the horizon, a nose rather longer than the norm.

Anthea looked up and Chris was there, solid and inscrutable, in front of her. She held out the drawing and he took it, then nodded in Camilla's direction.

Camilla was laughing at something Bob Sinclair had just said. Or else she was laughing at the spectacle, from Frank and Riza, and Julie, who had joined them, and was teasing Riza with the ball, to Cynthia Erwin waiting on Brian Laidlaw, and Laidlaw's look of amazed effrontery as he accepted a cake.

Anthea thought of comfort and compassion, and how they need not be withheld, and how these were moments worth preserving.

A week later, Chris was strolling along the bank of the Murray River, experiencing not the delighted surprise of his first encounter, but the more assured pleasure of a treat anticipated, one that would not let him down. Before making the trip to Swan Hill, he'd applied for, and been granted, six months leave. He knew why his application had been dealt with swiftly. He'd explained to Anthea that his decision was in no way a reflection on her, either as a colleague or a person. She'd listened and nodded, then made a face and said she'd miss him. He'd tried to joke about it, replying she couldn't get rid of him that easily. He did not want to think about his replacement, temporary or otherwise.

Lights winked on the far bank, the one belonging to New South Wales. They seemed to beckon him, humbly, reachably. A woman's body had been buried not so far along. He did not want to think about her any more. It was enough to carry the memory of Jack Benton standing over him with a gun, to feel again that contemptuous thrust of a boot against his bare back. It could well be that he was not cut out to be a police officer, and that all these years he'd been cushioned from the realisation by a small town which had accepted him as its keeper of the occasionally interrupted peace. He did not have to find an answer to that now. He had not lied to Anthea. He would come back, once his leave was over, and then he would decide.

Lights formed themselves into faces and dissolved again. There was his mother, whose grave would never be disturbed, or not in his lifetime. Her face split into two and was replaced by those of Anthea and Julie, laughing at him from the other side of their youthful energy and hope. And lastly, there was Camilla and that camel - words that ran together in his mind. Strange how the likeness hadn't occurred to him till now. Chris had booked himself a ticket to Europe with a stopover in Cairo. Its bargain price was only half the motivation. He would spend a few days in a country where Riza's ancestors were native, not a feral pest. He would take a trip along the Nile. Perhaps that would truly lift his spirits. Perhaps then he might even learn to see the world through a camel's eye.

Can't wait for more from Dorothy Johnston? Here's the first chapter from her second sea-change mystery, *The Swan Island Connection.*

All children were a mixture of innocence and guile, Chris thought, but the innocence had been squashed out of Bobby McGilvrey unnaturally young. Chris Blackie, senior constable in charge of the small, some would say redundant, Queenscliff police station, was in the habit of qualifying his impressions and his thoughts. He did so automatically; and for the last four months he'd lived mostly in his own company, with only himself to talk to and share impressions with, apart from the small practicalities of daily life. He'd been travelling in countries where, though everyone who dealt with tourists had at least a smattering, English was not a language in which they chose to express themselves. Though politeness ran deep, he'd too often watched the pained expression with which some poor river guide attempted to follow what he was trying to convey. He was sensitive enough not to continue inflicting embarrassment, so he'd given up. He wished now that he'd kept a diary, but it was too late for that.

Rivers of the World, he could have called his trip, and the irony would have been apparent to no one but himself. He'd become fascinated by the Nile, and, though planning only to make a stopover in Egypt on his way to Europe, he'd ended up staying in Africa for almost the whole of his leave.

Now Australian rivers looked like trickling drains, and Chris was back on the Barwon, a river he'd ignored for most of his life, trying to work out what to do about Bobby McGilvrey.

There'd been a dolphin in the estuary for almost two months. It happened from time to time that dolphins, seals as well, came upriver to fish; but none, in his memory, had stayed so long. Familiarity had led to mischief; or perhaps the boys who'd stoned the dolphin, then tried to run it down with Dad's borrowed boat, would have done so however long it had been there. Dealing with them wasn't his problem, thankfully, since Barwon Heads was in the next municipality. But Bobby lived in Queenscliff, and it was to Chris that Bobby had reported the attacks.

In retaliation, the boys had threatened to kill him. This was not surprising. Bobby was a loner who did not appear to be afraid of making enemies. He did what he pleased and took orders from no one, so far as Chris could see. He'd been paddling about on the bay and the river in his small red kayak since he was six years old. He'd rigged up a trailer for the kayak out of a discarded pram, and carted it about behind his bike the way other kids carted surf boards. Chris believed he'd stolen the money to buy the kayak. He could pass off the death threat as children's chatter, but something told him he had better not.

Bobby McGilvrey was not a boy to give away information, and there were aspects of the business with the dolphin that he was keeping to himself. Chris identified with the child's reserve, but the identification resided in a part of himself that he did not wish to examine closely. Examining uncomfortable emotions had been a large part of the reason for his extended leave, and he was aware that he'd returned with only a small amount of introspection having been achieved.

Bobby appeared without his bike or kayak, his dog Max walking close to heel.

When Chris said hello, Bobby regarded him solemnly and did not return the greeting. 'I'm worried about Max,' he said.

Max was a Kelpie cross, swift as black lightning and Bobby's only regular companion. The boys he'd dobbed in over the dolphin had threatened to kill him as well.

Chris knew that Bobby's house had no proper yard. The back gate was falling off its hinges, and, even if it hadn't been, the fence was falling down as well. The boy wasn't allowed to bring his dog inside.

'I could keep Max at the station for a while,' he said.

'He wouldn't stay there. He'd come looking for me.'

'I could tie him up.'

Bobby looked thoughtful, considering the risks.

Chris said, 'I expect the boys will forget about it after a while.'

He was about to add that boys did get sick of whatever torment they happened to be fixed on; something new always came along. But before he could frame the words, Bobby turned on his heel and walked away. Neither boy nor dog looked back.

Next morning, a Saturday, Chris was enjoying a mug of tea on the station's back veranda when he heard shouting and a dog barking wildly.

Max charged up the road pursued by a bunch of boys, their leader out the front, whooping and yelling, waving a flaming branch.

Chris opened the gate and Max ran in.

'You lot, in my office,' he told the boys.

He tossed the burning bit of wood into a damp garden bed, kicked earth over it and stamped it down.

Chris locked the five boys in - not strictly legal, but they deserved to be frightened and he wasn't having them run away. He and Bobby spent the next fifteen minutes soaping petrol off Max; they had to rinse and rinse to get rid of the stuff, and though they used warm water, Max would not stop shivering. Chris gagged on the smell, but Bobby, working with careful concentration, seemed oblivious.

He spoke only when necessary. 'Be careful not to get soap in his eyes, Mr Blackie.'

The boys were subdued by the time Chris got to them. He made them dictate separate statements while he typed. None was allowed to hide behind silence, or their leader. He made each one spell his name, although he already knew them all. These were boys who'd thought it would be fun to stone a dolphin and set a dog on fire. He talked to them about multiple offences while they affected boredom. Another hour or so and he would break that pose, Chris thought; but he had better things to do. He printed out copies and made each boy sign his name on all of them.

Chris would not necessarily have thought of Olly Parkinson as the one to help out with Max, but when he happened to bump into Olly outside the small supermarket, it seemed a sensible solution.

Olly hadn't lived in Queenscliff for long, and Chris had come into contact with him mainly as his assistant constable's boyfriend. He knew that Olly's cottage had a secure yard and that Olly worked from home. He was a keen kayaker and Chris had often seen him exploring the bay.

When Chris raised the problem of Max, Olly said he'd think about it. Chris said it would only be temporary and repeated what he'd tried to tell Bobby, that the gang would forget about Max after a while.

Olly had seen Bobby out kayaking, and they'd said hello to one another. Chris tried to indicate that this was a good start. Most newcomers, unless they went around with their ears gummed up, got to hear things pretty quickly.

Bobby's father beat him. Chris had reported the beatings and had alternately tried to persuade and threaten Phil McGilvrey into treating, not only Bobby, but all his children decently. He knew that neither his threats nor his attempts at persuasion had had the desired effect. He also knew that for Bobby to be put in foster care, away from Max, would be a worse punishment than being beaten by his father.

Chris watched Olly walk away and told himself that here was a man who could not be rushed; Olly would come to a decision in his own time.

Olly Parkinson and Anthea Merritt sat drinking a pre-dinner glass of champagne on Anthea's small balcony. Olly did not ask what the occasion was. It had been a pleasant surprise, as he got to know his neighbour, to discover that Anthea produced small occasions for celebration, that she had the gift of making ordinary evenings special. He feared the loss of his privacy, but this fear was gradually being replaced by pleasure in Anthea's undemanding company, pleasure in the feel and touch and smell of her, the way his days were coming to be shaped by anticipation of the night ahead.

Anthea never asked unwelcome questions. She wasn't at all his idea of a police officer. She laughed and flushed when he told her this, not quite pleased, but not offended either. He wondered what he would have to do in order to offend her. She never pushed him, or appeared, apparently by accident, when he was on his way somewhere. She'd given him to understand that she'd been hurt by a relationship that had ended not so long ago, and that her appointment at Queenscliff police station had been taken up reluctantly. But she seemed to have accepted where she was, and to be making a life for herself in the town.

Somehow or other, Olly had found himself on Anthea's balcony sipping champagne as the sun went down, and one thing had led to another. He refused to ask himself: what next? He simply enjoyed the quality of the wine, the food Anthea prepared, and the company, both in bed and out of it.

When they spoke about Bobby McGilvrey, Anthea was careful not to repeat her boss's request. She told him all she knew about the boy, which wasn't much.

Bobby's self-reliance appealed to Olly. He agreed that Max would be no trouble and the arrangement would be temporary.

Anthea sipped her wine, then bent forward to light two candles. She asked Olly if he felt like eating outside, or preferred to go in. It was cool, but windless on the balcony. Olly could smell the seagrass. From time to time he heard swans honking, very faintly. He noticed how the candles, perhaps because he had got used to the twilight, perhaps because his senses were more alert than usual that evening, played over Anthea's strong features. She wasn't smiling; indeed her expression might have been described as grave; yet there was a glow to it, a kind of promise or assurance that he couldn't name and didn't want to, yet felt drawn towards.

'Let's stay out here,' he said. 'Do you want any help?'

Anthea shook her head. This was already their custom. Olly would do the washing up.

She served linguine with local mussels in a spiced tomato sauce, and they ate for a few minutes without speaking, except for Olly's murmured praise.

A gunshot bounced over the water, echoing, fooling the ears, producing sensations that, while clearly auditory, seemed visual as well.

Olly looked up. 'They're practising again.'

Anthea lifted her chin in the direction of the gunfire, to the narrow beach which, in the gathering darkness, was all that could be seen of Swan Island.

The shot was followed, in quick succession, by four more.

She turned and looked at Olly. 'Apparently there's a special kind of snail that lives in the seagrass. It's important because the fish, the baby whiting, eat it. Well, the lead in the bullets has been turning all the snails into males. The marine scientists didn't know why their numbers were decreasing, so they did a study, and that's what they found.'

'I don't suppose they've listened to the scientists and started firing inland,' Olly said. 'I heard something related to that too. There's a huge problem with algae taking over and smothering the seagrass. The common assumption is that crop fertilisers and cattle manure are responsible, but those snails did their bit to keep it down. They live on algae. It's their main food source.'

'So we need the snails back. What are they shooting at anyway? I mean it's hardly cut-outs in the shape of terrorists when they're firing over the water, is it?'

Olly made a face and shook his head.

Anthea said, 'It might be time to move inside. It's a good thing my bedroom walls are thick.'

Olly smiled. 'Dessert won't spoil, will it?'

'Oh no. Not at all.'

Anthea listened with her head on one aside as a last shot followed them through the French doors. She turned over her shoulder to say, 'You know, Chris's lived here all his life, and he's been a policeman for the last fifteen years. But he doesn't have a clue what goes on over there. They never tell him anything.'   .

Olly related another story later, over coffee and citrus tart, which they ate sitting up in bed with the doona over their legs, and a small table beside them, holding a carafe and mugs, a jug of cream. The story concerned a rich yachtsman who'd arrived at the marina one weekend to find the sail of his ocean-going yacht full of bullet holes.

Anthea leant over to add cream and sugar to her coffee.

'Did he get compensation?'

'I doubt it.'

Anthea smiled. She knew what she did *not* doubt, with Olly's warm brown shoulder next to hers, Olly's easy way of being with her, and his way of showing, by small words and touches, that he liked her, and that liking grew each time they shared a meal and went to bed in the middle of it. Anthea was used to being criticised by men, but Olly never criticised her. He made her feel that what she did was right.

Because the buildings were so close, they couldn't avoid knowing when each other was at home. Anthea thought that Olly might be in flight from something, or someone. Sometimes a stillness came over his face, as if he was waiting for her to pry so that he could rebuff her questions. If she'd been a different kind of woman, she might have remarked to her neighbour that he never had any visitors. Then Olly would have made it plain that visitors or the lack of them were none of her business.